## Praise for Marta Perry

"Perry's s_____ _____ _____nny
ability to _____ _____ _____ith
contempo_____ _____ead."
—_____ _____ _____ on _Home by Dark_

"Perry skillfully continues her chilling,
_____ romantic suspense series with
_____ that features a sweet romance
_____ing of Amish culture."
—_____ _____ on _Vanish in Plain Sight_

_____ the differences between the
Amish community and the larger society with an obvious
care and respect for ways and beliefs…. She weaves these
differences into the story with a deft hand, drawing the
reader into a suspenseful, continually moving plot."
—_Fresh Fiction_ on _Murder in Plain Sight_

"_Leah's Choice,_ by Marta Perry, is a knowing
and careful look into Amish culture and faith.
A truly enjoyable reading experience."
—Angela Hunt, _New York Times_ bestselling author
of _Let Darkness Come_

"_Leah's Choice_ is a story of grace and servitude
as well as a story of difficult choices and
heartbreaking realities. It touched my heart. I think
the world of Amish fiction has found a new champion."
—Lenora Worth, author of _Code of Honor_

"Marta Perry delivers a strong story of tension, fear and
trepidation. _Season of Secrets_ (4.5 stars) is an excellent
mystery that's certain to keep you in constant suspense.
While love is a powerful entity in this story,
danger is never too far behind."
—_RT Book Reviews_, Top Pick

# SEARCH

*the*

# DARK

# MARTA PERRY

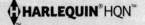

Recycling programs
for this product may
not exist in your area.

ISBN-13: 978-0-373-77786-0

SEARCH THE DARK

Copyright © 2013 by Martha Johnson

This edition published by arrangement with Harlequin Books S.A.

For questions and comments about the quality of this book, please contact us at CustomerService@Harlequin.com.

Printed in U.S.A.

www.Harlequin.com

This story is dedicated to my granddaughter, Greta Nicole. And, as always, to Brian, with much love.

Dear Reader,

I hope you'll enjoy this second book in my latest Amish suspense series. I certainly enjoyed revisiting my fictional community of Deer Run. If you happen to visit my area of north-central Pennsylvania, you'll find many small towns that look very much like Deer Run, nestled in the valleys with the wooded ridges rising above them.

The Amish practice of marrying within their religion is very strong, and parents hope their children will find love within the Amish community, since marrying an *Englisch* person often results in the child leaving the faith. The strong feelings aroused on both sides seldom lead to murder, however, except in suspense fiction!

Please let me know how you felt about my story. I'd be happy to send you a signed bookmark and my brochure of Pennsylvania Dutch recipes. You can email me at marta@martaperry.com, visit me at www.facebook.com/martaperrybooks or at www.martaperry.com, or write to me at Harlequin HQN, 233 Broadway, Suite 1001, New York, NY 10279.

Blessings,

Marta Perry

# SEARCH

*the*

# DARK

Trickles tend to become streams,
and streams become torrents.
—Amish proverb

# *PROLOGUE*

A THIN SHAFT of moonlight penetrated the shadows under the trees, turning the surface of the pond to silver. Strange, that the place should look so serene. No one knew; no one even imagined that murder happened here.

A shadow stirred within the densest shadows. Foolish to come here, but on sleepless nights the lure was too great. Stand here for a few moments, that was all that was needed. Remember.

It was safe enough. No one knew, no one watched. The darkness hid everything, just as it had hidden what had been done here twenty years ago.

*Accident,* they'd all said. Deer Run locals knew how dangerous the dam was where the stream emptied into the pond below. Only a few feet high, but in times of heavy rain the dam could produce a current as strong as any riptide.

The boy had been careless, people had said. An Amish kid, maybe drinking, maybe showing off, trapped by the dangerous water and drowned. The *Englisch* spoke of putting up a fence; the Amish said it was God's will. Tragic, but understandable.

The secret lay forgotten for twenty years, until

those two stupid women had come together again. They'd been children when Aaron Mast died, but they'd loved him. They talked, they wondered, they asked questions.

Well, for all their questioning, what they'd found was a good enough reason to call Aaron's death a suicide. Tragic, wasn't it? The village had buzzed about it again for weeks, but now even the talk slipped away like a leaf on the current.

No one thought of murder. No one would. But if the unthinkable happened… Well, there might have to be another death at Parson's Dam.

The shadow stirred, stepping toward the water for an instant, and then slid back into the darkness and melted away in the night.

# CHAPTER ONE

"YOU ARE THE only one who can find the truth, Meredith. You must do it."

Meredith King stared in dismay across the small café table at her cousin Sarah. With her hair drawn tightly back under her *kapp* and her simple Amish dress, Sarah seemed an unlikely person to be urging her cousin to investigate a death that had occurred twenty years ago. But worry had driven lines around Sarah's normally placid blue eyes, and she reached one hand across the table in pleading.

"I'm not sure what I can do." That came out sounding much less definite than Meredith had hoped. "Aaron drowned twenty years ago. There's probably nothing left to learn."

And a small-town accountant shouldn't be anyone's idea of a crusader. Her weekly coffee klatch with her Amish cousin had turned in a direction Meredith had never anticipated.

"But it was your looking into what happened that summer that brought about this talk of Aaron killing himself. Yours and Rachel's," Sarah added. "You've already found out so much—surely you can discover the rest of it."

Meredith couldn't argue that she'd resurrected the talk about Aaron Mast's death, no matter how she might want to. When her childhood friend, Rachel Weaver Mason, had come back to Deer Run several months earlier, they'd started reminiscing about the events of that summer when they'd been ten and had shared a childish crush on the Amish teenager.

Aaron had been the hero of the imaginary world they'd created that summer. But the world had come crashing down when Aaron died in the pond below Parson's Dam. What started as harmless wondering about the events of that summer had also ended in uncovering the probability that Aaron had committed suicide.

"I'm sorry we ever started poking into it," Meredith said, guilt settling across her shoulders like a heavy blanket. "We certainly didn't intend to cause grief to his family."

"Please, Meredith. I can't go asking questions among the *Englisch,* but you can." Sarah gestured to her Amish dress as if in explanation.

True enough. An action that would be unthinkable for an Amish matron was possible for Meredith.

"Besides, you know as much as anybody about that summer, following Aaron around like you did." Sarah must have sensed her hesitation and pressed on. "I know you were just a girl, but you didn't forget our Aaron, ain't so?" The possessive way Sarah spoke suggested that Aaron had meant something special to her.

"Aaron was a friend of yours, then?" She should have realized that Sarah, ten years older than Meredith, would have been about Aaron's age.

"Friend, *ja*." Sarah's gaze seemed to lose focus, as if she looked into the past. "More than friends, once." She shook her head, becoming again the mature Amish wife and mother. "But this talk of suicide hurts so many people. The Aaron I knew would not do such a thing."

"Sometimes we don't know others as well as we think." For example, she'd never guessed that there had been any love in Sarah's life other than her husband, Jonah. "Even if I can think of a way to find out more, you might not be happy with the result."

"If Aaron really did this thing, I will bear it." Sarah's voice was firm. "We all will. But we must know for certain sure."

Meredith was silent for a moment, trying to find a way to refuse. She didn't want to bring still more heartache to people who'd already suffered so much.

But Sarah was the closest link she had to her father and the Amish side of her family. For their sake, she couldn't refuse to do as Sarah asked, could she?

"I'll try," she said at last. "I don't know if I can help, but I'll try."

"*Denke,* Meredith." Tears shone in Sarah's blue eyes as she clasped Meredith's hand. *"Da Herr sie mit du."*

*The Lord be with you.* She'd certainly need the help if she were to solve a twenty-year-old mystery.

"Meredith?" Anna Miller called from behind the counter of the combination grocery store/tourist stop/coffee shop that had served the village of Deer Run as long as Meredith could remember. "Your mother has called, saying why are you so late and don't forget the goat's milk she wants. I have it ready for you."

"Thanks, Anna." She stood, wishing she could stay long enough to wipe the worry from Sarah's face, but knowing her mother was perfectly capable of calling every five minutes until Meredith showed up. That was why she'd muted the ringer on her phone.

"I'd better go." She touched Sarah's shoulder lightly as her cousin stood, gathering her purchases. "Give my love to Jonah and the children."

Sarah nodded. "I would say the same to your *mamm,* but I think it would not be *wilkom, ja?*" She gave a wry smile and turned toward the grocery section of the shop.

Since everyone in the valley knew of Margo King's antipathy to her late husband's Amish kin, there was little point in pretending it was otherwise. So Meredith just nodded and went to the counter to pick up the quart of goat's milk Anna had ready.

"Thanks, Anna."

"It makes no trouble," Anna said, although it had to be a bit of a chore to make a separate trip just to pick up the milk, especially when, like Anna, one drove a horse and buggy to do so.

"Well, I appreciate it." She handed over the money.

"You're a *gut* daughter," Anna said as Meredith turned toward the door. "Ain't so, Jeannette?" She appealed to the woman who'd just entered the shop.

Jeannette Walker's smile, as always, seemed to curdle a bit when she turned it on Meredith. "I'm sure she must be." Since Jeannette's bed-and-breakfast, the Willows, stood directly across the street from Meredith's house, she no doubt thought she had ample opportunity to judge.

"It's nice to see you, Jeannette." Meredith gave the expected greeting and attempted to reach the door, but Jeannette stood in her path, and she seemed in no hurry to move.

"Don't rush off yet," she said. "I haven't had a chance to tell you my news." Jeannette patted the tightly permed curls that made her look older than the fortysomething she probably was.

Funny, the difference between her and Sarah even though they were probably about the same age. Sarah, with no makeup, plain dress and her hair pulled back from a center part under her white *kapp,* still looked younger than Jeannette.

"Is something new in the bed-and-breakfast business?" she asked, even though she wasn't exactly panting to know.

"You might say that." Jeannette's gaze sharpened on Meredith's face. "I have a guest coming in today. An old friend of yours, I think."

"Really?" It seemed unlikely that one of her friends was coming to stay at the Willows, but she supposed stranger things had happened. "Who is it?"

"Well, you're just not going to believe it when I tell you." The faint look of triumph on Jeannette's face made Meredith vaguely uncomfortable. "I'm sure he was once a special friend of yours."

Meredith's fingers tightened around the milk bottle, and somehow she already knew whose name was coming out of Jeannette's mouth.

"Zachary Randal." Jeannette proclaimed the name loudly enough that everyone in Miller's Shop could hear it. "Now, tell me I'm not wrong. You two were an item once upon a time, weren't you?"

The smile on Meredith's face was probably frozen, but it had nothing on the icy hand that gripped her heart at the name. Zach Randal, returning to Deer Run after thirteen years? Surely not. He'd made it plain enough when he'd stormed away from her that he would never come back.

"Zach Randal?" Anna joined the conversation, diverting Jeannette's focus, thank goodness. "Well, that is interesting news. It'll be nice to see how that boy turned out after all these years."

Jeannette's expression suggested she smelled something nasty. "Not very well, I'm sure. If anyone had asked me, I'd have said he'd be in prison by this time."

Meredith discovered she was still capable of being

roused to anger on Zach's behalf. "If that's so, why did you rent a room to him?"

Jeannette shrugged, spreading her hands wide. "I run a business, after all. What can I do? But I'm surprised you didn't suggest he stay at your friend Rachel's little inn."

Rachel ran Mason House, a thriving new B and B that was giving the Willows a run for its money. But never mind the barb—Jeannette was fishing for a response. She was probably torn between wanting to be the only person who knew of Zach's imminent arrival and her desire to find out if Meredith was still in touch with him.

The thought of exposing her feelings in public kept Meredith's spine straight and her face composed. "There's no reason for Zach to contact me about his plans."

"So sad." Jeannette shook her head as if in sympathy, but her gaze was that of a robin with its eyes on a succulent worm. "When you were once so very close."

"Just casual friends," she said, knowing full well that everyone in the store probably saw that for the lie it was. Knowing, too, that she couldn't keep this front up much longer. "Excuse me. I must get home."

She brushed past Jeannette and hurried out the door, trying not to look as if she were running away.

She didn't run away. She'd never been able to. Running away was what Zach had done. She had just provided the reason.

ZACH HAD EXPECTED he'd have some time to adjust to being back in Deer Run before his inevitable first sight of Meredith King. He'd been wrong. As he pulled up in front of the Willows, Meredith was letting herself in the gate to her front yard, right across the street.

He could have stayed at a big, anonymous motel out on the interstate, but conducting this business had become a matter of pride to him. If he had to come back to Deer Run, he'd come, and nobody here could intimidate him again.

Including Meredith. He slammed the car door, making her face turn toward him, and started across the road. Sauntering, not hurrying. He'd greet her like any nearly forgotten acquaintance he hadn't seen in years. He'd show both her and himself that nothing remained of their long-vanished love.

That was easier said than done, given the fact that just the sight of her made him feel as if he'd been rammed full-on by a semi.

He came to a halt a few feet from her. Meredith stood still, just looking at him, her hand arrested with the gate half-open.

"Meredith." Luckily his voice came out as cool as he'd hoped. Undercover work had honed his acting skills. "It's been a long time."

He might have hoped to find that his first love had turned into a frazzled housewife carrying an extra twenty pounds and with a whining toddler in tow. She hadn't. If Meredith had added any weight since she was seventeen, it had certainly gone to the right places. The lovely girl she'd been had turned into a beautiful woman.

"Thirteen years," she said. She seemed to realize that she was gripping the gate tightly, and she let it swing closed, creating a barrier between them. "How are you, Zach?"

"Doing fine." He probably resembled the drug dealer he'd been posing as, with his tight, well-worn jeans, hair over his collar and stubble on his jaw. Fine. Let Deer Run think ill of him. It always had.

Meredith, on the other hand, looked like a polished professional woman with her shining brown hair worn in a sleek, just-below-the-chin cut, neat slacks and a soft coral sweater, with a touch of gold at ears and wrist.

Not on her hands, though. He'd seen that bare ring finger first thing.

"I just learned from Jeannette that you were coming." Those big brown doe eyes focused on his face. "I was surprised."

He managed a short laugh. "I'd say appalled was closer to the truth, right?" That came out sounding more bitter than he'd intended.

"Just surprised. Because I remember hearing you swear that Deer Run had seen the last of you." Those full lips might have trembled for an instant on the words.

"We talk a lot of nonsense when we're seventeen, right?" *Things like I love you. I'll always love you.*

He shrugged. "It was time I dealt with the property I own here. Had a few vacation days coming, so I figured I'd clear things up."

"I see." She glanced away, as if at a loss for something else to say.

He could remember when it seemed they'd never run out of things to say to each other. They'd walk around town in the summer twilight, sharing secrets and dreams as if they were two parts of a whole.

Meredith seemed to regain her poise after the momentary lapse. "I guess this visit won't be much of a vacation from work for you. What are you doing now?"

He raised an eyebrow, wondering how she'd react. "Police. Detective Zachary Randal, Pittsburgh P.D., believe it or not. I imagine most people in Deer Run expected me to end up on the other side of the bars."

"I'm sure that's not true." A faint flush touched her cheekbones, denying the words.

"Come on, Meredith." He put his hand on the gate, dangerously close to hers. "We both know what this town thinks of me."

"Deer Run has changed," she protested.

He took an obvious look down the street at the same lineup of century-old Victorian houses and small shops. A few cars were parked in front of the grocery store, an Amish horse and buggy was hitched at the side of the hardware store. The village snoozed under the shelter of the mountain ridge that seemed to cut it off from the rest of the world.

"Really? Looks the same to me." He raised an eyebrow and had the satisfaction of seeing a spark of anger in those brown eyes.

"You shouldn't judge what you don't know." Her chin came up, reminding him of the sensitive good girl who'd still had the courage to date the bad boy from the wrong side of the tracks.

The front door of the house rattled, and a high, sweet voice called out, "Meredith? Come inside, please. I need you."

The door closed again. Apparently Margo King had her daughter so well trained that she didn't need to call twice.

Meredith half turned away from the gate. "I'm sorry. I have to go in."

"Yeah. Right." Bitterness welled up, raw in his throat. "I see one thing hasn't changed at all."

Before she could answer he turned and walked away, his fists clenching as he tried to stamp down feelings he'd been sure had died a long time ago.

ANGER WAS MEREDITH'S only shield against pain, and she clung to it as she hurried into the house. If all Zach had to offer her was bitterness, so be it. He might at least have given her a chance to explain.

The thought drew her up sharply. What was there to explain? She'd said she loved him, but she hadn't had the courage to go against her family, her mother's imagined social status or the opinion of Deer Run to prove it. Zach knew that as well as she did. Their love was long since dead and buried, and it might have the decency to stay in its grave.

"What on earth were you doing, talking to that boy? Standing there at the front gate where everyone in town could see you—Meredith King, you should have better sense." Her mother waited in the entry-way, shaking with anger from the top of her carefully tinted hair to the tips of her neat leather loafers. "I can't imagine how he has the nerve to show his face in Deer Run again. What's he doing here, anyway?"

Meredith sucked in a deep breath and prayed for calm. "I'm not sure, Mother. I believe he has some business to take care of." She kept walking, head-ing for the kitchen. "I'd better put the goat's milk in the fridge."

It was too much to hope that her mother wouldn't follow her. "What kind of business? If he's come back here to moon after you again, he might as well go back where he came from."

"Don't be silly." That came out too sharply. "You know all that was over a long time ago."

"You shouldn't have talked to him at all." Her mother sank onto a kitchen chair, pressing her fin-gertips to her temples. "It gives me one of my head-aches just to think about Zach Randal, right at my front gate, looking like some kind of a hoodlum."

Zach had looked a bit rough around the edges, hadn't he? That had always been part of the allure, Meredith supposed. It was classic, a good girl like Meredith King falling hard for the boy who was bad to the bone, or so people said. And Zach, with his disdain for small-town attitudes, had seemed to enjoy shocking the denizens of Deer Run. If he wasn't cutting school, he was sauntering in late. And he'd been quick with his fists at the slightest opportunity.

"I understand he's a police officer now," she said, opening the refrigerator door to shield her face while hoping to head off some of the inevitable speculation.

"I suppose he told you so, and you believed him. Just like you always did." Her mother's voice went up an octave, and she stopped massaging her temples to clutch at her chest—never a good sign. "You believed him no matter what we said, causing your poor father so much grief."

Tears spurted from her mother's soft brown eyes, and her words came in little gasps. She was working herself into a state of hysteria, and if Meredith didn't intercede, she'd end up with a frantic call to the doctor, insisting she was having a heart attack.

"Now, Mother, that's all in the past. There's nothing to worry about anymore. Zach is only here for a few days, and then he'll be gone and we'll never see him again." Her heart seemed to lodge a protest at that, but she kept going. "I'm sorry his return upset you, but it doesn't need to. Why don't you come upstairs and have a nice rest before supper?"

Still soothing, Meredith led her mother gently to the stairs. They'd played this scene so often she knew it by heart. First it had been Daddy doing the soothing and comforting, and now it was Meredith's job.

Keeping her voice calm, her touch gentle, she guided her mother up to her bedroom, pulled the shades, tucked her under the coverlet. Experience had taught her that it was useless to try and reason with her mother—she was no more amenable to reason than the average two-year-old. And too much emotion led inevitably to the racing heartbeat that frightened her mother as much as it did Meredith.

According to the doctors, her mother's atrial fibrillation was not nearly bad enough or frequent enough to require anything other than the mild medication she was on. Their assurances had never comforted her mother.

Finally, after repeated promises that Margo would never be subjected to the sight of Zach Randal again, Meredith was able to get away. An easy promise to make, wasn't it? It was hardly likely that Zach would care to confront Margo King after what she had done to him.

Meredith had barely reached the kitchen when she heard a tapping on the back door. Through the window she spotted Rachel, who'd probably cut across the back lawn between their houses in the shortcut they'd developed in the past few months. The elderly Amish seamstress whose small house sat between the two didn't mind their frequent trespassing.

Meredith opened the door with a sense of relief. Here was someone she could confide in without the need to protect her feelings.

Rachel came in, handing her a package as she did so. "This was on your back porch."

Meredith glanced at the label as she led the way into the kitchen and sighed. "It looks as if Mother has been watching the Shopping Channel again. I can't seem to convince her that we can't afford every little thing that appeals to her." She'd have to have another of her futile talks with her mother.

Rachel nodded in sympathy. She knew all about getting by on a small income, since she was supporting herself and her young daughter by turning her former mother-in-law's house into a bed-and-breakfast. "She still doesn't understand that her investments aren't paying off the way they used to?"

"Understand? She won't even listen. Says it gives her a headache."

Meredith put the kettle on the stove with a little unnecessary force. Rachel was the only person in whom she confided, and Rachel was safe. Their childhood friendship had blossomed into a solid relationship since Rachel moved back to Deer Run.

"How is she taking Zach Randal's return?" Rachel lowered her voice, as if Margo King might be lurking around the corner.

"It's okay to talk. She's taking a nap." Meredith set two mugs on the counter. The late-September day was cool enough to switch from iced tea to hot tea for their afternoon break. "So the rumor mill is turning already, is it?"

"I'm afraid so." Rachel hesitated, her usual gentle expression concerned. "If you don't want to talk about it…"

"I'd rather talk to you than anyone. I just can't believe Zach has come back. I never expected to see him again after what my mother did."

"Your mother?"

"You didn't know? I guess you might not have." Rachel had still been Amish then, and their childhood friendship had faded by that time. Amish teenage girls were helping their mothers or preparing for marriage at a time when *Englisch* girls were engrossed in cheerleading and the latest hairstyles.

The kettle shrieked, a suitable sound for the way Meredith felt. She poured water over the tea bags.

"My parents didn't want me involved with Zach, as you can imagine. He was the rebel, constantly in trouble with everyone."

She had to smile. It had been such a classic story—like *Grease* without the music. Or maybe more like *West Side Story,* even though no one died.

"When we started getting too serious, my mother came up with a simple plan to get rid of him. I had let him into the house when she wasn't there, and she claimed money was missing from her desk drawer. She said Zach had taken it, and she threatened to prosecute if he didn't go away and leave me alone." The words were as dry as dust in her mouth. "He was ready to leave Deer Run behind, anyway, I suppose. He wanted me to go with him. I said no." She set the mugs on the table with a clunk and sank into her chair.

Rachel studied her face for a moment. "Did you love him?"

A fair question, wasn't it? In a similar situation, Rachel had run off to marry Ronnie Mason, to the dismay of both their families. It hadn't turned out well, but at least Rachel had her little Mandy by way of compensation.

"I thought I did." Meredith shook her head. No point in evading the truth. "Yes, I loved him. I just didn't have the courage to go with him."

"Maybe you did the best thing." Rachel's voice was gentle.

"I doubt that Zach saw it that way. He ended up branded a thief because of me." She sucked in a breath. "Now he's back, and he's…" She hesitated, trying to find the word to express what she'd sensed from him. "…bitter, I guess. I can't blame him. I just wish I knew what to say to him."

"Maybe you need to tell him how sorry you are. For your sake, if not for his." Rachel had a way of going to the emotional heart of the matter.

"I'm not sure he'd want to hear it." She saw again the dark intensity of his gaze.

"If he's not willing to forgive you, then that's his right." Rachel still had a typically Amish attitude toward right and wrong. "But you'll have cleared the slate, and you can move on."

Meredith stared down into the amber liquid in her

cup, as if she'd see an answer in its depths. "Suppose...suppose I find I don't want to move on. What if I still have feelings for him?"

Rachel didn't speak for a moment. "Either way, isn't it better to know the truth?"

The truth. The words were an echo of what Sarah had said to her earlier. Life seemed easier, somehow, if you could settle for a polite fiction that glossed over the difficult facts. But some people would only be satisfied by the truth, and she had an uncomfortable feeling that she might be one of them.

Rachel leaned back, sipping her tea, ready to talk or listen or forget, whatever Meredith needed. A wave of gratitude went through her. Maybe that was really the definition of a friend... Someone who could hear all the bad stuff, empathize and then let it slip away.

She took a gulp of her tea, letting the hot liquid dissolve the lump that had formed in her throat.

"I met with my cousin Sarah this afternoon," she said, abruptly changing the subject. "Apparently rumors are going around that Aaron Mast killed himself."

Rachel's clear blue eyes clouded. "Oh, no. We tried to be so careful not to let anyone know what we'd found."

"I'm beginning to think there's no such thing as a secret in Deer Run," Meredith said. "Sarah's so upset about it. And Aaron's parents, as well. She asked me to find out if it's really true."

"I can understand how they feel. Suicide goes against everything the Amish believe. But how are we supposed to come up with something new after all this time?"

Meredith appreciated the *we*. Rachel wouldn't let her deal with the problem alone. "At this point, I don't have a single idea. But I'd like to go through the scrapbook we kept that summer again. Would you mind if I picked it up?"

She, Rachel and their friend Lainey Colton had kept a scrapbook of their imaginary world that summer, filled with their observations and the illustrations Lainey had drawn. Meredith had already been through it several dozen times, but perhaps there was something she'd missed.

"I'll drop it off for you," Rachel said, still looking concerned. She glanced at her watch. "I didn't realize how late it was getting. I hate to cut this short, but I told Mamm to send Mandy home at four-thirty."

"No problem. At the moment, I don't have any idea of how to do what Sarah wants." She rose, putting the mugs in the sink.

"Maybe if we both think about it, we'll come up with something." Rachel touched her arm in silent sympathy. "As for the other…well, try not to worry too much about Zach. He's not a boy any longer. He's responsible for his own happiness."

*Or unhappiness,* Meredith added silently. Still, Zach hadn't seemed unhappy. Just bitter.

"Say hi to Mandy and your folks for me." Meredith walked with her to the back porch. The breach between Rachel and her family over her leaving the Amish faith had healed, and Rachel considered herself fortunate to live only a stone's throw from her parents' farm on the far side of the covered bridge over the creek.

Meredith stood for a moment on the back stoop, watching as Rachel cut across the intervening backyard. All of the backyards on this side of the road ended at the creek, which formed a boundary between the village on this side and the Amish farms on the other. Meredith kept her backyard mowed to just beyond the garage, as her father always had. A little farther on, a tangled border of raspberry bushes spanned the space to the trees that crowded along the creek banks.

If she went down the path behind the garage, it would lead her to the small dam that emptied into a wide, inviting pool. The pool where Aaron Mast died.

A breeze touched her and set the branches moving, a few leaves detaching themselves to flutter to the ground. The sun was just beginning to slip behind the mountain, but the shadows already lay deep under the trees around the pond.

She rubbed her arms, unaccountably chilled. She

hadn't liked going to the dam since that summer. It had figured in too many bad dreams.

She didn't believe it was haunted by ghosts. That was nonsense. But it certainly was haunted by memories.

## CHAPTER TWO

MARGO SLIPPED AWAY from the kitchen door, her terry-cloth slippers making no sound at all. But she wouldn't be heard in any event. Meredith had gone out on the back porch with her friend. She'd never know her mother had been out of bed at all.

A lady doesn't eavesdrop. It wasn't polite. But what was she to do when her own daughter kept secrets from her?

Margo's anger flickered as she made her way up the stairs, her hand on the railing for support. Really, Meredith should have better sense, but it certainly wasn't her fault. No one could say that Margo hadn't done her best to raise her only daughter properly.

It was a mother's duty to protect her child, even when that child was an unmarried woman of thirty. She winced, Meredith's age reminding her uncomfortably of just how old she was. Still, her friends assured her she didn't look a day over fifty.

Margo padded into her bedroom, sending a satisfied glance at her image in the mirror. Like a Dresden doll, her father had said of her the evening she'd gone to her first dance. Certainly the boys had agreed. She'd had her pick of boyfriends. If only she hadn't imagined herself in love with John King....

She fluffed up her pillows and settled back against them, frowning a little. The issue now was Meredith, and how she could be protected from her weakness where Zachary Randal was concerned.

Good riddance to bad rubbish—that was what people had said when he'd left town all those years ago. Margo had bathed in a glow of righteousness for weeks over her role in making his departure come about. Zach had left, and Meredith had been protected from him. Goodness only knew what might have happened if Margo hadn't intervened when she did.

She'd been so sure the incident was closed after all these years. Who could have imagined that Randal boy would dare to show his face in Deer Run again?

Her breath came too quickly, and Margo forced herself to relax. She mustn't upset herself or she'd bring on one of her attacks, and then she wouldn't be able to do anything to save Meredith from herself.

Meredith was still in danger of succumbing to Randal's dubious attractions. Margo didn't doubt that for a minute. There was simply something about one's first love that blinded one.

She glanced at the silver-framed photo of John that stood on the bedside table. John hadn't liked having it taken—some silly hangover from his Amish upbringing. But she'd had no patience with that foolishness and had insisted.

Enough of thinking about the past. She had to decide what to do now. Meredith and Rachel had brought up two distasteful matters in their private little chat.

Why were they so fascinated with Aaron Mast's death? It had been an accident, pure and simple. Everyone knew that. As for Sarah asking Meredith to look into it—well, that was just ridiculous, and no more than one could expect from her husband's relatives.

Meredith couldn't possibly know anything about what happened the night Aaron drowned in the pond. She hadn't even been at home. She'd spent the night with another of John's numerous cousins, at his insistence. If Margo had had her way, Meredith would have had no communication with those people. But John, usually so compliant and eager to please her, had stood firm on that subject.

Margo sifted through memories. Odd, how some incidents formed landmarks in a person's mind. She remembered that night clearly because of what had happened early the next morning. She'd gone downstairs to find Bill Kramer, his fishing rod still dangling from his hand, pounding on the back door and insisting on using the telephone because someone was dead in the pond.

Margo pulled the silky comforter up to her chin. The accident had probably happened in the late evening, people had said. Meredith hadn't been home, thank goodness. John hadn't, either. He'd gone back to the harness shop to work on an order.

Margo's lips tightened at the remembered grievance. All the men in her family had been professionals—doctor, pharmacist, teacher—but John had insisted on opening his harness business right here in Deer Run. Worse, he'd left her alone in the house the evening that boy had drowned.

Still, his callousness had an unexpected benefit now. If anyone in the family knew anything about the Mast boy's death, she would.

Margo glanced at the window, shielded by the shade Meredith had pulled down. It faced the driveway, down which someone might have walked to reach the creek. People shouldn't trespass, of course, but they did. And the window would have been open on a summer evening.

Memories began to stir and shift in her mind. Consider how satisfying it would be if Margo was the one who remembered something important about that night. It would certainly show Meredith she wasn't the only smart one in the family.

Margo leaned back against the pillows, indulging in a rosy daydream. Of herself, the heroine of the hour, graciously telling her story to a chosen few. Of Meredith, looking on admiringly.

As long as she was dreaming, she might just as well dream of a means of getting rid of Zach Randal again, this time for good.

ZACH ARRIVED RIGHT ON TIME for his meeting with the attorney the next day. *Evans and Son*. The gilt letters on the window of the office weren't exactly a surprise. Jake Evans had been slotted to go into his father's law firm from the day he was born, he'd bet.

Zach paused for a second, his hand on the doorknob, remembering. Jake had been in his class in school, so they were about the same age. There the similarity between them ended.

Jake had been one of the "in" crowd, the people who lived in the big old houses along Maple Street and Main Street, the ones whose fathers had worn coats and ties to work every day, who never had to wonder if there'd be food in the house.

The "in" crowd hadn't had much time for somebody like Zach Randal in those days. He didn't figure much had changed in that respect, not in Deer Run. He swung the door open and went into the outer office with a determined step.

The middle-aged receptionist didn't look familiar, but she eyed him as if his reputation had preceded him. Either that or he didn't look as good as he'd thought he did after a night's sleep and a shower and shave.

"Mr. Randal? One moment please. I'll let Mr. Evans know you're here."

Her finger moved to a button on her desk, but before she could push it, one of the two doors behind her desk swung open. Jake Evans stood there, giving him a quick, assessing glance before his face eased into a smile.

"Zach, come on in. It's been a long time. Good to see you."

Zach allowed himself to be ushered into the inner office, where the latest thing in computers seemed to argue with a heavy oak desk that would fit more readily with a fountain pen and legal pad. Zach swept the room with a comprehensive glance, accustomed to sizing up his surroundings swiftly.

The office was clearly a study in contrasts, with the taste of the elder Evans jockeying for control with that of his son. A small basketball hoop was attached to a black enamel wastepaper basket, and a Phillies ball cap sat rakishly atop a crystal vase on the corner of the bookshelves.

Jake waved him to a chair and folded his lanky, still-athletic frame into the black leather one behind the desk. He moved like the basketball star he'd been in high school.

"Is Jeannette Walker making you comfortable at the Willows?" Jake leaned back and seemed to restrain himself from propping his foot on the wastebasket.

"The place isn't bad." He couldn't blame the setting for Jeannette's blatant curiosity.

Just like all of Deer Run and everyone in it. He'd come back because he had to, but given the feelings Meredith had stirred up by a single conversation, he'd be better off to sign whatever papers Jake had for him, get rid of the house and head back to his real life.

Jake twirled a pen between his fingers, seeming in no hurry to get down to business. "What do you think of Deer Run? Does it look different to you after being away so long?"

"No." Zach said the word flatly. "Look, let's just take care of things so I can get out of here. You didn't have time for me in high school, and I don't see any point in making small talk now."

Jake was immobile for an instant, and then one eyebrow edged its way upward. "I hope I've grown up a little since high school," he said, apparently not taking offense. His grin flickered. "Not that my father would agree with that. He still looks at me and sees the kid who embarrassed him by asking both the Hamilton twins to the senior prom." He glanced toward the wall beyond which, Zach assumed, lay the senior Mr. Evans's office.

"That must have caused quite a stir." He remembered the Hamilton twins—identical daughters of the then mayor. But he didn't remember the prom. "Afraid I was gone by then."

"Right." Jake's gaze slid away from his, as if he was embarrassed he'd mentioned the prom. He shuffled through a file folder on the desk. "Well, to business."

Zach nodded, the movement curt. He didn't want any side excursions into high school memories. He had intended to take Meredith to their senior prom, going so far as to sell his beat-up old car in order to have enough money to do it right. But fate, in the shape of Margo King, had intervened.

"You know that the house went to your stepmother after your father's death, of course," Jake said, raising a questioning eyebrow.

He nodded. The only surprising thing was that Wally Randal had hung on to enough money to pay the taxes and keep from losing the place altogether.

"I'm not sure why the property comes to me," he said. "I'm not related to Ruth."

Jake shrugged. "I guess she didn't have any other family. Her will was clear enough. Everything goes to you. Unfortunately, as I mentioned in my letter, the house is badly run-down. If you want to sell—"

"Definitely," Zach interrupted him. "As soon as possible. Can you refer me to a real estate agent?"

Jake frowned, his frank, open face looking suddenly older. "To tell you the truth, I doubt you could find anyone to take it on. It's in such bad shape I don't know how you're going to find a buyer."

Zach could only stare at him. He'd ignored the place since he'd heard that he owned it. Now, it seemed, he was going to pay the penalty for that.

"You're telling me that I own a worthless piece of property, and I won't be able to get rid of it." He glared at Jake, who returned the look with interest.

"You'll recall that I sent you several letters asking you to come back and deal with the place. You didn't."

So it was his fault. He'd like to deny it, if he could think of anyone else to blame, but he couldn't.

"Okay." Zach blew out a long breath. "Where do I go from here?" If he stopped paying the taxes, the place would eventually go up for sheriff's sale, but he couldn't bring himself to do that. It would be proof that he was trash, just as the good people of Deer Run had always supposed.

"As I see it, you could either do the minimum amount of repair work to make the place saleable." There might be a trace of sympathy in Jake's face. "Or you could have the house demolished and try to sell the lot."

Either way, his legacy was going to cost him. The old man would be laughing his head off, if he knew about this from wherever he'd ended up.

"You have an opinion about which?" Zach raised an eyebrow.

Jake shook his head. Yes, that was definitely sympathy in his expression. "Sorry. That's not for me to make a recommendation. If you want the opinion of someone in real estate, you ought to talk to Colin McDonald. You remember him from high school, don't you?"

Zach nodded. Another one of the "in" crowd. Presumably they'd all stayed here, where they could be big fish in a small pond. "I'll give him a try."

Jake reached across the desk, holding out a set of keys. "In the meantime, I'd suggest that the first thing you ought to do would be to take a look for yourself."

Zach forced himself to take the keys, fighting down a wave of nausea. That wasn't the first thing he wanted to do. It was the last thing.

IF SHE CONCENTRATED on what Sarah had asked of her, Meredith decided, she might be able to keep her mind off Zach. She would not let herself wonder why she hadn't seen him since the previous day, or what he was finding to do in Deer Run.

Reminding herself of her good intention, Meredith walked quickly down Main Street and turned up Church. Church Street, named for the two houses of worship which faced one another on opposite sides, sloped gently uphill to Maple, where Victor Hammond, heir to the Hammond Grocery chain, had built a dream house for his wife, Laura.

There would be no taking over the comfortable old Victorian house where Victor's parents had lived. Gossip had it that Victor had been so surprised and pleased when Laura accepted him that he'd have given her anything, including the ultramodern home that now sat uneasily among its more traditional neighbors.

Since no place in Deer Run was too far to walk to, Meredith had walked. The problem was going to be finding Laura both at home and accessible. The secondary problem was having some believable reason for dropping in on her.

Well, she'd create some logical excuse for her presence. If she were going to find out anything else about Aaron's death after all these years, Laura was the obvious place to start.

The clearing at the dam had been the meeting place for Laura and Aaron's ill-fated romance. The curiosity of three ten-year-old girls had been more than up to unraveling that little secret. They'd known, and they'd been awed by the Romeo-and-Juliet story of Amish and *Englisch*—their golden knight involved with the most beautiful girl in the valley.

But Aaron had died at the dam, and Laura had never been the same since. That had to add up to something. Perhaps Laura had broken up with him and he'd taken his life in a moment of despair, or maybe he'd been showing off for Laura and had fallen, to be caught up in the treacherous swirling waters. Try as she might, Meredith couldn't come up with any other likely alternatives.

Meredith approached the wrought-iron gate and stopped, hand on the cool metal. The grounds surrounding the house were professionally cared for, she felt sure. She couldn't picture Victor cruising along on a riding mower, or Laura deadheading the chrysanthemums.

Meredith's breath caught. It looked as if the way had been paved for her. Laura, her face hidden by a floppy-brimmed hat and a pair of dark glasses, sat on a wrought-iron garden bench, motionless. Was she admiring the gold and bronze of the mums, or staring into space?

Even as she watched, Laura stood. She paused, as if she'd forgotten what she was about to do, and then drifted wraithlike along the path between the rosebushes.

She wouldn't get a better chance. Meredith slipped through the gate and hurried toward the rose garden.

"Laura?"

Laura turned at the sound of her name, her expression, or what Meredith could see of it with the barrier of the glasses and hat, oddly stiff. For an instant she seemed about to speak but instead made a gesture, which Meredith decided to interpret as an invitation to join her.

"I hope you don't mind my dropping by without calling first," Meredith said.

"Of course not." The polite words took a visible effort. "It's always nice to see you, Meredith." Laura pulled off the dark glasses, managing a smile. "I was just enjoying…" The sentence trailed off, as if it took too much effort, and she gestured vaguely at the roses.

"Your roses have been beautiful this year." They were about past their prime now, a sentiment that could apply equally well to Laura.

What had become of the prettiest girl in the valley? In recent years, Meredith had thought Laura resembled a child's fashion doll with her perfect face, perfect hair and perfect clothes. Today she looked…

empty. There seemed no life at all in the blue eyes half-hidden by drooping lids.

"Yes, lovely," Laura repeated. "The gardener does it all." She cupped one overblown blossom in her hand. "You wanted…" Again the sentence trailed off.

Fortunately the flowers had given Meredith a reasonable excuse for her presence. "The church women's group is having a flower stand at the Amish school auction tomorrow. If you'd like to donate some of your blossoms, it would be appreciated. I could come by early tomorrow and pick them up."

All of that was true, although not, strictly speaking, her reason for being here. Still, she was bending the truth for a good cause, wasn't she?

Laura nodded, her attention still on the rose in her hand. "Fine, fine." Her fingers tightened on the rose, and with a quick wrench she pulled it off. The flower disintegrated in her hand, petals scattering on the flagstone path.

The sudden violence of the gesture made Meredith's stomach twist. She tried to think of something to say, but came up empty. If she intended to bring up Aaron, she'd better do it.

"These are too perfect," Laura announced. She caught another of the full red blossoms and subjected it to the same fate.

"You…don't care for the red ones?" That was an inane question, but she couldn't think of a better one.

"Too perfect," Laura said again. She reached out as if to destroy another bloom, but then her hand fell to her side, the animation draining away as quickly as it had come.

"I wanted to ask you…" Meredith began.

"The little white roses grow wild along the edge of the field." Laura swung on her, frowning. "You know that, don't you?"

"Yes, of course," she said, feeling as if she'd stumbled into some dark version of Wonderland. Everyone knew the wild roses that grew with abandon if given a chance. They practically had to be firebombed to be gotten rid of.

"Those are real roses, don't you think?" Laura's expression turned dreamy. "Aaron brought me those." She smiled. "You remember. He'd scratched his hand on the thorns, but he said it was worth it. I kissed it to make it better. You remember, don't you?" Her tone demanded an answer.

"Yes, I remember," she soothed. "That's a nice memory."

Why was Laura so insistent that she remember? Maybe she was thinking of the three young girls following her and Aaron around that summer. They'd never given away those secret meetings between Laura and her Amish lover. Maybe that idea had planted itself in Laura's apparently scrambled thought processes.

"I remember a lot about that summer," she went on, watching Laura's face for a reaction. "Aaron really loved you."

"Yes." Laura's smile was dreamy, and she stroked

her cheek with one of the despised roses. "He loved me. We were going to get married. But then—" She stopped, her expression shifting in an instant. "It all changed. Why did it change?" She grasped Meredith's arm, her nails digging into the skin. "Why did it change?"

"I don't know." Meredith fought to keep her voice soft. "Why did it?"

"I don't know, either." Laura's face crumpled like the roses. "That last night…"

"What about that last night?" Her heart thudded in her ears.

"That night—" Laura's breath caught on a sob.

"It's all right, Laura. Don't worry about it." Meredith put her arm around Laura's waist.

She was ashamed of herself, tormenting this poor creature by asking questions. And yet, even though she'd come here for that reason, she hadn't had to bring up the subject. It was as if her presence was enough to send Laura's thoughts back to that lost summer.

"You have to know," Laura said. She pressed her fingers to her forehead. "You know, don't you?" Her eyes pleaded with Meredith.

"I'm not—"

"Well, Meredith. What a surprise."

She spun around to see Victor puffing across the lawn toward them, his round face caught between anger and worry, it seemed.

Meredith moved a step, aware of some insensible desire to shield Laura's tears from her husband.

"It's nice to see you, Victor." She managed what she hoped was a natural-looking smile. "Laura and I were just discussing the possibility that you might donate some flowers for the women's association stand tomorrow."

"That's tomorrow, is it?" He seemed to respond automatically while scanning Laura's face, perhaps gauging her emotional temperature. "Yes, I'm sure we'd be happy to do so. Anything for a good cause." He edged around her to take Laura's arm, patting it. "Isn't that right, Laura?"

"That's right," Laura parroted, her expression blank.

Meredith's stomach gave a decided wrench. Definitely time to beat a retreat. Laura wouldn't say anything else with Victor there, and judging by the way he grasped her arm, he had no intention of leaving Meredith alone with her.

"I'll stop by in the morning to pick them up," she said.

"No need." Victor waved his hand in dismissal. "I'll have the gardener drop them off first thing. Down at the fire hall grounds, right?"

"Right." Most outdoor events of any size were held there, and the twice-yearly auctions to support the local Amish schools were a fixture.

"Good, good." His attention on Laura, Victor began nudging her toward the house. "Time you were having a rest, dear. You know you'll get a headache if you stay out in the sun for very long."

Laura nodded, face empty. She walked toward the house next to him, as docile as a doll.

Poor Laura. Everyone in town knew about what Victor called "her visits to a spa." The kind murmured of a nervous breakdown, while others speculated on rehab, drugs, alcohol. No one knew for sure, but the woman was clearly hurting, lost in one tragic event in her past.

Meredith hurried to the gate. She'd made a mistake in coming here. Anything she did to uncover the events of that summer was bound to cause pain to someone. She should never have gotten into this.

## CHAPTER THREE

ZACH HAD COME to the conclusion that being back in Deer Run had turned him into a coward. He'd tried to walk over to the old house after his meeting with Jake Evans, but he'd wimped out. Twice.

Too many bad memories—memories he'd effectively buried for years but never quite gotten rid of. His boss had been right. He should have come back years ago to settle up with Deer Run once and for all.

He walked down Main Street, not sure where he was going but knowing he didn't want to go back to the bed-and-breakfast. He couldn't leave, and he wasn't ready to face the house yet. The tiny post office, its flag fluttering in the breeze, sat where it always had, and the imposing red brick of the bank still stood on the corner. There was a bench between them where a guy loitering to meet the girl he was forbidden to see could spot her coming out of her house.

He'd imagined that the years would make it easier—that he'd have forgotten Meredith and that he'd have come to terms with his father. Instead, the shadow of his old man could still turn his spine to spaghetti. And as for Meredith...

When he'd seen her, the years had telescoped and

he'd been a love-struck seventeen-year-old again. At least he hadn't let her see that, he trusted.

Neither of them was the same person now, and imagining anything else could lead to disaster. He had to figure out how to make peace with his memories, and he'd better do it fast, because Meredith was walking down Main Street toward him.

He sucked in a breath, telling himself to play it cool. She hadn't seen him yet. Her gaze was fixed on the sidewalk, and something had upset her usual equilibrium, setting a frown on her forehead and anxiety in the set of her jaw. It struck him that he might have been the cause, given how he'd spoken to her yesterday.

There was a difference between being cool and being cruel. He didn't have the right to hurt her for decisions they'd made when they were seventeen.

He stepped into her path and she looked up, startled. Color flooded her cheeks.

"Zach. I—I didn't see you."

"What's wrong?" They'd always been able to go to the heart of things with each other, and he didn't figure he'd start making polite conversation now.

"Nothing," she said quickly and then shook her head. "Well, nothing I can do anything about, in any event." She seemed to brush aside whatever it was, or at least table it until later. "Have you taken care of the business you had to deal with?"

"I've made a start." He shrugged. "According to

Jake Evans, you can't just toss a house in the trash if you don't want it."

Meredith studied his face, and he had the sense that she was seeing beneath the surface, just like she used to do. She'd always been able to glimpse the person behind the tough-guy façade.

"The house where you grew up, you mean?"

He couldn't keep from grimacing. "It came to me after my stepmother died, it seems. I don't want it."

"You don't want it because the property is a tie to Deer Run, I guess." Her direct gaze wanted the truth.

"Maybe." But that was putting too much of the burden on her. "But mostly because the place holds a lot of bad memories. My childhood isn't something I care to be reminded of."

That had been one of the best things about starting a new life in a different place. He hadn't had to deal with the constant reminders.

"What are you planning to do with it, since throwing it away isn't an option?" The curve of her lips invited him to see the humor in the situation.

He didn't. "I figured I'd put it on the market cheap and get rid of it, but according to Evans, it won't sell in the shape it's in."

Meredith nodded, the tiny frown line back between her brows, for his problem this time. She shoved a strand of hair behind her ear, and his heart jolted. She'd always done that when she concentrated on something.

"You can trust Jake to give you an honest opinion, I'm sure. Everyone says he's become a good attorney."

"He claims his father is the exception to that opinion," he said, just to see her face lighten.

Her smile flickered. "Jacob Senior is proud of his son, but of course he can't admit such a thing. His gruff predictions of imminent disaster when Jake takes over are just a smoke screen, and everyone knows it."

"Must be nice to have a father like that." His old man had meant every word of the things he'd said to him, most of it stuff he certainly couldn't repeat to Meredith, of all people.

As always, she saw behind his words to the meaning. Her hand moved tentatively, as if she wanted to reach out to him.

"I'm sorry." Her voice was soft.

"Yeah. Well, it's over and done with. I don't suppose there were many people who thought Wally Randal was much of a loss when he died."

"You didn't come back for the funeral," she observed.

"You were there?" That shocked him. He hadn't known about it in time, but if he had, he still wouldn't have come. But Meredith had gone. "Why?" Because of him?

"I...thought I should attend." She looked so uncomfortable that he let it go.

"I heard about your dad's passing." Courtesy of Jeannette, who seemed convinced he wanted to hear every scrap of news about what had happened in Deer Run since he left. "I'm sorry."

"Thank you." Her face was composed, but her eyes were shadowed. "It's been a long time, but I still miss him."

Zach's heart twisted. "I know you were close." He'd admired John King's devotion to his daughter, even though that devotion had once made him Zach's enemy.

Meredith stepped aside to let a woman carrying a shopping bag pass, nodding a greeting. She didn't speak again until the woman was well out of earshot.

"There was something I wanted to say to you, Zach." Her brown eyes were candid, fixed on his face. "Maybe I'd better say it now, since I don't suppose you'll be in town long."

He wasn't sure he wanted to hear whatever it was, but he nodded.

Meredith hesitated, and for a moment he thought she looked more like the girl she'd been than the polished woman she was now. That glimpse kicked him right in the heart.

"I want you to know how sorry I am for what my mother did to you." She seemed to force the words out. "She thought she was protecting me, but that's no excuse. She drove you away from your home, kept you from finishing high school…" Her voice trembled slightly. "And I hurt you, too. I can't expect you to forgive me, but I wanted you to know how much I regret what happened."

She pressed her lips together, and he knew that it had cost her a lot to say what she had. How much easier it would be for her to pretend the past had never happened, to greet him politely and then avoid him until he disappeared again. But Meredith had never been one to take the easy way. He'd admired that quality years ago, and he still did.

"It's all right. I mean it. Getting out of Deer Run was the best thing that could have happened to me. Your mother didn't intend to, but she did me a favor."

She managed a faint smile at that idea. "It's good of you to take it that way. But I let you down, too, and I'm sorry."

He had to take the guilt from her face, even at the cost of a lie. "Forget letting me down. What did we know about life at seventeen? The way I see it, you kept both of us from making a big mistake, right?"

Her face was immobile for a moment. Then her lips moved in a stiff smile.

"Right." She glanced around, as if to be sure no one was watching them. "I'd better get back to work. If I don't see you again, have a safe trip back."

She turned and walked quickly away.

As she headed up the steps to the wide front porch a few minutes later, Meredith couldn't help hoping that her mother wasn't back yet from her committee meeting. If the local rumor mill had already reported her conversation with Zach, she'd have to listen to her mother's laments, lectures and warnings all over again.

More importantly, Meredith didn't want her mother's sharp eyes zeroing in on how upset she was.

Her luck was out—Mom sat in her favorite upholstered rocker in the living room, her low-heeled pumps propped on the small ottoman. "Meredith, you're finally home. I was starting to worry about you."

What did she imagine could happen to Meredith in Deer Run in broad daylight? Maybe exactly what had happened—an encounter with Zach.

"How was your meeting?" Meredith paused in the archway. She wanted nothing so much as to disappear into her bedroom or her office and close the door, but that would be inviting her mother to follow her with questions.

"Fine, fine. We're all ready for the sale tomorrow." Her mother's lips tightened, accentuating the fine lines. "Though why Jeannette imagines she's in charge, I don't know."

"You know how she is." Meredith kept her tone soothing, fearing the subject of Jeannette would lead inevitably to Jeannette's current guest. "She thinks nothing will go well if she doesn't have her hand in it."

Her mother sniffed, not mollified. "She thinks she knows more than anyone else, too. She actually had the nerve to ask me if you'd talked to Zach Randal yet. Nosy woman. I can't stand gossips."

If her father were here, he'd be exchanging a secret smile with Meredith about now. He'd known perfectly well that Margo was fully engaged in the silent, secret battle that went on among much of Deer Run's female population to be the first to know what their neighbors were thinking and doing. Or thinking about doing.

There didn't seem to be any useful comment she could make. "I'm going to change clothes before I settle down to work." She turned toward the stairs.

"Wait." Her mother straightened, moving her feet to the carpet. "You didn't tell me where you've been." There was a slightly sharper edge to her voice than her usual curiosity.

"I was up at the Hammond place. I spoke with Victor." Since she'd set up the bookkeeping system for the Hammond grocery stores, her mother wouldn't be surprised. And she had spoken to Victor, after all.

"Did you see Laura? How is she?" Mom, along with most of the village, was insatiably interested in Laura's frequent visits to rehab.

"She seemed fine." That was really a whopper, wasn't it? Laura was definitely not fine. "She showed me her roses, and they're going to send some flowers for the stand in the morning."

A few more steps, and she'd be on the stairs.

"Wait," her mother said again. "There's a bag inside the door. Something Rachel dropped off for you. That scrapbook you girls kept when you were little."

In other words, she'd checked the contents. Well, stopping her mother's curiosity was about as likely as stopping the wind from blowing.

"Thanks, I'll take it up with me." She slid the scrapbook out, handling it cautiously. The pages were browned and brittle after all these years.

"I suppose this means you're thinking about the Mast boy's drowning again." Her mother stood in the archway, one hand on the brass latch of the pocket door. "I don't know what you think you'll find out after all these years."

Meredith tried to mask her surprise. Was that just a general comment, or had her mother somehow learned what Sarah had asked of her?

"I'd just like to hold on to the scrapbook." She cradled it in her arms. "That's all."

"You weren't even here that night." Her mother went on as if Meredith hadn't spoken. "Spending the night with some of your cousins, as I recall. So you couldn't know anything about what happened. Any more than your father could. He was out that night, too."

She'd heard often enough how her mother had been alone in the house the night Aaron Mast had died not more than a hundred yards away. It was a frequent refrain when her mother didn't want to be left alone in the evening.

"That's true. I don't know anything about it." And she was beginning to think it was best that way. What right did she have to probe into other people's private grief? She ought to tell Sarah there was nothing to find and let the past rest.

Her mother nodded, but she didn't return to her chair. "When is that Randal boy leaving?" she asked abruptly.

Meredith's heart clenched at the sudden introduction of his name, although she hardly thought the man Zach was now deserved to be referred to that way.

"I don't know."

"Why not? You talked to him."

"He didn't say. He has some business to take care of. I suppose he'll leave when it's finished." And that was another piece of the past that she should lay to rest.

She walked quickly to the stairs. "I really have to get to work now, Mom. We'll talk later." She hurried up toward the sanctuary of her room, relieved not to hear her mother's plaintive voice behind her.

Once the door was closed she leaned against it, closing her eyes. Strangely enough, now that she could cut loose, she no longer felt the urge to cry.

Zach had made his feelings clear—he was glad she had refused to go away with him. So all the guilt she'd been holding tight had been unnecessary. He apparently considered that he'd had a narrow escape.

She should be happy. Unfortunately, she didn't seem able to convince her heart of that fact.

Meredith crossed the room, carrying the scrapbook, and slid it into a drawer of the maple desk Dad had bought for her when she outgrew the frilly pink bedroom of her childhood. The desk, along with the maple sleigh bed and chest of drawers, had been made by an Amish furniture craftsman, and the star quilt had been a gift from Sarah's mother, a little touch of her Amish heritage in a house that was otherwise decorated in her mother's taste.

As for the scrapbook, she'd study it later. Or not. Without thinking, she looked out the back window toward the dam, catching just a glimpse of the water through the trees.

Hadn't she already decided that poking about in the past was too hurtful? It was time she buried the events of that summer.

Meredith reached out, automatically straightening the milk-glass vase her father had won for her at the county fair when she was ten. It had stood on her desk ever since, filled with pens and pencils. Her hand rested on the desk blotter, and she frowned. She always kept it aligned with the front edge of the desk, but now it was pushed a good two inches back.

Still frowning, she let her gaze scan the desk surface, the bookcase, the dresser with its embroidered scarf. Her mother thought she was too methodical, too organized, as if that was a fault, or too masculine a trait. But she liked order, and she found it soothing to see things in their proper places...things like the hand mirror, which belonged on the right side of the dresser, not the left. And she'd never leave the top drawer slightly open like that, caught on a frill of lace.

She went to the dresser, her heart thudding uncomfortably, and yanked the drawer open. Someone had been in her room. Someone had disarranged things in his or her search.

She glanced at the window again, feeling as if a shadow had reached out of the past to touch the present.

But that was ridiculous. She didn't have to look very far to find out who had searched her room. No doubt it had been her mother, looking for evidence of her nonexistent affair with Zach.

She closed the drawer firmly. Irritation burned in her, urging her to confront her mother about this invasion of her privacy.

She fought back the indignation. Did she really want to open that subject with her mother? And did she want to deal with the inevitable consequences of a scene with her mother?

Better to do what she always did. Better to swallow her annoyance, put on a pleasant face and deny her feelings. She was getting almost frighteningly good at that.

MEREDITH CHECKED TO BE SURE there was still decaf in the coffeepot, in case anyone wanted a second cup, and switched off the light over the kitchen sink. Her image, reflected in the window, disappeared, and she stood looking out at the lawn and the strip of woods beyond as dusk drew in.

From the living room she could hear the chime of her mother's laughter. Dr. Bennett Campbell had stopped by, and the two of them were playing a game of dominos. As good an excuse as any, Meredith supposed, for an exchange of local gossip and the mild flirtation that had gone on between the two of them for years.

Bennett had closed down his medical practice a few years ago, but he was always ready to listen and sympathize with Mom's complaints. He'd describe himself as a family friend, probably, but Meredith had always believed he didn't care much for her. She was too sensible and practical, too much like her father. Bennett, ridiculously old-fashioned for his age, liked women who were frilly and flirtatious, and who at least pretended to be a bit helpless when there was a man around.

Still, she had to be grateful to Bennett for tonight's visit, since it removed the temptation to confront her mother about searching her room.

A flicker of movement from outside caught Meredith's eye, and she leaned forward for a better look. Someone had come down the drive, apparently, and was headed toward the path to the pond. A faint uneasiness touched her, moving like a breeze across her skin.

People did come through this way, even though it involved walking across their property. She wouldn't ordinarily say anything, but something about the way that figure drifted silently along…

Her breath caught. She recognized the shape and the movement. It was Laura Hammond.

What was Laura doing here? She rarely went out at night, and certainly not alone and on foot. The unease strengthened to concern. With a quick glance toward the door to the living room, Meredith slipped out onto the back porch.

Dusk drew in earlier now, and the air had cooled down from this afternoon's balmy seventies. She should go back for a flashlight and jacket, but something insisted she hurry. Laura was already disappearing into the trees.

Meredith walked swiftly across the back lawn. Daylight lingered enough here to make the way easily visible, but shadows gathered beyond, where the path wound toward the dam.

Laura had every right to go there, but at the risk of appearing a hopeless busybody, Meredith knew she couldn't ignore this visit. Certainly Victor didn't know Laura was heading for the spot where she used to meet Aaron, the place where Aaron died.

The woods closed around Meredith once she reached the path. She could call to Laura, but the same impulse that had compelled her to follow also urged her to silence.

A thought struck her, nearly taking her breath away. What if Laura was meeting someone else there, where she'd once met Aaron? Her step faltered. Well, if so, Meredith would have to hope she could slip away undetected.

Her sneakers made no sound on the soft earth, and only the faint rustle of the weeds on either side of the path disturbed the stillness.

A branch snapped somewhere off to her left, and her heart stuttered. *Foolish.* An animal, probably.

She could see the surface of the pool now, gleaming through the trees, and she slowed, coming to a cautious halt when she reached the edge of the clearing. She drew in a breath. Where was Laura? The path didn't lead anywhere else, but the clearing lay empty before her.

A sound drifted through the air—a kind of tuneless humming that started and stopped. As Meredith's eyes adjusted to the dark she spotted Laura, sitting on a log in the shadow of the big oak that overhung the dam. Her arms were wrapped around her knees, and she rocked back and forth, as if in time to some music only she could hear.

Meredith approached slowly, trying not to startle her. "Laura?"

Laura didn't turn, but the slightest movement of her shoulders acknowledged Meredith's presence.

"What are you doing out here by yourself?" Some instinct kept her voice soft, her movements slow.

She sat down next to Laura on the log, feeling the rough bark even through her khakis. Laura was wearing a short-sleeved sweater and a soft, full skirt—hardly the apparel for walking in the woods.

"I come…sometimes." Her words were as soft and fragmented as the tune she'd been humming. "I…" She seemed to lose focus for a moment. "I'm waiting."

Meredith pressed her hands against the log, grateful for the bite of the texture grounding her. If she really wanted to find out what Laura knew about Aaron's death, this might be the only opportunity she'd have.

"What are you waiting for?"

Laura's forehead puckered. "I don't remember."

She was on something, Meredith felt sure. The slightly slurred speech, the unfocused stare… Still, it might be a medication that had been prescribed for her. Even so, she shouldn't be out here alone, and the pity Meredith felt for her overwhelmed her desire to question the poor woman.

"It's getting chilly, and you don't have a jacket. Why don't you come in the house with me? I'll make you a cup of tea."

"That's very kind of you." From somewhere, Laura pulled up the appropriate response. "But I can't go yet. I have to tell him something."

"Tell who?" She thought she already knew the answer, and a chill settled inside her.

"Aaron, of course." Laura looked at her, an expression of surprise on her face. "You know that. You know I have to tell him."

Was Laura imagining that Meredith was one of her high school friends? Jeannette, maybe, who'd always been her best friend, even when they were teen-agers. She'd always thought Jeannette an odd choice of best friend for the most popular girl in the valley.

"I don't think he'd want you to wait out here in the cold, would he?" She took Laura's arm, attempting to get her to her feet. "Let's go back to the house."

"I can't." Laura rose, but her voice rose, too. "You know I can't. It's important. I have to tell him. It changes everything. I have to tell Aaron."

The chill seemed to expand, surrounding Meredith's heart. Laura wasn't talking about whispering a message to Aaron in the place he'd died. She was back there, twenty years ago, waiting for Aaron to meet her.

"Aaron? Where are you?" Laura called out, taking a step toward the dam and the foaming water.

Meredith caught her arm. "He's not here. He couldn't come tonight. You can tell him later." She tugged at her, suddenly desperate to get Laura back to lights and warmth and other people.

Laura strained toward the dam. Meredith held on, afraid of what Laura might do if she let go. She needed help, she couldn't cope with this alone—

The pressure on Meredith's hand stopped. Laura stared at the water. And then she buried her face in her hands, her body trembling as she began to weep soundlessly.

Meredith wrapped an arm around her and hustled her toward the path. "It's all right. Really. We'll soon get you home. Everything will be all right."

Nonsense words, and false besides. She didn't think everything was going to be all right for Laura for a long time, maybe not ever. But the words were meant to comfort, and maybe they did that, at least.

They stumbled up the path. It wasn't really wide enough for two, but Meredith was afraid to let go of the woman, so she walked through the weeds. Berry brambles caught at her pant legs, but she kept forging ahead, absurdly glad to see the lights of the house still on and even to see her mother and Bennett seated at the card table in the living room.

Bennett was a doctor. Maybe she should ask him for help with Laura.

But Bennett was also an incurable busybody, and if her mother saw Laura like this, it would be all over Deer Run by morning. Better just to put Laura in the car and run her home. Her mother would hear the car going out, of course, but Meredith could think of some explanation by the time she got back.

But she didn't have her keys. She'd have to go in the house for them, risk having her mother hear what was going on—

A light stabbed her in the face, and she lifted one hand to shield her eyes, clutching Laura with the other.

"What are you doing with Laura?" Jeannette lowered the flashlight she held, rushing toward them like an avenging angel.

"Keep your voice down unless you want my mother and Bennett Campbell out here," Meredith said in a furious whisper. "I was about to run Laura home."

Jeannette shielded the flashlight with her fingers, letting out enough light to examine Laura's face. The tears had stopped, thank goodness, but her face was still wet with them, and she'd begun humming again. Meredith's heart clenched with pity.

"My car's still out," Jeannette said abruptly. "I'll drive her."

Meredith nodded. She had no desire to face Victor with explanations. "I'll help you get her to the car."

Laura's humming had been replaced with a soft murmur of words Meredith couldn't understand. Did Jeannette? She glanced at Jeannette in the circle of light from the streetlamp as they crossed the road, but Jeannette's face was expressionless. Maybe she was used to this. Being Laura's best friend couldn't be an easy task.

Jeannette steered them to her car, which was parked at the curb, and opened the rear door. Wordlessly they helped Laura inside. She promptly slid over to lie down on the seat. Jeannette closed the door.

"I'll take it from here." She yanked the driver's door open. "Thank you." The words were an afterthought, apparently. She started the car and drove off.

Meredith shivered, rubbing her arms as she watched the red taillights recede down the nearly empty street. It didn't look as if anyone had noticed them. She'd better get inside before she was missed.

When she reached her own driveway again, she couldn't help glancing at Jeannette's place, and she sucked in a breath. She'd been wrong. Someone had noticed them. Zach stood in the upstairs window, and he was looking right at her.

Meredith turned and fled for the back door.

## CHAPTER FOUR

Zᴀᴄʜ ᴘᴜsʜᴇᴅ ᴀsɪᴅᴇ the frilly curtain in his bedroom to stare out at the street again. Frills—the place was full of them. Jeannette's taste ran toward what he supposed was High Victorian—fine for those who liked it, but he didn't.

The street told him exactly nothing. Meredith had vanished into her house. Really hers, as Jeannette had informed him over breakfast. Meredith's father had left everything to her, along with the responsibility of taking care of her mother. In any event, she hadn't reappeared since that little scene he'd witnessed earlier, and Jeannette hadn't come back.

Not that he cared, but it was odd. It was in a cop's nature to notice odd.

Meredith and Jeannette didn't care much for each other—that much was evident from the way Jeannette spoke of her. Yet they'd come out of the driveway next to Meredith's place together, supporting a third woman between them. They'd put her into the backseat of Jeannette's car and exchanged a few words. Jeannette drove off.

That was all, except that when Meredith looked

up and saw him, she'd run like a scared rabbit. Or like someone with something to hide.

Okay, he could call it a cop's instinct if he wanted to, but he suspected he was just too interested in anything to do with Meredith King. Just as he'd been back in high school, noticing her, but not letting her see that he was. At that point in his life he'd figured someone like Meredith was as far out of his reach as the moon, but it hadn't turned out that way. When she'd turned those big brown eyes on him and looked, really looked, at him, he'd been sunk.

Impatient with himself, he grabbed the room key and headed for the stairs. He'd been cooped up too long. He needed some exercise to help him get his mind on other things.

Deer Run was the kind of place where they rolled up the sidewalks at ten o'clock. Nothing was open at this hour except for the village's lone bar, and even it didn't seem to be doing much business for a Friday night. He passed the fire hall grounds, already set up for the auction tomorrow. Those Amish auctions had been going on when he was a kid—everybody in town turned out for them. The auction tent had already been erected, fluttering ghostly in the dark.

Zach turned aimlessly at the corner and headed along a residential street where the houses sat back from the road, their windows warm yellow rectangles behind which families went about their business.

Jeannette could have turned up one of these streets. He'd had no way of seeing her route from his vantage point. If she'd been taking someone home from Meredith's… But what sense did that make? And why had she and Meredith been supporting the woman between them?

He hadn't been able to identify the third woman, not at that distance and in the near dark. Anyway, he'd been gone too long to remember most of the denizens of Deer Run.

At least he could return Jeannette's curiosity about him with a few questions of his own, he supposed. Somehow he had a feeling it would enliven the breakfast table if he were to ask what she'd been doing.

Zach stepped off the curb, and then did a quick leap back when a car screeched to a halt right in front of him, close enough that he could feel the heat of it. A cop car, he noted.

He waited, tension running through him, not sure what was happening. A moment's pause, and then a big guy in uniform slid out of the driver's door. He stepped into the circle of light from the streetlamp, and Zach recognized him. Ted Singer. A year or two ahead of him in high school, a jock, inclined to resent or bully anyone who was different.

Zach had had his share of run-ins with Ted in those days, usually when he'd found the guy picking on someone who couldn't, or wouldn't, fight back. Ted had outweighed him, but Zach'd been quick, and he liked to think he'd given as good as he'd gotten.

Strange, that someone like Ted had ended up a

cop. Still, maybe he'd outgrown his bad habits since high school. After all, Jake Evans hadn't treated him as he'd expected.

A flashlight beam hit him in the face. "What are you doing here?"

Maybe Ted accosted every stranger to Deer Run that way, but somehow he doubted it.

"Taking a walk. How're you doing, Ted?" Zach made an effort to keep his tone easy, tamping down the temptation to snap back.

Singer took a step closer. He had a couple of inches on Zach, and if anything was even beefier than he'd been in high school. "Do I know you?"

Ted was pretending not to recognize him, even though everyone in town had to know he was back by now. If it wasn't pretense, Ted wasn't much of a cop. But no, he could feel the antagonism flowing toward him.

"Zach Randal." He waited, sure he knew what was coming next.

"Randal." Singer ground out the name. "It seems to me there's an outstanding theft charge against you, Randal. You come back to face the music?"

If he hadn't been so annoyed, he'd have laughed. Singer was doing a hackneyed imitation of a tough cop in an '80s film.

"If you remember the complaint, you must also remember that it was dropped." He considered pulling out his shield, but with the mood Singer was in, that might make things worse.

"Not sure I do." Singer jerked a thumb toward the patrol car. "Let's go back to the station while I run a check."

His jaw tightened, and it took an effort to unclench it. He held up both hands, palms open. "In that case, I'll just pull out my cell phone and call my attorney, Jake Evans. It'll be like old home week. We can talk about old times while Jake draws up a complaint against you. Should make for interesting reading for the chief when he comes on duty in the morning, right?"

Singer's hands clenched into fists. Zach could see the desire to take a swing and braced himself, fighting down the urge to react. *Don't start it. Whatever you do, don't start it.*

Singer loomed over him a moment longer. Then he moved back. "You take one step out of line and I'll land on you. That's a promise."

"I'll keep it in mind." Zach forced his voice to stay casual.

"You always were trash." Singer stalked to the car, slid in and pulled out with a shriek of tires. "People don't change," he called out over the noise.

Zach didn't move until the taillights disappeared around the corner. Funny. Singer certainly hadn't changed.

Zach's desire to take a walk had vanished, but he went on to the end of the block before turning back, just to prove he could.

He'd made an enemy. Not surprising, but that

hadn't been his intent in coming back. He'd wanted to clear the slate and walk away. Maybe he'd been naïve to think he could.

MEREDITH FOUND HER THOUGHTS straying as she tried to focus on the spreadsheet in front of her the next morning. Her mother had taken an early shift at the flower stand, so she was already at the fire hall grounds. She'd be in her element, sitting in the booth surrounded by flowers, chatting with everyone who passed by.

So this was a perfect time for Meredith to get caught up on her current project, if she could just manage to keep her thoughts on the figures and not on last night's curious events.

She couldn't help glancing out her office window. The room had once been a back parlor, and it had the same view as the kitchen window from which she'd spotted Laura last night. A shiver traced its way down her spine.

Was Laura recovered today? Would she even remember the things she'd said in Meredith's presence? Somehow she doubted it.

Jeannette's reaction hadn't surprised her. She'd been protective of Laura for as long as Meredith could remember. It was second nature for her to spring into action at the sight of her friend.

As for the discovery that Zach had been watching them... Well, she wouldn't have to explain the situation to Zach, because the chances were that she wouldn't see him again. He'd find some way of getting rid of the house that seemed such an albatross around his neck, and he'd leave.

If she did run into him— The pealing doorbell cut into her thoughts. She closed the file automatically, always aware of her clients' privacy concerns, and hurried toward the front door.

Victor Hammond stood on the porch, his image distorted and magnified by the glass medallion in the front door. Meredith's breath caught. Maybe she should have expected a visit from him after the incident with Laura. An echo of the panic she'd felt at the dam shivered through her. What was she going to say to Victor? Awkward didn't cover it, even with someone she'd known as long as Victor.

She swung the door open, mustering up a smile. "Victor, good morning." She stepped back. "Please, come in."

He stepped inside, running his finger around the collar of his sport shirt. His round face wore an expression of reluctant determination, like a kid about to climb into the dentist's chair.

"Thank you, Meredith. I won't take up much of your time. I noticed your mother was already at the stand when I dropped off the flowers."

"Yes. She always enjoys working the opening. I'm scheduled for a little later."

Was the implication that he wouldn't have stopped by if her mother had been here? Meredith led the way into the living room and gestured toward the sofa.

Victor adjusted the knees of his slacks as he sat, and then linked his hands loosely in a posture that should have looked relaxed but didn't.

"I wanted to thank you. Jeannette told me that it was you who found Laura last night." Somehow his tone invited her to explain just how that had come about. Well, that was natural enough, she supposed.

"I happened to glance out the kitchen window when I was doing the dishes, and I saw her going down the path." She paused. Explaining why she'd followed Laura was a bit touchier. "I was concerned. The dam..." He could fill in the blanks, couldn't he?

"The dam." He said the words heavily, and his somewhat pudgy face was drawn with strain. "I was afraid of that. It's always a sign that her condition is worsening when she becomes obsessed with the dam again."

"I see." Well, she didn't, not really. How could she? The only things Meredith knew about Laura's condition were the things everyone whispered about—the drugs, the alcohol, the visits to the rehab center.

Victor took out a handkerchief and mopped his forehead, then stared blankly at it as if not sure how it had come to be in his hand. The gesture shook Meredith. She'd been guilty of thinking about Laura as a piece of the puzzle to be solved, disregarding the widening circles of pain that still radiated out from Aaron's death.

"If people knew what grief their suicide would

cause, they'd never resort to it." His words were nearly an echo of Meredith's thoughts.

A wave of sympathy had her reaching across the space between them to pat his hand. "I'm so sorry. I didn't realize Laura was still so affected by Aaron's death."

That wasn't entirely true, was it? Well, she'd wondered about it, but she hadn't known for sure until last night.

"Is that what Laura said?"

The question had a sharp edge that startled Meredith, and she drew back. "She...she didn't really say anything that made much sense. I just had an impression that she was grieving."

"For Aaron?" Victor's jowls still drooped sadly, but his eyes focused on her with laserlike intensity.

"Well, I..." *Careful,* she told herself. *Tread lightly.* In addition to his place in a difficult situation, Victor was also one of her most lucrative accounts. "She didn't actually say that, but of course I know Aaron Mast died there, and that they were close at the time."

"Yes." Victor's gaze dropped, and he contemplated his hands. "Yes, they had a little romance that last summer."

A little romance. Laura and Aaron would have hotly denied that description, she suspected, sure that theirs was a love that would last a lifetime.

"It does seem odd that Aaron would kill himself, doesn't it?" she said tentatively.

Victor drew himself back against the sofa cushion. "No one knows for sure that it was suicide. But if it was, it certainly wasn't Laura's fault."

"No, of course not," she said hastily. "But you know how intense teenagers can be. If she felt she had to break up with him—"

"Laura had nothing to do with it." Victor's eyes flashed. "If anyone is saying she did, that person is lying."

"I'm sure you're right," she murmured, more than a little startled by his reaction. In company with the rest of Deer Run, she'd always thought Victor a bit inane—diffident and never quite sure of himself, either in regard to his wife or the business he'd inherited.

"Yes, well…" Victor seemed to subside into his usual vacuity. "I suppose it's possible that Aaron himself realized their relationship would never work. Amish and English isn't a happy mix." He stopped, flushing slightly as he obviously remembered that her parents' had been just such a mixed marriage. "I'm sorry. I didn't mean—"

"It's all right. Believe me, I know my parents' marriage wasn't entirely successful."

Victor fidgeted, as if he'd gotten himself into a situation he didn't know how to get out of. "If you do remember anything specific that Laura said, please give me a call. Her doctor would find it helpful, I know."

"Of course I will." Meredith's heart twisted for him. Poor Victor. He might seem ineffectual in most areas of his life, but who was she to make a judgment like that? At least Laura had inspired his devotion.

Victor stood. "Thank you, Meredith. I knew I could count on your good sense and your discretion."

Was that a plea? She had a feeling it was. "You can trust me not to gossip about Laura's visit to the dam."

"Thank you," he said again. He seized her hand quite suddenly and squeezed it, tears forming in his eyes.

Shame flooded through Meredith when she thought of the questions she'd asked Laura. She couldn't go on like this, creating problems for people who already had enough of their own. She'd have to tell Sarah that finding out more about Aaron's death was impossible.

THE FLOWER BOOTH was a good vantage point from which to watch all the comings and goings at the auction, Meredith realized. She perched on the kitchen stool someone had brought and propped her elbows on the booth's counter. During the morning rush there'd have been two or more people working, but the auction was in full swing now and she was alone in the booth. Things would pick up later, as people stopped to buy flowers on their way home.

Gawkers and serious bidders alike crowded the auction tent, leaving few customers at the moment for any of the other booths. Across from her, the white-haired woman running the Civic Club's hot dog stand was working a crossword puzzle, and the two teenage girls who'd been left in charge of the PTA's soda booth had their heads together, giggling.

Meredith could easily hear the rhythmic tones of Timothy Byler, the auctioneer, carried by the loudspeaker system. The two Amish schools would be well provided for if Timothy had anything to say about it.

The Amish bishop had thought long and hard before he'd given the okay for an Amish auctioneer to use the speakers. New technology was always studied carefully for its possible negative effect on the family or the church. But eventually the bishop had agreed, and Timothy's cheerful banter echoed through the fire hall grounds.

A couple walked slowly from the parking area toward the auction tent, and Meredith blinked. Victor and Laura—that was a surprise. She hadn't anticipated seeing Laura out in public after last night's misadventure.

Dismay flickered through Meredith at the thought of speaking to her. But after a quick glance, the couple started around the semicircle of booths in the opposite direction. Laura was probably no more eager for an encounter than she was.

There was a flutter of movement at the open flap of the auction tent—an Amish woman, tossing a quick word over her shoulder to the person behind her.

Not just any Amish woman. It was her cousin Sarah. She stopped a few feet from the tent, seeming intent on saying something to Samuel, her next older brother. The family always teased the two of them about being twins, close as they were in age.

Samuel would have known Aaron Mast well, having been in the same *rumspringa* group as the teenager. He'd probably be as disappointed as Sarah when Meredith told her there weren't going to be any answers about Aaron's death.

Still, it had to be done, and the sooner the better, so she could stop brooding about it. She was trapped in the flower booth at the moment, but if Sarah looked her way...

She didn't. Instead, Sarah turned sharply away from her brother and disappeared back into the tent. Samuel, his face set in a frown, followed her.

"What's wrong? Flower sales in the pits?"

Meredith jumped at the sound of the once-familiar voice. While she'd been concentrating on Sarah and Samuel, Zach had appeared, seemingly out of nowhere.

"Don't sneak up on me." She'd have busied herself with the flowers, except that it was painfully obvious that there wasn't a thing to do.

Zach's eyebrows slid upward. "Walked, not sneaked. There is something wrong, isn't there?"

"No." She brushed a dried leaf off the counter. "Can I sell you some mums to brighten up your room at the Willows?"

"It's bright enough already, thanks." He gave a fleeting grimace. "Does your problem have anything to do with what happened last night?"

"What do you mean?" She tried looking innocently unaware and suspected he saw right through her attempt.

"You and Jeannette—an unlikely pair if ever I saw one. You were helping a woman into Jeannette's car."

Her mind scrambled for a convincing story. Unfortunately she'd never been very good at lying. But if he didn't know who it was...

"Is this a sample of your police interrogation skills?" Maybe offense was the best defense.

Her question didn't seem to bother him. He just responded with the smile that still slid under her guard.

"A little friendly interest, that's all. What was Laura Hammond doing at your place, anyway?"

He'd seen them come out of the driveway, then. "I'm surprised you recognized her after all these years."

He shrugged. "I didn't at first, but it came to me after I thought about it. She and Jeannette were always great friends. Why was she at your house?"

"Were you watching my...my house?"

Zach's eyes flickered slightly at her question. "She wasn't at the house, was she?" He seemed to be putting the pieces together at lightning speed. "Was she at the dam?"

"How did you know? You've been gone for years. Has someone been talking?" Victor would hate it if word got around about Laura's visit to the dam, and he'd probably assume the rumor came from her.

"Relax, Meredith." He eyed her quizzically. "Even I remember where Aaron Mast drowned, and you told me once about the world you and Rachel created around him and Laura when you were kids."

She could feel her cheeks grow warm. "I can't believe I told you about that. It's like talking about an imaginary friend."

That made him smile again, and something that had been tense inside her began to relax.

"We told each other a lot of things," he said. He spoke lightly, but a shadow crossed his face, and she knew he was thinking about his father.

He'd talked, only once, about his father's abuse. They'd gone swimming at the county park, and she'd noticed the scar on his upper arm when he came out of the water. She'd asked him about it, light-hearted, expecting some tale of a crashed bicycle. The truth—that his father had slashed at him with a steak knife—had stunned her into silence. She'd been naïve, hardly realizing that such things happened, let alone in Deer Run.

"I guess we did." No doubt he still had that scar. If she touched his arm, she might feel it through his sleeve. She restrained herself, not sure where that simple gesture might lead.

"So Laura's still obsessed with Aaron's death after all this time." Zach would no doubt rather talk about Laura and Aaron than the other secrets they'd once shared. "I take it she has problems? Drugs? Alcohol? Psychological?" One eyebrow arched.

"I'm not sure what it is. Victor pretends she's going to a spa or to visit friends, and we all play along. She's been in some sort of treatment facility I don't know how many times. She'll seem all right for a while, and then something trips off the memories, and she slips back into whatever hole she's dug."

"What did it this time?" Zach was interested. He couldn't know that his question caused her pain.

"I did, I'm afraid." She took a breath, steadying herself. "Rachel and I, actually. Rachel came back to town in the spring, and when we got reacquainted, we started talking about that summer. Wondering about Aaron's death. There seem to be so many unanswered questions."

A frown wrinkled Zach's forehead. "The cops called it an accident, right?"

"They did." She shrugged. "When you're ten, you accept what grown-ups say at face value. But once Rachel and I started remembering that summer... well, it just seemed so unlikely. What could Aaron possibly have been doing alone there that would result in his drowning? It would be understandable if it was a gang of kids partying, maybe daring each other to do something stupid, but there was never a hint that anyone was with him."

"What was his blood alcohol?"

She blinked, staring at him. "I have no idea. No one ever said he'd been drinking. We certainly never saw him take a drink. After he was found, Chief Burkhalter called it an accident."

"Surely there must have been some investigation. I know Deer Run doesn't have the most up-to-date police force, but even so…" He stopped and gave her an apologetic smile. "Sorry. I'm reacting as a cop instead of a friend. Even if you and Rachel started talking about Aaron's death, I don't see how you can blame yourself for Laura's problems."

"We asked questions." Her fingers linked together, twisting. "And Rachel found a note someone had left for Aaron in the hiding place he and Laura used, telling him that Laura was going to break up with him. We tried to keep it quiet, but you know how word gets around in Deer Run." She pressed her hands flat on the counter, forcing herself to stop twisting them. "Sometimes I think there must be microphones in the walls."

"I could almost believe it." His lips curved just a little. "But even if word got out about the note…"

"It seems to give Aaron a reason for suicide, you see. Sarah, one of my Amish cousins, says that now his parents fear he killed himself, and it's causing them so much pain. She wanted me to try and find something that would reassure them."

"You talked to Laura?" His cop's mind leaped ahead of hers, following the trail to its obvious conclusion.

"I'm afraid my meddling stirred it all up again for Laura. When I found her at the dam last night…" A shiver went through her despite the warmth of the afternoon sun. "Honestly, she was talking so wildly it frightened me. I can't do it. I'm going to tell Sarah there's nothing else to try."

"There's always something to try, even in a cold case," he said, and she could practically see his mind ticking away. "I'd love to get my hands on whatever records exist from the time."

"I'm afraid that will never happen." She could just imagine Chief Burkhalter's response if she asked for such a thing. But still, Zach's expression of interest moved her. "And I can't be responsible for hurting anyone else. But thanks." She smiled at him, all the enmity vanished and she actually thought they might be friends again.

A flicker of movement caught her eye, resolving itself into Jeannette Walker, who was bearing down on them intently. Zach seemed to sense her approach at the same time and drew back from the counter.

"I see you two are getting reacquainted." Jeannette's comments always sounded acidic, and this was no exception.

Meredith gave her a cool smile. "It's always nice to renew old friendships."

"Victor stopped to see you today." Jeannette was abrupt. If she intended to repeat Victor's thanks, she was going about it oddly. "If he didn't tell you this, I will. Leave Laura alone."

Meredith could only gape at her for a moment, unprepared for a frontal attack. "I don't know what you mean. If I hadn't gone after her when I saw her headed for the dam last night—"

"She wouldn't have been there at all if you and that friend of yours hadn't stirred up memories that are better forgotten." Jeannette clutched her oversized bag in one hand as if she'd like to take a swing with it. "I'm warning you. Stop poking your nose into what happened to Laura and Aaron, or you're likely to find out something you won't want to know."

Meredith stiffened. "I'm sorry if I reminded Laura of a painful episode in her life." She ought to tell Jeannette she had no intention of pursuing the subject, but Jeannette might think she'd succeeded in intimidating her. "But there's nothing I fear about the past."

Fear, no. Regret, maybe. She carefully didn't look at Zach.

"Don't you?" Jeannette's penciled eyebrows lifted. "But then, you don't know everything there is to know about your sainted father, now, do you?" She turned and stalked away, leaving Meredith staring after her, mind reeling.

"Merry?" Zach's use of his pet name for her nearly shattered her precarious control. "You're not taking that poisonous female seriously, are you?"

She could only stare at him. "What did she mean? My father didn't have anything to do with Laura and Aaron. And he never did anything that I'd be ashamed of."

"Forget her." Zach's hand closed over hers in a

firm, comforting grip. "She's just trying to scare you into dropping it. And since you've already decided to do just that, it doesn't matter what she says."

Meredith shook her head, the truth crystallizing in her mind. "No. Don't you see? I can't give up on it now, not after what Jeannette implied. I have to prove my father didn't do anything to be ashamed of."

Jeannette probably had no idea what she'd done, but she'd just made it impossible for Meredith to stop searching for answers, no matter how much she wanted to.

## CHAPTER FIVE

ZACH TOLD HIMSELF it was time he pulled back. Meredith's choices weren't his business, and maybe they never had been. He couldn't let himself get sucked into this particular drama.

All logical thoughts. But the chanting of the auctioneer and the hum of the crowd receded to a muted background, and the only reality seemed to be the hurt in Meredith's face. His hand moved without volition, touching hers where it was clenched on the countertop.

"You can't let Jeannette's poisonous attitude push you into something you don't want to do." The counter was a barricade between them, reminding him of all the other barriers that existed. "The woman's an expert at saying what she knows will sting."

Meredith's eyes seemed to regain their focus. "Do you remember her, or are you just that good a judge of character?"

"A little of both." If he kept Meredith talking, maybe he could banish that lost look from her eyes. "I've run across enough people like Jeannette to know better than to take her seriously. She's the type who relishes knowing the negative about others, just so she can feel superior."

He'd certainly always given the people of Deer Run plenty of fodder for looking down on him. Skipping school, fighting… A little petty theft when there hadn't been any food in the house. And then there were the things he'd been blamed for even if he hadn't done them. *Stay detached,* he reminded himself.

"I don't care what she says about me, but I won't let her get away with slandering my father." Anger sparked in Meredith's eyes. "How would you feel if it was your father?"

His lips twisted wryly. "There's nothing she could say about my old man that wouldn't be true."

Meredith sucked in a breath. "I'm sorry. I shouldn't have said that."

"Forget it." He made an effort to shrug off the words. "Being here just brings up a ton of bad memories."

She stared at him for a long moment. "I hope they aren't all bad."

"No." His voice roughened. Their eyes met. Held. Awareness seemed to shimmer in the air between them.

"I hope I'm not late, Meredith." The woman who bustled up to the booth was vaguely familiar. Elderly, her hair done in tight white curls and her eyes bright with curiosity, she looked from him to Meredith.

"Helen." Meredith's smile was artificial, but

maybe the woman didn't recognize that. "No, you're right on time. It's been pretty quiet." She lifted the flap in the counter, allowing the woman to go behind it as she slipped out. "It's all yours. Unless you need me to help..."

"Goodness, no. You young people go and enjoy yourselves." She waved her hands at them, shooing them away. "I'm sure you need some time to catch up. It's nice to see Zach after all these years."

Did everyone in Deer Run remember him? Apparently so. He caught Meredith's gaze and they exchanged a look of complete understanding. It startled him. Apparently they could still achieve that instant, wordless communication.

For an instant he thought Meredith was going to embark on something—explanation or denial, maybe? But then she smiled and turned away from the booth.

Zach fell into step with her. "Okay?"

"Helen didn't mean anything. Or at least, it was kindly meant."

"Just intrusive," he said. "But she didn't seem to be assuming I'm a bum."

"Of course not." She glanced at him. "Sorry you got caught up in this difficulty with Laura. I've been friends with these people for years, and I can't detach myself. But it's not your concern."

Just what he'd been telling himself. It was his cue to walk away and keep on going. He didn't want to.

"No problem. How about sharing a funnel cake, for old times' sake?"

Her step slowed, and he could almost read the emotions that skittered rapidly across her face.

"Still embarrassed to be seen with me?"

"I've never been embarrassed." Meredith shot the words back.

No, she never had been, even when people stared and whispered when they walked into a school dance together.

"All right. One funnel cake." She nodded toward the cement-block fire hall. "It's over by the building."

They fell into step again, and he ignored the small voice in the back of his mind that insisted that this was a bad idea. "While we're eating, you can tell me why Jeannette's so hell-bent on protecting Laura Hammond."

Meredith's lips pressed together, and she strode toward the food stand. He kept up, biding his time.

The funnel cakes were being made by an Amish woman who gave him a wary look before greeting Meredith warmly.

"I can make you two funnel cakes, *ja?*"

"Just one, thanks, Sarah. I couldn't eat more than half." Meredith glanced at him. "Unless you want a whole one."

He disclaimed any desire to eat an entire plateful of fried, sugar-dusted dough on his own.

The woman began pouring batter through a funnel into the bubbling oil, turning it in a circular motion to produce the twisty confection. His memories moved sluggishly. Meredith had a bunch of Amish relatives. This must be one of them, apparently the cousin who'd stirred up Meredith's need to know about Aaron Mast's death.

He studied her face as she drained the golden treat, transferred it deftly to a paper plate and sifted powdered sugar over the whole thing. It wasn't always easy to judge an Amish woman's age, but he'd guess her to be about ten years older than Meredith. Of an age, then, to have been Aaron Mast's contemporary. Meredith hadn't really explained what her interest was in that long-ago tragedy.

A question he should ignore, he supposed, except that he couldn't turn off his cop's brain any more than he could stop the instincts that went along with it.

He waited with as much patience as he could muster until they'd moved beyond earshot of the booth. One bite of the funnel cake reminded him both of how sweet and how messy they were. He tried without success to brush the powdered sugar from his fingers.

Something that was almost a giggle escaped Meredith. "Resign yourself to being covered with sugar. I have some wipes in my bag for just this contingency."

"You're like the Scouts, always prepared." He watched her face, enjoying her answering smile. Too bad to spoil the moment with questions, but he couldn't seem to stop himself.

"So that was your cousin, the one who expects you to prove Aaron didn't kill himself."

Meredith nodded. "Sarah. I don't suppose you would have known her."

"No. But I remember that your mother was always trying to keep you away from your father's side of the family."

"She still is." Meredith pressed her lips closed for an instant, as if she regretted voicing that particular truth. "Sarah just wants to know what really happened."

"Why?" He asked the question bluntly. "I mean, why does it matter so much to her after all this time?"

"People have been talking about what happened to Aaron again, and this rumor of suicide has been gaining strength. It hurts people—his parents, Sarah—"

"Again, why Sarah? What was her connection with him?"

Meredith blinked. "He was a friend. More than a friend, before Aaron became infatuated with Laura. Her first love, I suppose. They say you never forget your first love." She looked suddenly as if she'd like to unsay those words, and her color heightened.

In his case, the old saying was right, but maybe he'd better not go there. That would really be playing with fire.... Another cliché that was rooted in truth.

Meredith was staring intently at the nearly forgotten plate of funnel cake. He suspected she was relieved when he didn't respond.

When she glanced up again, the color had faded.

"You mentioned something earlier about there being ways to investigate a cold case."

"Maybe I should have kept my mouth shut."

She shook her head, smiling a little. "You may as well tell me. I can't give up on it now, so if you have any ideas, I'd like to hear them."

He could read between the lines easily enough where Meredith was concerned. She had adored her father, and she wouldn't let Jeannette's implied accusation rest.

"If I were looking into it, I'd start with anyone who might have seen something that night." He raised an eyebrow. "Your house is the only one that directly overlooks the dam, though."

"I wasn't there. I was staying overnight with one of my cousins. And Dad had gone back to the store to work."

"Your mother never mentioned seeing anything?"

Meredith shook her head. "Whenever she spoke of Aaron's death, it was only to fret about having been left alone in the house that night."

He could imagine. "What about your neighbors? Have you ever talked to them about it?"

"No, I haven't. But I will. What else?" She seemed to have a renewed sense of purpose.

Much as he distrusted where that might lead her, Zach couldn't help admiring her perseverance. Along with a few other attributes.

He forced his thoughts back to business. "Lacking the ability to look at the reports of the investigation, I suppose I'd want to talk to Aaron's friends. He must have confided in someone about his relationship with Laura."

Meredith nodded. "I can find out from Sarah who he was close to. As far as Jeannette is concerned—"

"Why don't you let me tackle Jeannette?" He heard himself making the offer even as one part of his mind told him he was crazy.

"You... That's good of you, but I'm sure you don't want to get involved in this."

Right. "She'd just try to needle you if you talk to her. Let me see if I can get an idea of what she's thinking about, if anything."

"Thank you." She looked into his face, as if searching to be sure he was being honest. "I'm not sure how I'd confront her." She glanced past him and stiffened. "There's my mother. I should go."

He grasped her hand. "Meet me tonight. I'll let you know how I made out."

"I can't." She tugged at her hand, and he suspected she was frantic to avoid the kind of scene her mother was capable of putting on.

"Would you rather I came and knocked on the door?" He'd get a certain amount of pleasure out of doing just that, except that he knew Meredith would be the one dealing with the aftermath.

She looked as if she'd argue, but then she shrugged. "Where?"

"How about the dam, around nine? I'd like to have

a look at the spot." He almost said crime scene, but it wasn't that, as far as he knew.

Meredith nodded, pulling her hand free. In a moment she was gone.

He strolled on in the direction they'd been headed, detouring to toss the paper plate in a trash can. He would not look back to see Meredith with her mother.

But that didn't keep him from visualizing Meredith's face. Or from wondering how he'd gotten so far away from what he'd intended to do.

FORTUNATELY HER MOTHER hadn't caught a glimpse of Meredith talking to Zach, so Meredith was able to get home from the auction without a hassle. Determined to follow up on Zach's suggestions as quickly as possible, she found a skirt of her mother's that needed to be hemmed. That would make a reasonable excuse. Meredith cut through the gap in the hedge between her house and Rebecca Stoltzfus's, her mind busy with every possible approach to Lainey's great-aunt.

Not that Meredith needed an excuse to drop in on the elderly Amish woman. Rebecca loved company, and she was always so happy to see Meredith that she felt guilty for not stopping by more often.

Rebecca was in her usual seat—a rocker placed close to the front window, where she got enough light for hand sewing and also had a fine view of the comings and goings on Main Street. She beckoned for Meredith to come in, smiling broadly.

The front door stood wide to the warm September

day. Meredith pulled the wooden screen door open and stepped inside.

The Stoltzfus house was smaller and simpler than theirs, but it dated from the same era, with its wide woodwork and floors faded to a honey brown. An archway led into the living room where Rebecca spent most of her time these days.

"Ach, Meredith, it's so *gut* to see you. I didn't think to have company until after the auction." Rebecca put aside the small black pants she was mending, no doubt for one of her countless relatives. "*Komm,* sit." She gestured to the second rocker that was conveniently placed next to hers for a chat with her frequent visitors.

"I slipped away after I finished working in the flower booth," Meredith said, bending to kiss Rebecca's cheek, still as firm as a small red apple despite her eighty years. "I wanted to drop off a skirt of my mother's to be hemmed if you have time."

"For sure," Rebecca said, smoothing the tweed wool in her hands. "A pretty color. Your *mamm* always wears such nice shades."

The skirt was a soft coral, much lighter and brighter than the dark maroon of the plain dress Rebecca wore with her black apron. Like most Amish women, she'd switched to the darker colors in midlife.

"I thought maybe I'd see you at the auction today." Meredith leaned back in the rocker, wondering how she was going to get the conversation headed in the right direction.

"So many people offered to take me, but you know my legs just don't work so well as they used to." Rebecca rubbed her knee. "I'd just as soon sit here and watch the folks go by."

Rebecca used her windows the way most *Englisch* used their televisions—to provide constant entertainment. That was all the more reason why Zach's comment had been spot-on. Rebecca was more likely than most to have seen something the night Aaron died.

Meredith could hardly plunge into questioning her without some buildup, though. "I think I spotted one of your quilts up for sale today. A Tumbling Blocks pattern, wasn't it?"

"*Ja,* I sent along two quilts for the sale. A Tumbling Blocks and a Nine Patch." Rebecca's eyes twinkled. "With all the *kinder* my great-nieces and nephews keep having, I must support the school, that's certain sure."

"I'm sure the quilts will bring a good price with all the people who are there." She hesitated for a moment. "Have you heard anything from Lainey recently?"

Lainey had been ten the last time Meredith saw her—sent to Deer Run to stay with a virtually unknown Amish great-aunt while her much-divorced mother embarked on matrimony once again. Most Amish had kin who had jumped the fence to the

*Englisch* world in search of another life, just as her father had done.

"Ach, *ja,* I had a letter from her chust last week." Rebecca's face brightened, her keen blue eyes shining. "She is living in St. Louis now, doing some work in advertising, she says."

"I hope it's something that uses her gift for drawing." That was what she remembered most about Lainey from that summer—a vivid imagination coupled with a pencil that could create a scene in a few lines while she and Rachel looked on in amazement.

"She was *sehr gut* at drawing, wasn't she? I remember that from the summer she was here." Rebecca's eyes grew misty as she seemed to look back through the years.

"I wish we'd stayed in touch. We did write for a time, but it seemed she kept moving around." Probably Meredith should have tried harder, but life had moved on, even though that summer had never entirely faded from her memory.

Rebecca opened the drawer of the sewing cabinet that sat against the wall. "I don't keep this out, but I like having it here where I can look at it." She drew out a photograph and handed it to Meredith.

No, she wouldn't keep it out. The Amish didn't display things "for pretty" and they didn't believe in having photographs taken. But Rebecca obviously cherished this recent image of her *Englisch* great-niece.

Lainey leaned back against a cluttered desk, her

face caught in a half smile. Her mass of curly dark hair was pulled back from her face and fastened at the nape of her neck, and that was surely a drawing pencil tucked behind her ear. She wore jeans and a print tunic in vivid colors, and her silver-and-turquoise earrings dangled nearly to her shoulders. She was a far cry from the ten-year-old tomboy Meredith had known, and yet she felt she'd have recognized her anywhere.

"She's beautiful. And she looks happy." Meredith glanced at Rebecca, hoping she'd said the right thing.

"*Ja,* she is." Rebecca took the picture back, caressing it with a wrinkled hand before returning it to the drawer. "I wish St. Louis wasn't so far away."

Not far on a plane, Meredith thought but didn't say. It wasn't her business whether or not Lainey visited her great-aunt.

"It would be nice to see her again." Again she hesitated, not sure how to go on. "I've been thinking a lot about that summer we spent together."

"*Ja,* because of Rachel coming home." Rebecca nodded, obviously seeing through what she didn't say. "The three of you were inseparable that summer, following Aaron Mast around like puppies."

"You knew that? We thought we were being so sneaky."

"Ach, for sure I knew it. And I knew you wouldn't come to any harm with Aaron. He was a fine young man, even if he was foolish enough to take up with that *Englisch* girl." Her face was touched by sorrow.

"Rachel and I were saying it seemed as if our summer ended when Aaron died," Meredith said. "And you're right, it was Rachel coming back to Deer Run that made me remember so much." She forced herself to go on. "And to start wondering about what happened to Aaron."

Rebecca eyed her with a certain amount of reserve, it seemed. "Aaron's drowning was an accident. It was God's will."

That was the Amish response to sorrow. It was God's will. She hated to mention the possibility of suicide, but if the Amish community was talking about it, surely Rebecca would have heard.

"I understand from my cousin Sarah that there's a rumor going around that maybe Aaron killed himself."

"*Ja,* I have heard that." Rebecca's gaze focused on Meredith's face. "People are saying there was a note of some kind that Rachel found."

Meredith nodded. Better to tell the whole thing than to talk around it. "We discovered that Aaron and Laura used to leave notes for each other behind a loose board in the covered bridge. A note was still there after all this time, but it was an anonymous one. It was written to Aaron, telling him that Laura was going to break up with him."

Rebecca stared down at her lap, absently smoothing her apron. Then she glanced up at Meredith. "Why have you come to me?"

For a moment Meredith couldn't speak. Then

she found her voice. "People are saying that maybe Aaron was so distraught he killed himself. Sarah asked me to look into it. To try and prove that he didn't, for her sake, and for his parents' sake."

Rebecca seemed to be waiting for something.

"I thought there might be something you remembered from that night," Meredith said. "Your house has as good a view of the dam as ours does. If you saw anyone coming or going, it might help me find answers."

Still Rebecca didn't speak. She seemed intent on the movement of her fingers, pleating and repleating her apron. Finally she looked up.

"I did not see anything that night. Sarah and the Mast family must accept what happened as God's will." She sounded as if she'd made up her mind.

"Even if they never know the truth?"

"Even then. Even not knowing is trusting God."

Somehow she'd thought Rebecca was going to say something that would lead to an answer. It seemed she was wrong.

But Rebecca wasn't finished. She leaned forward to put her hand over Meredith's. "It's right for us to bear one another's burdens. But we can't blame ourselves for the decisions other people make." She leaned back again, closing her lips into a firm line.

That was an odd bit of philosophy coming from an Amish woman, and Meredith couldn't help feeling that there was something left unsaid.

But Rebecca turned the subject firmly to the proper length for the skirt, and Meredith knew that whatever Rebecca might suspect, she wouldn't speak of it.

# CHAPTER SIX

MEREDITH STEPPED OUT the back door and eased it closed behind her. Her mother had been tired from the auction, and it hadn't taken much persuading to convince her to let Meredith tuck her into bed to watch her favorite sitcom. When Meredith checked on her a half hour later, she'd been sound asleep, the remote still in her hand.

Meredith pulled her tan jacket around her against the chill evening air and slid a flashlight into her pocket. Her mother was unlikely to wake. Still, it was wise not to switch the light on until necessary.

Going down the steps to the lawn was like descending into a dark pool. Annoyed with herself, Meredith shrugged away the image. Her eyes were adjusting already. Fitful clouds obscured the quarter moon and then moved on. She could do without the flashlight until she reached the path.

Next door, Rebecca Stoltzfus's house was dark. Rebecca kept Amish hours—early to bed and up with the sun. Beyond her place, a glow came from Rachel's bed-and-breakfast, most likely from the family room in the rear of the house. Colin might be there with Rachel, planning their future together although he, like Meredith, had an ailing parent to take care of.

Meredith crossed the lawn, moving more confidently as shapes emerged from the darkness—the birdbath, the circular bed of dwarf marigolds, the lawn chairs she hadn't put away for the winter yet. She was a bit early, but Zach might be there already, waiting for her. She felt a bit like the teenager she'd been, sneaking out to meet him in the first rebellion of her otherwise responsible life.

Zach had struggled not to laugh at her nervousness the first time she'd slipped out to meet him under the screening branches of the weeping willow tree in the back yard. But when he'd seen how upset she was, he'd put his arm around her, snuggling her close, and her guilt had evaporated. She'd tried to be open about her friendship with Zach, but her mother hadn't listened. She'd had a choice between giving him up or seeing him behind her parents' backs, and it still surprised her that she'd found the courage to disobey.

She'd nearly reached the garage when she heard… what? Meredith froze. There had been some alien sound she didn't expect on an autumn night, but it was gone before she could identify it. She waited, but there was no recurrence. An animal, she told herself, as afraid of her as she was of it.

The cloud passed over the moon's face again, so Meredith switched on the flashlight, letting the light seep through her fingers. It was unlikely that Mom could spot the light from her bedroom, even if she woke and looked out, but Meredith had no desire to set anyone else in town talking.

Odd, that she and Zach had never met here when they were teenagers, probably because the dam was linked too closely in her mind to Laura and Aaron's tragic love. Still, it made sense to talk there tonight. She could be back at the house in minutes, and no one was likely to spot them together.

Darkness gathered under the trees as Meredith reached the woods. Shivering a little, she turned the flashlight on again. Its yellow beam seemed feeble against the dark, as if the air was dense enough to repel it. Rachel had talked once of seeing a light flickering at the dam from her bedroom window. Though Rachel denied it, Meredith knew it had frightened her. They were both easily spooked by the place.

She and Lainey had sneaked out one night and followed Aaron to the dam, tiptoeing and whispering, trying not to giggle. Funny, how the giggling had died when they actually spotted Aaron and Laura. They hadn't been kissing. They'd just been standing, looking into each other's eyes, holding hands.

Lainey had nudged her, she remembered. They'd exchanged one look and then scurried back the way they'd come. Even then, they'd sensed that some things weren't meant for other people's eyes.

The path ended at the clearing. Meredith half expected Zach to be there waiting, but a quick flash

of the light showed her otherwise. Well, he'd come
soon. She eyed the sullen surface of the pond and
fought back a shiver. She didn't like it here.

A branch cracked, the sound as sharp as a shot
in the still night air. She spun toward the path. It
would be Zach.

He didn't appear, and she moved a few steps toward the entrance to the trail. "Zach?" She kept her
voice low, not eager to advertise her presence. "Is
that you?"

No one answered, but a faint swish sounded, as if
someone had brushed against a branch. Meredith's
fingers tightened on the flashlight. If it was Zach—
But Zach wouldn't be playing games with her.

A shiver went down her spine. Who was there
with her in the dark?

The silence stretched until she couldn't stand it.
Better to move than to stand there frozen and wait
for someone to come to her.

She took a few quick steps down the path, swinging the flashlight up. Something moved ahead of her,
a figure, dark clothes, face invisible.

Meredith choked on a gasp, trying to focus the
light on the figure's face, trying to think which way
to run—

A hand grasped hers, turning the beam of light
aside. She yanked at it, unable to find her voice, she
should scream, she should run—

*"Was ist letz?"*

At the sound of the soft Pennsylvania Dutch words

the fear went out of her, leaving her limp, and she knew who it was. "Samuel? What are you doing?"

The grip on her wrist didn't loosen, and her tension seeped back. Samuel was her cousin, but how well did she really know him as an adult? She tugged at her wrist.

"Samuel, let go."

He ignored her words. "I must talk to you."

"So talk." Fear made her voice brittle. "You don't have to scare—"

Her words were lost as Zach shot out of the dark, barreling into Samuel and yanking him away from her.

"What happened? What's going on? Did he hurt you?" The urgency in Zach's voice touched unexpected depths of response, and Meredith sucked in a breath before she could speak.

"I'm all right. It's just my cousin Samuel." She discovered she was still holding the flashlight, and she flicked it on. "Samuel, you remember Zach Randal, don't you?" Ridiculous, to be standing here in the dark performing introductions.

Samuel gave a curt nod. "*Ja.* I remember."

"You said you wanted to talk to me," she prompted, every trace of fear gone now that Zach stood so close.

"To tell you something," Samuel said. "To tell you to drop this foolishness of looking into why Aaron Mast died."

She could only stare at him for a moment. "But…

Sarah is the one who involved me to begin with. She asked me to find out."

"She shouldn't have." Samuel's voice was gruff, and she wished she could see his face more clearly.

"She wants to be at peace about Aaron," she said. "You and Sarah have always been so close. You must understand that."

Even in the dim light she could see his face tighten as if in pain. "No. Sarah will be better off if she never knows the truth." He turned away, brushed past them and disappeared down the path.

ZACH DECIDED HE'D be better off not looking too closely at why he'd reacted so strongly when he'd seen that dark figure looming over Meredith. "Look, maybe we should put this conversation off. If you're upset—"

"I'm fine. Samuel just startled me, that's all. He certainly didn't mean to scare me."

"You sure of that?" He reached out to touch her arm and then thrust his hand into his pocket instead.

"Positive." She seemed to be trying hard to convince herself. "I've known him all my life. He was practically Sarah's shadow since they were so close in age."

"He's a man now." Big, hefty, with the kind of muscles men developed when they did hard physical labor every day.

Meredith seemed to shrug that off, or maybe she didn't catch his meaning. She glanced toward the house, visible from where they stood. "We'd better go. I don't want to be out too long."

Zach followed her through the trees toward the dam, his memories of the place hazy. It was funny that the local kids hadn't hung out there, even when he was a teenager. Nobody talked about it—they just didn't go there.

His foot kicked something that rattled metallically, and he bent to pick up a beer can. Maybe times had changed. He tossed it into a thicket of brambles.

They stepped from the band of trees into the clearing by the pond, and Zach swung the beam of his flashlight around. The water flowing over the three-foot-high dam made a ruffle of white even in the dimness, and the pond was an ominous patch of darkness beneath it. But even as he thought that, the moon slipped from behind the clouds and laid a silvery path across the water.

Meredith made her way to a rough wooden bench. He sat down next to her and patted it. "Was this always here?"

"It's fairly recent. Colin McDonald's dad comes down here to fish since he retired, so Colin knocked this together to give him a place to sit."

He remembered Colin from school. One of the "in" crowd—the kind of person who had it easy. Like Jake, his father had had a business all ready for him to step into.

"I hear Colin's running the real estate office now," he said, keeping the rest of his thoughts to himself.

Meredith nodded, staring out at the pond. "It wasn't exactly what Colin had in mind for his life, but after his mother died, his dad started to go downhill quickly, so Colin came home to take charge."

Maybe even the golden boys like Colin didn't always get everything they wanted. He studied Meredith's face, relaxed now. He didn't want to bring the strain back to her expression, but he wasn't satisfied with her explanation of Samuel, not by a long shot.

"Look, we need to talk about your cousin. What was he doing sneaking around here at night if he just wanted to deliver a message?"

"Avoiding my mother." Meredith turned from her study of the pond to focus on his face instead. "Like us. Maybe you don't remember, but my mother prefers to ignore the Amish side of the family."

"Not posh enough for her?"

"Something like that. Anyway, I did see him at the auction today, but he had his family with him, and he wouldn't have been able to talk without them hearing. He probably intended to come to the back door and attract my attention, but saw me out here."

That made sense. It was what they were doing, after all. Avoiding Margo King was apparently a popular sport in Deer Run.

"Why wouldn't he want you to do what Sarah asked?"

Meredith's forehead wrinkled with concern. "I don't know, unless he's afraid that Sarah will be even more upset by the answers, assuming I actually find any. He's always been protective of her."

"What was his relationship with Aaron?"

Meredith blinked. "What are you implying?"

"Nothing. Relax. I'm not accusing your cousin of anything. I'm wondering if he knows more than he's saying, that's all. Would Aaron have confided in him?"

She seemed to accept that at face value. "I wish I knew. Obviously I'll have to talk to Sarah again." She ran her hand back through her hair, pushing it behind her ear in the familiar gesture. "I can't do it tomorrow, because Sarah is busy with church and family on Sunday. Monday I have to be in Williamsport on business, but I can stop and see her on the way back."

"I thought you worked from home." Where her mother was a constant interference, he'd guess.

"Mostly, yes, but I have to make some site visits. I'm doing an employee health and welfare handbook for a new client, and that means spending hours at the company."

"You like doing that?" She didn't sound especially enthused.

"It's not my favorite part of the job, no. I'd rather work with figures." Her smile flickered. "They're easier to understand."

He studied her face. Was this life really what she wanted? "Why here?" he said. "With your skills, you could work anywhere. Why Deer Run?"

"Why not Deer Run?" She said it lightly, but her eyes evaded his. "It's home."

"I remember a girl who dreamed of seeing the world. What happened to her?" A girl who had encouraged him to dream big plans for the future. He remembered that, as well.

Her expression didn't change, but he thought she winced very slightly.

"She grew up." She turned, looking out at the water again, and linked her hands around her knee. "I was in my freshman year of college when my father got sick. Mom couldn't cope, so I had to come home." Her voice trembled a little on the words, and she seemed to steady herself. "He wanted to die at home, so I had to make that work."

"You. Not your mother." That was Margo, shoving her responsibility off on her daughter.

"She has a heart condition. She couldn't manage." Defensiveness threaded Meredith's voice. "Anyway, I wanted to." Her lips pressed together for a moment. "He left everything to me, and he asked me to promise I'd take care of my mother, just as he had."

Zach wanted to rage at her—to insist that John had had no right to ask her to give up her life for Margo's sake. But he knew it wouldn't do any good. She was held here as tightly as a princess in a tower, shackled by her own sense of responsibility.

Meredith straightened, seeming to feel there was nothing else to be said on that subject. "What about

Jeannette? Were you able to get anything out of her about my dad?"

"Not much. She doesn't trust me—no reason why she should. Even when I hinted that I had reason to dislike your father, she didn't say much." And what she did say would only make Meredith feel worse.

"Was that really necessary?" Her eyes narrowed.

"Can you think of a better way to get her talking? She was ready to believe I'd come back nursing a grudge for the way I was treated here."

Meredith studied his face. "That would be a logical assumption."

"Only if I were still a love-struck kid," he said deliberately.

Meredith drew back. "What exactly did Jeannette say to that? You may as well tell me. I can see there was something."

His jaw clenched. So he'd hurt her with his comment to push her away from the subject, but he was still going to have to tell her.

"You know Jeannette. She'll put the worst possible interpretation on anything."

"What did she say?"

Clearly Meredith wouldn't let it go. "It was more implication than an outright statement. She hinted that John hung around the teenagers. That he kept trying to talk to Laura privately. That he was too interested in her."

"That's ridiculous." Meredith snapped the words,

her hands clenching into fists. "My father would never do anything like that. How can you say that?"

"I didn't say I believed it," he protested. "I'm not even sure Jeannette does. She claimed all the kids noticed it, but I doubt that, since the rumor would have surfaced before now."

He watched her draw in a breath, fight for control and deliberately unclench her fists. "If she starts spreading that lie around, I'll sue her."

"Relax, Meredith. Jeannette was just using the threat to make you give up on learning anything about Aaron and Laura." He was beginning to sympathize with Samuel in his need to keep his sister from being hurt.

"If that's what Jeannette intended, she's wrong. I'll make her eat those words before she's done."

Meredith looked like some avenging fury at the slight to her father. She'd reacted with that same kind of passion when he was the accused, but it hadn't done any good. They had been kids, easily outmaneuvered. But they weren't kids now.

"Look, forget Jeannette. The truth is the best weapon against someone like her. What did your neighbor have to say?"

Meredith seemed to wrench her thoughts back. "Rebecca? Not much, unfortunately. I did get Lainey's address from her, so I could contact her if necessary, but I'm not sure she can help." She frowned. "Rebecca insisted she didn't see anyone that night, and she wouldn't lie. Still, I had the feeling she was holding something back."

"It seems like a lot of people in Deer Run are doing that."

She nodded, running her hands up and down her arms.

"You're cold." He yanked down the zipper on his jacket. "Take my jacket."

"No, I—"

He draped it around her shoulders while she was still trying to argue, and he flashed back to another moment, another time, when he'd done the same thing. They'd been up at the lake, sitting on a bench, talking, and he'd realized she was cold. He'd slipped his jacket around her, and…

Her gaze caught his, startled and aware, as if she knew what he was thinking.

She drew away quickly, but she hugged the jacket around her. "I…I suppose you need to be getting back to your job soon."

She was putting up barriers, reminding him that his life was elsewhere.

"My boss told me to take the time I need. He seemed to think I had things to settle here." He skipped on, not sure he wanted to explore that with Meredith, of all people. "I haven't even gone to the house yet."

"Why not?" Her steady gaze didn't let him duck away from the question.

"Too many memories, I guess. I have to make a decision about it soon."

"Let me go with you." She reached out to clasp his hand, momentarily depriving him of speech. "Please. I could meet you there tomorrow afternoon."

He should say no, but he wasn't going to. "Sounds good. Around three?"

"I'll be there." She stood, slipping the jacket off and handing it to him. "I'd better get inside."

Was she regretting her offer or that impulsive touch? He couldn't tell. "I'll walk you."

"I'm fine. Don't worry about me."

"Now you're asking the impossible." He lifted his hand to touch her cheek lightly, meaning it to be the briefest bit of encouragement and comfort. But her skin warmed under his hand, and he couldn't seem to break the contact.

Meredith was the one who spun away. "Good night." The word floated out behind her, and she was gone.

He stood immobile for a long moment, trying to get himself under control. He'd better stop kidding himself. The feelings he'd had for Meredith years ago were back, twice as strong, and he hadn't the faintest idea what he should do about it.

"I'M PERFECTLY FINE, MEREDITH." If she *wanted* Meredith to stay with her on a Sunday afternoon, Margo thought, her daughter would be eager to leave. "Go and visit your friend Rachel for a while. I'm just going to sit here and do the Sunday crossword or maybe take a little nap." Margo flipped up the footrest on her recliner and settled the newspaper on her lap.

"If you're sure." Meredith grabbed her handbag and jacket as if she expected Margo to change her mind. "Call my cell if you need anything."

"Of course, dear." Margo bent convincingly over the newspaper, pretending to study the crossword grid. She held the position until she was sure Meredith had walked past the windows and disappeared in the direction of Rachel's bed-and-breakfast.

Finally. Margo put the footrest down with a thud and tossed the paper aside. Ordinarily she might feel a little bereft at being left alone, but the idea that had come to her during church this morning required privacy.

Margo took a cautious look out the window to be sure Meredith wasn't coming back for something she'd forgotten and then started up the stairs, her thoughts returning to the morning's worship service.

She'd sat with Meredith where they usually did and watched as first Laura and Victor Hammond and then Jeannette Walker paraded down the aisle to the pews where their families had sat for generations. Their names might not be engraved on the seats, but no one else in Deer Run would think of sitting there. Even Meredith's friend Rachel, who was raised Amish and had no background at all, sat in the Mason pew by reason of her disastrous marriage to the Mason boy.

Deer Run's version of royalty, that's what they were, just because their people had been here since the Year One. Lording it over others who were just as good as them, if not better.

Like Jeannette, standing in worship this morning to accept thanks for her role in organizing the flower stand, nodding graciously as if she were solely responsible for its success.

Margo paused at the top of the stairs to catch her breath. It didn't do to hurry. She didn't want to get one of her spells.

She'd done every bit as much to make the flower stand a success as Jeannette, and certainly more than Laura, who'd simply donated some flowers that her gardener grew. But they looked down on her, just because she'd married an Amish man who'd worked with his hands. For years she'd longed to get the upper hand on them, just once. And now— Well, maybe now she had a chance.

Meredith's bedroom was as neat as always. Why on earth her daughter preferred this cool green space to the profusion of pink and ruffles that made Margo's room so charming she surely couldn't imagine. But she wasn't here to question the decorating. She wanted to have another look at that scrapbook Meredith and her friends had kept the summer that Amish boy drowned.

Something was going on about that incident after

all these years. Meredith imagined that she could keep secrets from her mother, but she couldn't. Margo opened one drawer after another, searching for the scrapbook, frustrated at Meredith's secretiveness. If Meredith would just be open with her, as a daughter should, she wouldn't have to make these recurrent searches.

Finally she found it, tucked into the center drawer of Meredith's desk beneath some folders. She pulled the scrapbook out, settled into the desk chair and opened it.

Margo clucked to herself as she flipped through the brittle pages, trying to make sense of them. If only she could remember something about the night of the accident, something no one else knew....

She paused, hand on the page, imagining herself the center of a crowd, congratulated and honored for resolving the mystery surrounding the boy's death. And she remembered the night very clearly. She hadn't wanted to be left alone, but John had insisted he had work to finish, leaving her by herself when that boy was drowning not a hundred yards from the house.

Margo turned another page and stopped. The scrapbook was filled with drawings, but this page had photographs, taken with the little camera Meredith had been given for her tenth birthday. Blurry and faded, they had been taken at the fire company fair that summer. Most were different combinations of Meredith, Rachel and Lainey, but one...

She bent over, studying it, wishing she had a magnifying glass. There was a teenage Laura, the center of an admiring group, as always. Jeannette stood a bit in the background, also as always.

The rest were boys. That had to be Aaron with his back to the camera, identifiable by his blond bowl-cut hair and straw hat. The others she wasn't quite sure of. Victor and Dennis Sitler were there. That tall boy they'd called Moose, who now ran the gas station at the edge of town. Two other boys, their faces young and unformed. Laura's followers, all of them. That girl had been the center of attention her entire life.

Margo flipped the page and discovered she was nearly at the end. There was another picture with some careful cursive writing in Meredith's hand— a story, it seemed. And then a final page, a clipping from the local newspaper pasted in the center. Amish Youth Dies in Pond.

She read through the article quickly, phrases lingering in her mind. Accidental drowning, gone there alone for some unknown reason…

Memory opened a door in her mind. The house had been stuffy that night, so she'd raised the windows. She'd stood at the window in the upstairs hall for a moment, enjoying the cool breeze, looking out at the moonlit lawn. Listening, and hearing voices carried through the still night air.

Voices, coming from the path that led to the dam.

She'd leaned out, catching a quick glance of dark figures moving into the woods.

Aaron hadn't been alone when he went to the dam that night. Margo stared down at the newspaper clipping, letting it sink in. She knew something important—the answer to a question no one had ever asked her.

Should she tell Meredith? But Meredith had been keeping secrets from her. Why shouldn't Margo keep one of her own?

Not forever, of course. She felt a righteous glow. Just until she could figure out a way to be certain who'd been out there with Aaron that night. And then... Well, maybe then certain people would realize they weren't so superior, after all.

## CHAPTER SEVEN

MEREDITH PAUSED FOR a moment in front of Rachel's bed-and-breakfast before heading on down the street. Evading the truth was more complicated than she'd expected. Now she had to walk over to the Randal house instead of taking the car.

Still, she could predict what would have happened if she'd told her mother she was meeting Zach this afternoon. Margo would have become agitated, and that in turn would lead to palpitations. She'd become short of breath and dizzy. Meredith would end up calling Bennett Campbell or possibly the rescue squad if the attack was bad enough. And she'd never make it to see Zach.

Meredith had never been sure how much control her mother had at the start of an attack, but she was very sure that the situation could spiral out of control in a hurry. Meredith had no wish to see that happen. It was far better to stay clear of the subject.

Zach would be gone in a few days, and she wouldn't see him again. In fact, she was probably hastening his departure by helping him with his decision about the house.

She frowned, realizing she'd covered half the

route to the Randal house without noticing a thing she passed because she was so deep in thought. Deer Run, however, drowsed in Sunday-afternoon torpor. People took naps, watched football, read the Sunday paper, cooked dinner. It was too early in the season to rake leaves and too late for backyard picnics.

She turned the corner at Pine Street and headed toward what Zach had called "the other side of the tracks." The train tracks were long gone, and several modest new homes sparked a more positive air to the block. The old Randal house was the exception, slumping to the side with an air of defeat. A broken window had been covered with plywood, and it looked as if the lawn was recently mowed. That was Jake Evans's doing, no doubt. He'd feel responsible as executor.

Someone moved on the front walk, and her heart did a little stutter step at the sight of Zach waiting for her.

The memory of that moment when he'd touched her cheek flooded back with a vividness that had her skin warming. The truth was like a punch to the heart. She still cared for Zach. That was the real reason she'd never been able to get serious about another man in the years since. She'd loved him. But that love was destined to go nowhere, because he couldn't wait to shake the dust of Deer Run from his feet for good.

She was here to help him achieve that, right? So

she'd keep her feelings to herself and her attitude friendly but casual.

Zach smiled when she approached, the same smile that had captured her heart at seventeen. Her breath caught. The casual attitude was going to be tough to achieve.

"I hope I haven't kept you waiting."

Her words sounded needlessly formal. Why couldn't she be natural with him? It didn't help that his snug-fitting jeans and leather jacket, combined with the strand of hair that fell onto his forehead and the glint in his eyes, made him look just as desirably dangerous as always.

"No problem." He held up a key ring. "Jake gave me these, so we don't have to break in."

She studied him, not reassured by the belligerent set to his shoulders. "You wouldn't, would you?"

He shrugged. "Sure I would. But I don't have to, so stop worrying. I won't ruin your standing as a good girl."

"I…" She wanted to come up with a snappy retort, but unfortunately she couldn't think of one. "Aren't you supposed to uphold the law?"

He grinned. "I'd just be bending it a little. After all, I am the owner." The smile faded. "Jake Evans called to see if I'd made a decision. Guess he's as eager as everyone else to see the last of me."

"That can't be true." She hated the note of bitterness in Zach's voice. "Jake was just following up.

That's his job. And there are people in Deer Run who'd be happy to see you hang around."

He quirked an eyebrow. "Such as?"

*Me*. "Anna Miller, at the store. She told me she was looking forward to seeing you."

"Anna and her husband are still there?" His face softened. "She caught me trying to shoplift a can of tuna fish once. She made me sweep out the store, then paid me with four or five cans."

Meredith's heart twisted. At least he had a few decent memories from Deer Run. "They're good people. You ought to stop in and say hello. It would please her to be remembered."

"Maybe I will." He was noncommittal, making her think perhaps he didn't want to revisit old times.

"Should we get this over with?" She gestured toward the door.

"Let's do it." Zach's expression hardened. He strode to the door and shoved the key in the lock. In a moment they were inside.

She'd never been here before, of course. Zach wouldn't have considered it when his father was alive.

There was no entryway. The door opened into what was probably meant to be a living room, empty now, with no identifying features. To the left was another empty room and beyond it a door stood open into the kitchen.

Zach had come to a halt a few steps in and stood there, his face frozen in an unreadable expression. He looked around as if he saw something other than the empty, dusty rooms. Instinct urged her to speak—to say something that would move him past the painful memories.

"The house doesn't seem to be in such bad shape," she ventured. "Was it rented after your stepmother died?"

Zach shook his head.

"There are some broken windows, and the plaster isn't in very good shape." One hole looked as if it had been made by someone's fist. And she sounded like an overeager real estate agent trying to make a sale.

"Can't figure out why she stayed on here after the old man died," Zach's voice grated. "I'd have expected her to sell up and get out."

"Your stepmother? Well, older people often want to stay in familiar surroundings."

"Wish she'd left it to someone else," he muttered. At least he was moving now, but it wasn't much of an improvement since he was prowling around the two front rooms like a caged panther.

"Were the two of you close?"

"Close?" He looked at her as if she was crazy. "Not likely. She didn't have a motherly bone in her body, and a stepkid was just a nuisance."

Meredith studied his face, looking for… Well, she didn't know what. Some sign that he could accept and leave the past behind instead of running from it, maybe.

"Whether she liked you or not, she did leave the

house to you. Let's have a look at the kitchen." She moved briskly toward the door, just glad to leave these empty rooms with whatever ghosts they held.

Unfortunately the kitchen was in worse shape, with the refrigerator door hanging drunkenly from a broken hinge and a rusted, filthy range.

Oddly enough, Zach seemed less haunted here. "Not much of a housekeeper, was she? I have to hand it to Ruth—she did know how to handle the old man. She taught me, though I don't suppose she intended it."

"What do you mean?"

He nodded toward the indescribable stove. "He came at her one night when she was cooking. Usually he was content with knocking me around, but that time he went after her. She swung away from the stove with a cast-iron skillet in her hand and whacked him with it. He went down like a log. Far as I know he never tried to touch her again."

Zach's face had actually lightened at the memory, even though it made her feel rather sick. "You said she taught you how to deal with him."

"Yeah. That was the lesson. I had to be big enough and strong enough to fight back. No more cowering like a scared kid. I flattened him against the wall and gave him my terms. I'd keep my hands off him, and he'd do the same for me. I was staying until I got my diploma, and then I'd get out and he'd never see me again." He paused. "Things didn't quite work out like that, though."

That diploma had been snatched out of reach when her mother said Zach had stolen money from the desk. Because of her.

"I'm sorry," she murmured, her throat tight.

He looked at her with what seemed honest surprise. "It wasn't your fault. I even understand your parents' attitude. If I had a daughter, I wouldn't want a kid like I was anywhere near her, either. They saw me like everyone else in town did—a piece of trash discarded on the street."

She made an instinctive sound of protest, unable to find words.

"Well, except for one person," he said, giving her a crooked smile. "Remember the day you were late to school?"

She nodded. She'd come rushing toward the building, knowing the bell had already rung, panic-stricken at the thought of being tardy for the first time in her life. Everyone had already gone inside, except for Zach. He lounged against the railing as she rushed up the stairs.

"I don't know what made me stop. I was late already." But she had stopped. Had looked at him. "I asked you why you weren't scared of getting in trouble."

"And I told you I was always in trouble, so it didn't worry me."

"I'd never met anybody who just didn't care." She had to smile, remembering her astonishment at his attitude.

"And I'd never met anybody who looked at me without seeing trouble." His gaze lingered on her face, and it was as if he touched her. Her cheeks warmed. She moved toward him without planning it, just knowing—

"What are you doing in here?" The loud voice from the front room made her jump, instantly guilty. Heavy footsteps thudded toward them.

ZACH FIGURED HE should have realized he wasn't finished with Ted Singer yet. The guy had a one-track mind, and right now it was settled on Zach Randal.

"You looking to add breaking and entering to your rap sheet, Randal?" Singer appeared in the doorway, and his voice suggested he was enjoying this.

Singer couldn't see Meredith from where he stood. She was shielded by the angle of the door. He'd just bet Singer's tone would change once he knew who else was there.

"It's not breaking in when I have a key." He held up the ring and let the key dangle from his hand. "I own this place."

"Prove it or I'll—" Singer stepped through the doorway and shut up as if the door had smacked him in the face. He'd seen Meredith.

"I can assure you it's true." Meredith's voice was icy. "But you knew that before you came in here. Everyone in town knows."

Ted looked as if he couldn't decide whether it was better to admit it, thus confessing he was just hassling Zach, or better to deny it and appear the worst-informed cop on earth.

"I...uh, I was just checking," he muttered, his face flushing. "Wouldn't want anyone breaking in, with the house empty and all."

Zach found his temper rising and knew perfectly well it wasn't because Ted was being Ted. He didn't like Meredith seeing anyone treat him that way. He'd been used to it when he was a kid, but he wasn't a kid any longer.

"Someone breaking in on a Sunday afternoon? Vandals must be getting pretty bold." He let his skepticism show in his voice.

Ted's face darkened, but before he could answer, Meredith broke in.

"I'm sure Zach appreciates the fact that the police are looking out for his property. In fact, I ought to tell Chief Burkhalter how conscientious you're being, even coming in to check when the owner is looking around."

Zach had never heard Meredith sound quite so cool and contemptuous. It seemed the good little girl wasn't naïve any longer.

Ted stared at her for a moment, maybe trying to figure out exactly what she meant. He had never been the sharpest knife in the drawer. Finally he shrugged, turning away.

"No need for that. I'll get back on patrol." He left, more quickly than he'd come.

The tension in the air dissipated with Ted's exit.

Unfortunately, so did the sizzle that had been alive between Zach and Meredith. Or maybe that was for the best. He raised an eyebrow.

"You amaze me. When did you develop that lofty way of dealing with the Ted Singers of the world?"

Meredith turned those doe eyes on him. "I had to grow up sometime. If I'd done it a little sooner, I might have been able to stop what my mother did to you. I'm—"

"If you apologize again, I might have to do something drastic," he threatened. "It wasn't your fault."

She wasn't diverted. "You must wish you'd never talked to me outside school that day."

He reacted before thinking, catching her hands in both of his. "There are a lot of things I regret in my life, Merry, but never you." He searched her face, willing her to understand. "You taught me how to dream about a better future. Nobody can get along without dreams."

Meredith's lips trembled, and that was all it took. He pulled her into his arms and kissed her. After a startled second she responded, her arms sliding around him. He deepened the kiss. He was falling, and he had no desire at all to catch himself. *Meredith...*

Rational thought hit like a splash of cold water. *Meredith.* He wasn't here to let history repeat itself. There was no possible future for them, and it was far better to stop this while it was just a spark, before someone got burned.

He drew back, trying to pretend he was in control of the situation. "Should I be apologizing about now?" He fought to keep it light.

The hurt in her eyes was quickly masked. "Of course not. We're both adults. If we want to kiss, it's no one's business but ours." Her smile trembled. "Still, maybe it's not the best idea in the world. You'll probably be leaving soon, and I...won't."

That about summed it up, didn't it?

MEREDITH DROVE UP the lane to the farmhouse where Sarah and her husband, Jonah, lived with their children. It had belonged to Jonah's parents, but they now lived in the *daadi haus,* connected to the main farmhouse by a breezeway. His father wasn't actually retired, since at that moment she could see him and Jonah out in the field, making one last cutting of hay.

At least that would keep the men out of the way so she could chat with Sarah.

Meredith parked under a black walnut tree, her tires crunching over some of the fallen nuts. Sarah wouldn't mind that—it was a time-honored method of getting the tough husks off the nuts. Small yellow leaves fluttered down as she got out of the car, one landing in her hair. She brushed it away and headed for the back door. With any luck, she and Sarah would be able to talk before the kids came home from school. It was time she knew more about Aaron Mast than her childhood image of a golden hero.

Sarah saw her coming and held the back door

wide. "Meredith. I'm wonderful happy to see you. *Komm*. Sit." She waved her into the kitchen.

An Amish kitchen was definitely the heart of the home. Sarah's was warmed by the sunlight streaming in the west windows, laying a path across the faded linoleum on the floor. The countertops and gas range shone with constant scrubbing, as did the long rectangular pine table.

Sarah pulled out one of the ladder-back chairs and gestured her toward it. "Sit down. I already have the kettle on, so it will just take a minute to make tea. You'll have some oatmeal cookies, *ja?*"

"The way they smell, I could hardly refuse." The cookies were spread on cooling racks next to the range. "Maybe you'd better not tell the kids I've been dipping into their after-school snack." Meredith slid one off the rack and nibbled. "Wonderful."

Sarah ducked her head with the usual Amish humility in the face of praise. "The *kinder* will be happy to share, as well you know. The big ones won't be home from school for another half hour, and the two little ones are napping, so we can have a nice talk."

She poured steaming water into a brown earthenware teapot and set it on the table. Meredith slid into the chair. No matter how much time had elapsed between visits, she always felt at home in Sarah's kitchen.

Maybe she'd better ease her way into asking questions. "I see Jonah and his dad are getting a cutting of hay in."

"*Ja,* the last one, I think. Jonah's *daad* says he thinks we might have an early frost, so we're eager to get the new barn finished."

Meredith nodded, her mouth full of cookie. "I noticed they have everything ready to start building. When is the barn raising?" Building a new barn was a job for the church, not a construction company, in the Amish community.

"Saturday, if the weather doesn't turn bad." Sarah sent a glance toward the window, as if assessing the chances, but surely it was too early in the week to know. "You will come, *ja?*"

"If I can." If her mother didn't think of a dozen other things she ought to do that day.

"And bring your friend, Zach." Sarah's lips curled in a mischievous smile.

"I don't know if he'll still be in town on Saturday." Meredith prayed she wasn't flushing. "How do you know about Zach?"

"I saw you at the auction, remember? And Samuel mentioned seeing the two of you together the other night." Sarah's forehead furrowed as she spoke.

"Did Samuel also tell you why he came to see me?"

Sarah nodded, looking distressed. "He tried to get out of it, but I made him tell me. He said he wanted you to stop looking into Aaron's death. He said I'd be better off forgetting about Aaron."

As annoyed as she was with Samuel, Meredith hated seeing Sarah so upset with him. "He just doesn't want to see you get hurt."

"That is foolishness." Sarah's tone was tart. "The truth is always better, even when it hurts."

She'd said something like that to Meredith once before. Sarah clearly believed it. But was it always better to know? Could the cost of the truth be too great? Maybe, but in this case she, like Sarah, couldn't settle for less.

"I was hoping you could tell me a little more about Aaron. Much as I thought I knew him that last summer, I only saw him through a child's eyes." A child's eyes that saw only the golden knight of a fairy tale.

"*Ja,* sure, but what do you need to know?" Sarah lifted her tea mug, holding it cupped in both hands. "I'll tell you anything that might help, but I don't know what it would be."

"Just start with what he was like. In real life, not a child's imagination." She smiled. "We always thought he was a hero."

"*Ja,* I know you girls followed him around that summer, making up your stories. He knew, too."

Of course he'd known. They hadn't been nearly as subtle as they'd thought they were. "What did he say about us?"

"He was kind. Aaron was always *sehr* kind." Sarah put her hand against her cheek, remembering. "He said you three could be doing something worse, and it didn't trouble him. He'd look after you."

"You see? He was a hero." She tried to smile, but remembered sorrow interfered.

How devastated the three of them had been when they'd learned of Aaron's death. It had put an end to their summer, in a way. Parents were suddenly watching their children more closely, and Lainey had been collected by her mother. Once school started, she'd been back in public school while Rachel was in the one-room Amish schoolhouse, and they'd stopped seeing much of each other.

She cleared her throat, trying to concentrate. "How did Aaron get involved with Laura and her friends to begin with?"

"I don't know for sure, but I know he went to some parties at someone's hunting cabin that summer." Sarah frowned. "*Englisch* and Amish kids both went. Most likely he met Laura there."

He'd have gotten involved with the other *Englisch* kids through Laura, of course. She'd been the center around which everything revolved.

"Did you ever talk to him about his relationship with Laura?" Sarah must have been hurt, seeing a boy she cared about getting involved with an *Englisch* girl.

Sarah looked down at her cup, maybe seeing the past there. "I tried. Before that, I was the one he'd taken home from singings. But more than that, I was afraid he'd be hurt so badly. Either Laura would break his heart, or he'd run off with her and lose who he was."

*Lose who he was,* Meredith repeated silently. Was that what her father had felt he'd done when he married her mother?

"What did Aaron say when you talked to him?" she continued.

Sarah smiled sadly. "That I didn't understand. That their relationship was different. That they would make it work because they loved each other so much. But they didn't succeed, did they?"

Apparently not. If Aaron had killed himself... But Meredith didn't know that for sure. And there was another question she had to ask, even though she feared the answer.

"Did you ever hear anything about my father taking an interest in that group of kids?"

"John?" Sarah looked startled. "I wouldn't know about that, would I?"

Because John King had left the Amish community behind when he married her mother.

"He wasn't under the *bann,* since he left before he was baptized into the church," Meredith pointed out. "We still saw a lot of your family. I just thought you might have heard something."

Sarah considered, frowning a little. "We were not the same generation, you see. But now that you ask, I did hear something, although it wasn't from John. It was from Aaron."

Meredith's heart was suddenly thudding against her ribs. "What did he say?"

"I'd forgotten that until just this minute." Sarah

pressed her fingers to her forehead. "Aaron said that John warned him away from Laura. That was it. He warned him away from her."

Meredith felt as if an elevator had plunged downward, carrying her with it. She'd hoped to hear that her father had never shown the slightest interest in Laura. Instead, what she'd heard just added to her doubt.

## CHAPTER EIGHT

MEREDITH STEPPED OUT onto the back porch of Rachel's house that evening, pausing to zip up her tan windbreaker. It had gotten dark while she was inside, and the breeze that whistled down the valley had a cold edge to it.

She'd come to Rachel's back door after supper, feeling as if she'd burst if she didn't talk to someone about her concerns. She should confide in Zach, but she'd become wary of being alone with him after that kiss. Or rather, after her response to it.

She'd always taken pride in being the calm one, the person who didn't let her emotions drive her. What had happened to that logical, sensible woman?

Rachel had been reassuring, as always. She'd pointed out that Sarah's story didn't necessarily imply there was anything untoward between Meredith's father and Laura. It might simply be that he'd been trying to keep Aaron from making the same mistake he had.

Rachel hadn't put it quite that bluntly, but that was what it amounted to. John King's marriage to an English woman had been an unhappy one, and he'd hoped to save Aaron from a similar fate.

Meredith stepped down off the porch, her eyes beginning to adjust to the dark. Through the family-room window she could see Rachel and Mandy talking. They headed toward the stairs, Mandy's arm around her mother's waist.

A pang pierced Meredith's heart. She'd never considered herself especially nurturing, but the love and trust between Rachel and Mandy made her long for something so nebulous she wasn't sure she could put a name to it.

Shoving her hands in her pockets, she started across the lawn. A flashlight would have been a good idea, but all she had was the tiny penlight on the key ring she'd stuffed in her pocket. Still, she'd come this way so many times that she'd be able to do it blindfolded. There was nothing to bump into.

The back of Rebecca's house was dark, but a glow came from the front room, where she was probably sewing or reading. Meredith's thoughts flickered again to Lainey. She could write to Lainey, but she wasn't sure how to broach the subject of Aaron's death in a letter.

After all this time, Lainey would think—well, she didn't know what Lainey would think, but it was unlikely she could know any more than she and Rachel did. Besides—

A sound came from the shed at the back of Rebecca's lawn. Meredith stopped, peering into the shadows, looking for the source of the metallic clink.

Nothing, but she almost felt as if eyes peered out at her from the shadows.

Stupid. No one was there. She took another step and heard it again—a faint clink, as if someone had brushed against something metal, a trash can, maybe.

Meredith's fingers closed on the key ring, and she pulled it out, feeling better for having something in her hand. She fingered the penlight, knowing she'd have to get closer to the sound for it to be of any use.

"Is someone there?" Her voice sounded loud to her, and she didn't like the slight quaver it contained. "Hello?"

Nothing. Silence. But she wouldn't be a coward. If someone was getting into her elderly neighbor's shed, she had to investigate. Gripping the keys, ready to switch the penlight on, she moved toward the shed, her sneakers making no sound on the grass.

The shed door was closed, but a whisper of noise came from beside it. Steeling herself, she rounded the corner. She switched on the light and nearly cried out when four red eyes stared at her, reflected in the feeble beam.

Catching a shaky breath, she waved the penlight at the two raccoons who were busily attempting to open Rebecca's trash can. They stared back at her, undeterred.

"Shoo!" A rake leaned against the wall of the shed and she grabbed it, brandishing it at the raccoons. Finally impressed, they scrambled down and waddled quickly off toward the woods.

One of the lids was tilted. In another minute they'd have had it off and been scattering trash in their search for food. She put the lids on both cans firmly and ran the handle of the rake through them. Hopefully that would discourage a repeat performance. In the morning she'd find a couple bricks to weigh down the lids for Rebecca.

The little adventure with the raccoons had banished whatever imaginings she'd been building about someone watching from the dark. She strode briskly to her own back door, finding the right key as she mounted the steps.

The lock resisted the key for a moment before it slid into place and turned. She opened the door, stepped inside and jerked back as she caught movement from the corner of her eye. A broom just missed her shoulder and clattered to the kitchen floor.

"Mom! What on earth are you doing?" Meredith swung the door closed, staring at her mother, who stood behind it.

"Lock the door again, quick, quick." Mom's eyes glittered almost feverishly, and her hands fumbled with the lock.

*What on earth?* "It's all right, Mom. The door's locked." Meredith took her mother's hands in both of hers. "Calm down and tell me what's wrong."

"Someone was out there!" Her mother's voice cracked, and her breath came too fast. "I heard someone outside the house."

Meredith's thoughts flashed back to that sense

of someone watching, but she pushed the fear away and spoke softly. "It was probably just me. I had to scare off some raccoons that were trying to get into Rebecca's trash cans. I'm sorry if the noise frightened you."

"Are you sure?" Her mother's fingers tightened on hers. "Really?"

"That's all it was." She put her arm around her mother. "Why don't we get you settled in your chair? I'll make you a cup of tea, all right?"

Her mother let herself be led into the living room, her breathing returning to normal as she settled into her favorite chair, her book and the television remote close at hand.

"You know I can't have caffeine at this hour of the night."

"Some chamomile tea." Meredith tucked the granny-square afghan over her mother's knees. "That will help you relax."

"I suppose. Be sure you put honey in it, not that artificial sweetener." Anxiety was slow to fade from Margo's eyes.

"I will. I'm sorry the noise alarmed you."

"Really, Meredith, you might have been more considerate. You know it worries me when I'm alone after dark."

"I know."

Her mother leaned back, switching on the television. She was calming down, and with any luck, the chamomile tea would complete the process. Meredith headed for the kitchen, realizing that her own nerves were jumping. Maybe she should have a cup, too, but she was already awash.

What had possessed her mother to be so alarmed she'd attempt to brain someone with a broom? Meredith would have expected her to lock herself in the closet with her cell phone, not go on the attack.

Carrying the electric kettle to the sink, she started the tap running, looking out the window over the sink automatically. The kitchen lights turned the window into a mirror, showing her face looking a bit the worse for wear.

But beyond the image, out in the dark— She froze, the water overflowing the kettle as her stomach clenched.

A flashlight flickered through the trees. Someone was at the dam, the beam of the light moving back and forth.

Water splashed on her hand. She turned the tap off, emptied the excess from the kettle and set it on its stand, never taking her eyes from the light.

Maybe her mother *had* heard something, then. And maybe that feeling she'd had of being watched had been genuine, as well, as someone had been waiting for her to go inside, out of the way.

Should she act? If it was Laura at the dam, having slipped away from her keepers again, something should be done. But would Laura bring a flashlight? Would Laura try not to be seen? That seemed unlikely.

She could go and see for herself. Or call the police. She could call Zach and ask him to check it out. And end up looking like an idiot when it was someone who had a perfect right to be there.

Wrestling with it, she brewed the tea and carried it to her mother, who had become absorbed in one of her endless game shows.

"I'm going to work in the office for a little while, Mom. If you want anything else, just call me."

Her mother nodded, not taking her gaze from the screen.

Meredith headed for the office and stopped at the door, frowning. The desk lamp was on. But she hadn't been in the office this afternoon, and she wouldn't have walked away and left it on if she had.

She chased away a flicker of what might have been fear. If anyone had been in here, it must have been her mother. She glanced back toward the living room.

"Mom? Were you in my office while I was out?"

For a moment the only reply was silence. "Well, what if I was?" Her mother sounded peevish. "I just needed a pencil to work my puzzle. You don't need to act as if I was snooping."

"I'm not." Whether she thought it or not, she hadn't implied it. "I just wondered why the lamp was on, that's all."

She paused for a moment, but her mother didn't respond. Well, she couldn't get into any of the work files, since Meredith had never shared the passwords, so it didn't really matter.

Meredith took a quick glance through the desk drawers, but nothing seemed disarranged. She settled in front of the computer, dismissing her mother's rampant curiosity from her mind.

She wasn't going to wander down to the dam in the dark, and she wasn't going to call Zach, either. She'd sit here and get some work done while keeping her ears pricked for any noise from the driveway that ran right past her window. If someone came up this way from the dam, she'd know it.

ZACH FOUND IT hard to believe that he was on his way to spend Saturday at a barn raising with Meredith at her invitation. He'd had the distinct impression that she'd been scared off by that kiss.

In fact, he'd told himself that it was a good thing. It was foolish to try and rekindle what they'd once had. Their lives were too far apart to make anything work between them. Then she'd called, and he'd forgotten all his good resolutions and jumped at the chance.

Meredith sat next to him, directing him along the narrow blacktop road that led to her cousin's farm. He glanced at her. She looked relaxed, sitting with her hands loosely linked in her lap, but he suspected that was an illusion.

Well, if you wanted to know something, the best

way to find out was generally to ask. "What made you ask me to come along today?"

She looked up, eyes somewhat guarded. "Well, I… When I talked to Sarah, she invited you. I just thought you might be interested."

Somehow he didn't think that was all, but he suspected the rest of it would come out eventually. "How did you make out with Sarah? Did she shed any light on your concerns about your father?"

He'd hit a sore spot. He could see it in the way her face tightened, feel it in her slight wince.

Meredith stared down at her hands. "I asked Sarah if my father had ever shown any interest in that group of kids. She remembered something she thought was odd. It seems Aaron told her that my dad had warned him away from Laura." Her voice was tight and colorless.

"That could mean a lot of things," he said quickly, trying to think of some. "Maybe he realized that Aaron was getting in too deep and was trying to keep him from…" He let that sentence peter out when he realized where it was going.

Meredith's lips tightened. "Trying to keep Aaron from making the same mistake he had," she said.

"I didn't mean that exactly." He sounded lame, he suspected.

"It's all right. Rachel said the same thing. And I don't have many illusions about my parents' marriage."

He rejected several soothing platitudes. "Maybe it makes sense that he'd try to get through to Aaron."

"Maybe. But saying he warned Aaron away sounds like something else."

"Is that what your cousin implied?" He could read the answer in her face before she responded.

"Of course not."

"Well, then, maybe you ought to give your dad the benefit of the doubt." And maybe it was time to get away from the touchy subject of her father. "Did Sarah ever talk to Aaron about his relationship with Laura?"

"She told me she'd tried, but didn't get anywhere. I suppose the fact that she'd been sweet on Aaron made it awkward for her. I did ask who Aaron's closest friends were, and she said Samuel was his best friend."

"Samuel," he repeated. "Does that have anything to do with why we're going to a barn raising?"

Her face relaxed into a smile. "It might. It's not easy for me to corner Samuel for a chat, but he's bound to be at the barn raising. I ought to be able to find some time when I can ask him a few questions about Aaron."

Zach turned that over in his mind, discovering that he was not pleased with the idea of Meredith confronting her cousin. "Why don't you let me ask the questions?"

"You?" She was clearly startled. "I don't think

so. You're a virtual stranger to him. Why would you do it?"

"I am a cop, after all. Asking questions goes with the territory."

"All the more reason why you shouldn't attempt asking him anything. The Amish are the most law-abiding people in the world, but they don't believe in getting mixed up with the law. If you start acting like a cop, everyone will clam up."

"And if you question Samuel, you'll make him realize you're not following his advice." He still didn't like it, even though what she said made sense. His one encounter with Samuel hadn't left him with a positive impression of the man.

"I'll just have to take that chance. We can't let anyone think this is a police matter. You understand that, don't you?" She made a tentative gesture toward him and then clasped her hands again.

"I guess so. But that doesn't mean I'm happy about it."

"I can see that." She seemed to study his face. "How did you get to be a police officer anyway? It seems an unlikely choice—"

"For a troublemaker like me?" He finished the thought for her.

"I wasn't going to say that. But we had talked about how you wanted to go into the military, and I always thought that's what you'd do."

He shrugged. "Not without a high school diploma." Which her mother's accusations had scuttled. "When I left Deer Run, I was ripe for any kind of trouble. Hitched my way to Pittsburgh, where I fell in with a gang of guys who were about as angry as I was. We got involved in some petty crime. Then they decided to rob a construction site."

He fell silent, remembering how he'd felt. Reluctance at doing something so irrevocably against the law had fought with his need to belong somewhere.

"You did that?" Shock laced Meredith's voice even though she probably tried to prevent it.

"Not exactly. Oh, I went with them. They really weren't very good at it. We got caught almost immediately by a night watchman. One of the guys took a swing at him, and the next thing I knew, they were all ganging up on this old man. I thought they were going to beat him to death."

He didn't like remembering that moment, seeing Joe lying on the ground, his head bleeding, someone's leg drawn back to kick him... "So anyway, I jumped in. Fought them off long enough for the man to radio for help."

He risked a glance at Meredith, not seeing any condemnation in her eyes.

"You saved him." She didn't even sound surprised.

"Yeah, well, I ended up arrested for my trouble. But Joe—that was his name, Joe Tedrow—was a retired cop. He had a lot of friends on the force, and he wouldn't give up on me. Got me out of jail, got the court to wipe my record clean, gave me a place to live. He badgered me until I went back to school."

"He sounds like a remarkable man."

"Yeah, he is." He couldn't talk about what Joe had done for him without his throat turning to gravel. "So I ended up wanting to be a cop like him. He still claims he knew I was meant for the job from the minute he saw me."

Meredith didn't speak for a moment. "It sounds as if life gave you a new father, as well as a new chance."

"Maybe so."

Meredith was the only one he'd even talked like this to, and the only one who understood. He'd never met another woman who could do that, and eventually he'd stopped trying.

She seemed to sense his feelings, because she didn't ask any questions. She leaned forward a moment later, pointing to an even narrower road to the right between two pastures. "That way. It's only a couple miles."

He nodded, making the turn. "Anything else turn up since the last time we talked?"

"N-no, not exactly."

"Not exactly what? Are you going to make me drag it out of you?"

"No." Her smile flickered. "Something a little odd did happen last night." She paused, seeming to organize her thoughts. "I had gone over to Rachel's, and I was coming home across the backyards when

I thought I heard something, but it was nothing. Just a couple of raccoons trying to get into my neighbor's trash cans."

"If that was all that happened, you wouldn't have mentioned it."

"Well, no. It was probably my imagination, but it felt as if someone was watching me." She sounded as if she were trying to reassure herself. "But then when I went in the house, my mother almost hit me with the broom."

"What? Why?" He nearly veered off the road.

"She said she heard someone outside. She was convinced someone was out there, but I persuaded her it was just me, chasing the raccoons away."

He eyed her face, hands gripping the wheel. "You don't think so."

"When I looked out the kitchen window a few minutes later, I saw a light moving through the trees down by the dam. Someone was there with a flashlight."

"Why didn't you call me?" He was instantly alarmed at the thought that she might have tried to investigate on her own.

"I…I thought that would be making too much of it. I mean, we don't own the area around the dam, just the path that leads down to it. Anyway… Well, I didn't. And I wasn't about to go check it out alone."

"I'm glad you had that much sense." Why couldn't she just have called him? He could have been there in a couple minutes.

She looked annoyed at his comment. "I decided I'd work in my office, where I could hear anyone who came past on the driveway. But no one did."

He considered that. "It's not the only way to get to the dam. Just the easiest one."

"True." She nodded, pointing to a lane that branched off to the right. "There's the farm."

The lane was wider and better tended than he'd expected, probably because the milk trucks used it.

"There's another explanation," he said, drawing up at the end of a long line of parked buggies and a few cars. "Someone could have intentionally kept quiet going by so that you wouldn't hear him."

He'd rather he hadn't thought of that, because it put an unpleasant image in his mind—an image of Meredith, sitting at her computer in a lighted room, in full view of anyone out in the dark. Of someone standing out there, watching her, before creeping silently away.

## CHAPTER NINE

MEREDITH SLID OUT of the car, taking a deep breath of crisp fall air and freshly cut wood. Being in the car alone with Zach even for the short ride to Sarah and Jonah's farm was disturbing to her equilibrium. Maybe she shouldn't have asked him to come today, but the urge to have a little more time with him before he left had overcome her better judgment.

Well, this was business, in a way. It would give Zach a better sense of the complex web of Amish relationships as well as give her the opportunity to question Samuel.

"Wow." Zach stood next to her on the lane, staring at the raw framework of the barn. Already it towered skyward, the bare ribs giving an impression of power. Men swarmed over it like ants, almost indistinguishable in their black pants, solid-colored shirts and straw hats.

"They'll have started hours ago," she said. "My onkel Simon, Sarah's father, is generally recognized as the person in charge of design. He'd have laid it out last week, so they could be ready to start at dawn. That's him over there, by the apple tree." She gestured toward the lanky figure who surveyed the workers with a practiced eye.

Zach glanced at her uncle, then at her. "He's your dad's brother?"

She nodded. "They were always very alike in looks, though Dad didn't have the beard, of course." Simon's beard was down to midchest now, and more gray than brown, but otherwise he'd changed very little over the years.

"If you want to help with the work…" she began a little tentatively, not sure Zach realized what he'd gotten himself into when he'd agreed to come today.

"Sure. I've pounded a few nails in my time. As long as someone tells me what to do, I'll be fine."

"Sarah will expect me to help with the lunch now, so I won't have a chance to corner Samuel until later." She started walking toward the house, and Zach fell into step beside her.

"I didn't realize you were so involved with your dad's Amish relatives," he said.

"It was harder when I was younger," she admitted. "My mother made it…well, difficult."

"And now?" His glance was questioning.

"She knows I'll come anyway, so we both pretend she doesn't know about it." It was one of the compromises she made to keep the peace, but it sounded a little ridiculous to say it out loud.

"Your mother hasn't forgiven them for objecting to your parents' marriage?"

"That's part of it." She hesitated, but Zach knew

so much about her family that there was no reason not to speak. "She looks down on the Amish. Thinks they're somehow inferior socially." It sounded even worse said out loud. "It doesn't make sense, but that's how she is."

"Trust me, nobody knows that better than me." His smile was wry, and he shook his head when she would have spoken. "Don't apologize."

She couldn't help but feel embarrassed. She'd inadvertently reminded Zach that Mom had felt the same about him.

Sarah came hurrying to meet them, smiling. "Meredith, Zach, *gut,* you're here. *Wilkom, wilkom.*"

"Thanks for inviting us." Meredith gave her cousin a quick hug. "Zach's ready to go to work."

*"Ja?"* Sarah seemed to size him up. *"Komm.* We'll talk to Daad. He'll give Zach something to do."

She led them toward the apple tree where her father stood. Simon beamed, bending to plant a kiss on Meredith's cheek.

"Ach, it has been too long since I've seen you."

Meredith's throat tightened. "For me, too."

"This is Zachary, Daadi," Sarah said, shoving Zach forward. "Meredith's friend. He's here to help."

*"Ja?"* Onkel Simon sized him up with much the same look Sarah had had. "You know how to use a saw and a hammer?"

Zach nodded. "I worked construction one summer. Hope I know enough to be of some use."

*"Gut."* Onkel Simon gave a short nod. "We'll get you started."

There was no chance to remind Zach not to ask questions about Aaron. She tried to put a warning in the glance she sent him, but he looked back blandly.

Sarah caught her arm. *"Komm.* These men will be wanting lunch before long. You can talk to Zach again later."

Meredith eyed her cousin as they headed for the kitchen. "You're not matchmaking, are you?"

Sarah's blue eyes twinkled. "Maybe a little. Somebody needs to, ain't so? Here's your first love come back to town. You can't pretend you don't feel anything."

"I hoped it didn't show." That was probably a futile hope, especially with those who really knew her, like Sarah and Rachel. "Even if I do feel something, it's still complicated. We've both changed."

"That can happen," Sarah said. "I know now that Aaron wasn't the one for me. Sometimes the first love is just meant to get you ready for the real thing. But sometimes it is the real thing. If it is, just be sure you don't let it slip away."

Meredith followed her gaze toward the barn. Zach was working beside Jonah, the two of them hammering in unison, it seemed. Zach looked as if he belonged, despite his jeans and T-shirt.

But he didn't, any more than he belonged in Deer Run. So she'd better concentrate on how she was going to talk to Samuel and stop wishing for the stars.

It was one thing to decide to confront Samuel and another to find the time to do it. Meredith was caught up in lunch preparations immediately, talking all the while with cousins and second cousins and others whose relationship was more distant on the family tree but recognized, nonetheless.

The other women switched effortlessly from Pennsylvania Dutch to English in her presence, as they always did. She had a rudimentary understanding of the language, but she'd never be able to keep up with the quick exchange of gossip, allusions and teasing that went on among women who'd known each other all their lives.

Sarah handed her a platter of sandwiches to carry out to the table in the yard and then took a second look at her face. "Something is wrong?"

Meredith shook her head. Given the tangle her emotions had been in lately, she was glad to know one solid truth. "Just thinking how fortunate I am to have family like you."

Sarah's quick smile lit her face. "We are wonderful glad that you are part of our lives. Onkel John would be pleased."

Meredith nodded. Her father would be happy, and maybe a bit relieved, to know that the bonds he'd fostered for her with his family were still strong.

Meredith joined the exodus of women and girls from the kitchen, carrying food out to the tables.

She'd been to enough of these things to know the routine. The men and boys who were working on the barn would be served first, so they could get back to work. Then the women would settle down to have a leisurely meal before cleaning up.

The lunch break finally gave Meredith the opportunity she'd been watching for. Zach stood talking with a knot of men that included Onkel Simon, Jonah and a few others. Samuel was alone by the barn, bending over a stack of boards.

With a murmured excuse, she slipped away from the table and approached him, waiting until she was at his elbow to say his name.

"Samuel."

He jerked at the sound of her voice, fingers closing on a plank, and he hefted it to his shoulder before turning to face her. "I must get back to work." His gaze didn't meet hers.

"The others aren't ready to start yet," she pointed out. "You can spare me a few minutes, can't you?"

He looked faintly mulish, but he nodded. "What is it?"

She'd have to be blunt and quick, or he'd be gone, she suspected. "Sarah told me that you were Aaron's best friend when you were teenagers."

"*Ja,* I guess. What of it?" He was just short of belligerent.

"You know how much it means to her to know Aaron didn't kill himself. If you'd just tell me about him—"

"Nothing I can tell you will help one way or another." He took a step away, and she stopped him by grabbing his arm.

"Come on, Samuel. You can at least tell me what his mood was those last few days before he died. Was he upset? Did he think Laura was going to break up with him?"

Samuel's eyes widened slightly, just for an instant, before he looked with a show of impatience at the ladder that leaned against the barn. "I don't know. He knew I thought he was *ferhoodled,* getting involved with an *Englisch* girl like that. So he wouldn't tell me."

Something about her question had surprised him, Meredith felt sure. But what? Surely it was a question he'd have expected. Frustration gnawed at her. Zach would be doing this much better.

"You must have had some idea of what he was feeling, even if he didn't talk to you about Laura," she persisted. "What did you feel when you heard he'd been found drowned? You must have wondered how it could happen."

Samuel's arm relaxed slightly under her hand, as if he no longer felt an urgent need to get away from her. "*Ja,* well, I thought it was odd. Aaron was sensible, not like some of them *Englisch* kids. He didn't take stupid chances. So how did he come to drown? He knew that creek like the back of his hand." A thread of anguish wove through Samuel's words, as if the pain was still fresh after all these years.

"You don't think it was an accident, then."

Samuel yanked his arm free, glaring at her. "I didn't say that. I think it is best left alone, before it causes still more trouble."

"Sarah wants to know the truth, whatever it is."

"Sarah is wrong," he said flatly. "But I'll tell you one thing. It never would have happened if Aaron had stayed with his own kind. You should take a lesson from that. Stay with your own kind. You're not one of us, and you never will be."

He spun away from her, the long plank he carried swinging out, missing her head by inches as she ducked away. Samuel was up the ladder and out of sight in the rafters of the massive barn by the time she could take a breath.

Zach raced across the lawn and grasped her by both arms. "Did he hit you? Are you all right?" His voice was low but urgent, his concern washing over her in a warm wave.

"It was nothing. The plank never touched me."

"No thanks to him." Zach swung toward the ladder, and Meredith grabbed him.

"Don't." She lowered her voice to a whisper with a quick glance around. "No one else noticed. Don't make a scene." Clearly Zach had been watching her with Samuel when she'd thought him absorbed in conversation.

"Maybe a scene is just what's needed." Zach ground out the words. "Did he tell you anything before he nearly brained you with that board?"

"Not really," she admitted. "He insisted he didn't know anything—that Aaron didn't talk to him about Laura because Samuel didn't approve of Aaron's relationship with an English girl."

"Did you believe him?" Zach's dark gaze probed her face.

"Not entirely." She said the words slowly, trying to recover the feelings she'd had in the moment. "I asked him if Aaron thought Laura was going to break up with him. After all, that's the idea that started the rumors he might have killed himself."

"And?" Zach sounded as if he was thinking he'd have made a better job of it.

"It wasn't his answer that was odd." She struggled to put her finger on the cause of her uneasiness. "It was more his reaction to the question. As if he'd expected me to ask something else. But I don't know what it would be."

Zach looked up at the barn, but Samuel was no longer visible. "We have to talk to him again."

"I don't know if that's even possible." She seemed to hear again Samuel's final words. Apparently Sarah had been wrong. Not everyone in the family thought Meredith had a place here.

Zach studied her face, frowning. "Look, Meredith, I know these people are important to you, but one thing is clear. Cousin or not, Samuel isn't behaving like an innocent man. He's acting like a person who has something to hide."

"I'm sure he's just trying to protect Sarah," she

said, but she wasn't sure at all, and she was afraid that showed in her voice.

"Maybe." Zach was grim. "And maybe his disagreement with Aaron over Laura turned violent. Did you ever think of that?"

She hadn't. But now that Zach had said the words, she suspected she wouldn't be able to stop.

As SHE'D IMAGINED, Meredith couldn't stop thinking of the situation with Samuel as they drove back toward Deer Run later. Zach had to be wrong about Samuel. He had to be. The cousin she knew could never have harmed his friend, even unintentionally. The Amish prohibition against violence was engrained so deeply that even a teenager—

The car slowed, tires crunching on gravel, and Meredith looked up, startled. Zach had pulled into the parking lot of the county park.

"What are you doing?" She glanced at her watch. "I should get home."

"Your mother can do without you for another half hour." Zach switched off the ignition and slid out, then looked back at her. "Come on. We need to talk, and I'm not going to do it while driving. Let's take a walk."

A little shiver went down her spine, and she wasn't sure whether it was apprehension or anticipation. She got out and followed him to the head of the path that led in a gradual slope toward the creek.

Zach started down the path, and after a moment's hesitation, she followed him.

"I thought you wanted to talk," she said to his back.

"I remember a bench by the stream. Is it still there?" He tossed the question back over his shoulder.

"I think so." She hadn't been down this way in some time, although it had been a popular hiking trail when she was younger.

The path emerged into the cleared area by the creek, leveling out and continuing on for another hundred yards or so before curving up into the woods. Zach caught her hand and pulled her onto the rustic bench that overlooked the water.

"This is better." He half turned to face her, propping his elbow on the back of the bench so that his hand was an inch or so from her shoulder. "Now, talk to me. What has you so upset?"

She shrugged, evading his gaze. "Nothing. Everything—Aaron's death, Samuel's secrets, the rumors about my dad. Take your pick." She hated sounding needy. "But I'll deal with it."

His fingertips brushed her shoulder, and she felt the touch even through her jacket. "I made a decision about the house."

It was such an abrupt change of subject that she almost asked: What house? His stepmother's property, obviously.

"What are you going to do with it? Not bulldoze it, I assume."

His smile flickered. "I talked to your friend Colin McDonald. He did a walk-through of the place and made a list for me of what I'd have to do to put the place on the market." He paused, glancing out at the stream. "I never thought too much of Colin in school, but he's turned into a good guy. Even put me in touch with the contractor and electricians I'll need."

"He is a good guy, or Rachel wouldn't be in love with him," she said. "So you're fixing it up to sell. Won't that be expensive?"

"I can manage, and it's the best option." He focused on her face, his fingers closing on her shoulder. "Thing is, if it hadn't been for you, I'd probably still be avoiding the place."

She could feel her skin warm under the intensity of his gaze. "You'd have come to grips with it eventually. Maybe I just pushed it along."

"You helped me. Now I want to help you. Don't tell me you can handle it. Tell me what's going on inside." His voice was low, compelling, and she couldn't help but remember how she'd once told him all her dreams, the things she didn't say to anyone else. He'd never betrayed her trust.

She blew out a long breath. "I just… I feel as if I've opened such a can of worms. If Rachel and I hadn't started talking about that summer to begin with, none of this would have happened. Now Sarah is desperate to learn the truth, and Aaron's parents are grieving all over again thinking he might have killed himself. My friendship with Samuel is gone, probably beyond repair, and these rumors about my dad just eat at me." She didn't realize she'd been twisting her hands together in her lap until Zach clasped them firmly in his. She shook her head. "Sorry." Her voice choked on the word.

"No need to be sorry. It's not your fault."

"It is." She couldn't absolve herself that easily. "What if it turns out Samuel is somehow involved? It would destroy him, as well as my relationship with my dad's family. I wish I'd never started this. I should have thrown that scrapbook away the day I found it."

"If you had, the truth would have come out some other way. That's the thing about the truth—it always does surface."

"You can't be sure of that." She had a flash of anger at his uncompromising tone.

"It's what I believe. And it's what you believe, too, Meredith, no matter how you try to deny it. Am I right?"

She closed her eyes for a second, wishing she could see a way out, but she couldn't. So she focused on Zach's face. His words might have been blunt, but his eyes were filled with compassion.

"Yes, I guess you are. But what do I do now?"

"We," he said. "We follow the evidence. That's all we can do. It's too late to go back to before you knew any of this."

He was right—annoyingly so. "I guess the only

way out is straight ahead, no matter how guilty I feel."

His fingers brushed her cheek, setting up a trail of warmth. "Plenty of people go through life never feeling guilty for anything. Thinking the bad things that happen to them are always someone else's fault. Not you."

"No." She hesitated, wanting to tell him a memory she had never told anyone. "When I was little…" She stopped, staring unseeing at the water, her courage failing. Better to leave it unsaid.

Zach touched her chin, tilting her face so that she couldn't help looking at him. "When you were little," he prompted.

"My parents used to argue after I was in bed at night. Well, my mother argued. My father just tried to avoid it. They didn't realize I could hear them."

"Don't stop." The words were barely more than a whisper, but they seemed to move across her cheek on his breath.

"My mother was yelling at him over something. She said that I was the only reason he'd married her. The only reason he stayed with her. He didn't deny it. They made each other so unhappy, and I was responsible." She shook her head before he could speak. "I know, in my head, that it's not my fault. I couldn't have done anything about being born. But in my heart… Well, my heart gets in the way of logic."

"Hearts seem to do that." His voice was husky. "Believe me, I know." Without warning he kissed her, pulling her close, his lips alive and warm and urgent on hers.

Her arms slid around him, feeling warm, solid muscle. She held on, letting sensation wash everything else away. She didn't want anything else but this.

Finally Zach pulled back a little so that he could see her face. He was smiling, and she suspected she looked stunned.

"You know what I want?"

She shook her head, almost afraid to ask.

"I want to stop sneaking around with you as if we were teenagers again. I want to go out on a real date with you, like any two normal adults would. You think we could manage that?"

Maybe it was a good thing that was all he asked. She wasn't in any shape to say no to anything. "I guess so." She pushed thoughts of her mother away firmly. She'd handle it somehow.

"Good." He rose, taking her hands to pull Meredith to her feet. "Monday night, around seven. We'll have one evening out and pretend we're like anyone else. Okay?"

"Okay." She suspected he could read her feelings written all over her face, and right now she didn't care.

## CHAPTER TEN

WAITING UNTIL THE latest possible moment to tell her mother about her dinner date with Zach was only sensible, Meredith kept telling herself. It would give Margo less time to work up a head of steam, less time for her endless reproaches. On the other hand, maybe she was just being a coward about it.

Well, time was up now. Zach would be coming for her in a little more than an hour. She had to get ready. Taking a deep breath, Meredith walked into the house with what she hoped was a confident stride. Work had taken her out all afternoon, but now she had no excuses left.

"Mom?" Meredith paused in the hallway to set down her laptop bag. Her mother wasn't in the living room, but cooking aromas wafted from the kitchen. She followed the smell.

"Meredith, there you are." Her mother closed the oven door on what looked like a chicken casserole, her cheeks pink from the heat. "Supper will be ready in fifteen minutes or so."

"It smells wonderful." Her mother was an excellent cook, but often she preferred soup and a sandwich for supper, saying it was too much trouble to make a whole meal just for the two of them.

"Chicken with mushrooms and rice. How was your afternoon? You were at Hammond's, weren't you?"

Her mother seldom showed an interest in her work, but clearly she was in a good mood today. Was that going to make it easier or more difficult to tell her something she wouldn't like?

"Victor wanted me to look over the computer files and be sure his clerk was entering the figures properly. She still acts as if the computer is going to bite her, I'm afraid."

Victor had actually looked surprised to see her, as if he'd forgotten she was coming. He'd given her a quick nod and scuttled away, shutting himself in his office, leaving her to deal with Betsy Long, the computer-shy clerk.

Her mother sniffed. "He should know better than to expect Betsy to master something new at her age. She never was very bright." Her mother tossed her oven gloves on the counter. "Was Laura at the office today?"

"Laura?" As far as Meredith could recall, she hadn't ever seen Laura take an interest in Hammond Groceries. "No, she never seems to come in. Why would you think that?"

Mom shrugged. "No reason. I just stopped by the Hammond house this afternoon, and the housekeeper said she wasn't home."

The housekeeper might be a convenient buffer if Laura didn't want visitors, or if Victor didn't particularly want her to have visitors, for that matter.

More surprising was the fact that her mother had gone anywhere this afternoon. Usually she took a nap, unless one of her several card clubs was meeting.

"What did you want to see Laura about?"

"The Historical Society is doing our fall membership drive. I thought Laura might like to join us. It's not as if she has anything else to occupy her time."

Meredith recognized the slightly peevish tone with which her mother said the words. Nothing would convince her that people like the Hammonds didn't look down on her, and it was a battle Meredith didn't want to start. Not now, especially.

"I suppose you could have left a note for her," she murmured, trying to think of the right way to frame what she had to say. It was all very well for Zach to talk about how she should be firm with her mother. He didn't have to live with her.

"A note? Certainly not." She opened the oven door to check the casserole again. "If Laura Hammond thinks she's too good to answer her own door, I'm not going to pander to such foolishness."

"You don't know that Laura was there. And even if she was, she might not have been up to visitors." She hesitated, but since no comment was forthcoming, she went on. "It's sad that she has so many problems. She was very popular and outgoing as a teenager."

"If by that you mean that everyone made a fuss over her, you could call it that. It's no wonder she was spoiled. Everyone was fooled by that sweet act she put on, even your father. I remember him buying an ad in the yearbook just because she asked him and batted her eyelashes."

That really wasn't what Meredith had wanted to hear. "I didn't realize Daddy knew her that well."

"He was just as foolish over a pretty face as most men," her mother said. She pulled on the oven mitts. "You can set the table. This is ready."

Time was up. "I'm not eating in tonight, Mom. The casserole looks wonderful, though. Maybe we could—"

"Not eating in?" Her mother slammed the oven door. "Why not? The least you could do is let me know in advance so I wouldn't have to go to all this trouble. Where are you going?"

*Be firm, remember?* "Zach is taking me out to dinner."

Her mother stared at her for a long moment, and Meredith braced herself for an explosion. To her amazement, it didn't come.

"I suppose it won't do any good to tell you how foolish you're being. If you won't consider my feelings about that man, there's nothing else to say."

Meredith knew her mother too well to suppose

that she wouldn't find something else to say, despite her words.

"Just don't come complaining to me when he breaks your heart again."

"I won't." Her mother might well be right about the state of her heart, but it was already too late to prevent that from happening. "I'd better get ready." She fled for the stairs, relieved that the anticipated storm from her mother had been so mild.

An hour later Meredith came down, feeling as excited and nervous as a teenager going on her first date. Come to think of it, it had been a long time since she last went out with anyone. She smoothed her palms down the skirt of the rose silk dress she'd bought on a whim and never had an excuse to wear. Eligible males tended to be thin on the ground in Deer Run.

She glanced warily into the living room, half expecting to see her mother stretched out with an ice bag on her head. But Margo sat in her usual recliner, her slippered feet propped on the ottoman, an afghan spread over her legs. She looked settled for the evening.

"I'm going now, Mom." She hesitated, hardly believing she was going to get out this easily.

Her mother's gaze never left the television screen. "Lock the door when you go out. You know how I feel about being left alone here at night. Anything could happen."

Useless to point out that no malefactors could possibly know she was alone. "I'll lock the door."

Headlights glanced off the glass of the front window as a car pulled into the drive, and her heart gave a ridiculous leap. She grabbed her bag and jacket and sped out the door, hurrying off the porch and looking for all the world as if she were escaping.

By the time she reached the car, Zach had come around to the passenger side.

"You don't need to open the door for me," she said. "I'm not helpless."

His hand closed on the handle, keeping her from opening it. "If I let you get in yourself, the inside lights would come on," he said. "And then I wouldn't be able to do this." He bent and kissed her, a long, leisurely kiss that left her breathless. "Now we're ready to go." He whispered the words against her lips and then opened the door.

She slid in, trying to control her racing heart. She'd been wrong. It wasn't a matter of escaping. She was running toward something, not away.

MARGO PULLED ON a sturdy pair of outside shoes, checking the clock as she did so. She had plenty of time until her appointment. She surveyed herself in the full-length mirror on the back of her bedroom door. Black slacks and a dark sweater ensured that she wouldn't easily be seen by someone who might wonder what she was doing.

Meredith's plans had saved her the trouble of

sending her off with some excuse. Margo headed down the stairs, aware of a pleasurable sense of excitement.

Of course, nothing might happen. Still, she had a good feeling about this. She'd spent several days practicing the wording of her note. This would work.

It had given her an unpleasant jolt when Meredith realized she'd been in the office, but she'd needed the scrap paper Meredith kept there to formulate her thoughts before she wrote the note. And she'd been careful to print the final draft on an ordinary notebook page and use plain envelopes. No point in giving herself away before she had to.

Margo headed for the kitchen, leaving the television playing to make it appear she was inside. A little shiver went through her as she took the flashlight from the drawer and checked to be sure it was working.

She'd have preferred to set up this meeting in another place, at another time. But if what she suspected was true, then that truth would come out most easily at the place where it had happened.

She opened the back door, stepped outside and just as quickly stepped back in. She hadn't realized how chilly the nights were getting. Meredith's tan windbreaker hung on a hook by the door, so she pulled it on. She was ready.

Once outside, she went down the porch steps carefully. She didn't want to switch the flashlight on before she had to. No point in rousing the attention of the neighbors.

The sound of her footsteps on the driveway was lonely, and she darted a quick glance around. She seldom went out after dark other than to a meeting or social event, and then she was in the car. But she was perfectly capable of doing this, and it would be worth it to know the truth.

Not that she'd do anything with it, necessarily, but it was high time certain people in this town realized they weren't so superior, after all. Margo smiled, picturing the scene. She might be gracious, promising to keep the secret, but still, they'd always know that she knew.

Or maybe she'd tell Meredith, show her that her mother could be just as clever as she was. If she were the one who exposed the truth after all these years, everyone would realize they'd been underestimating her.

That pleasant picture gave her the courage to go on when the path wound through the brush. She had to turn the flashlight on there, but she shielded it as best she could with her hand.

A loud rustle in the weeds off to her right had her swinging the light around wildly. It was nothing, but her heart was beating too fast. She pressed her hand against it, forcing herself to be calm. It wouldn't do to get excited. She was in control. She took a deep, even breath, waiting a moment before she went on.

Stepping into the clearing under the trees took

courage, but no one could say that Margo King was a coward. She swept the beam of the flashlight around, searching the dark places under the trees.

"Are you here?" she called softly.

No answer. Well, she'd expected to be first to arrive. She advanced toward the pool, drawn irresistibly to the smooth, dark water. It looked so peaceful, with a sliver of moonlight making the surface shimmer like a mirror. People found it hard to believe it was so dangerous.

Margo focused the light on the water coming over the dam, looking as innocent as a frill of lace. A breeze ruffled the surface of the water, and Margo shivered. She checked her watch. It was time.

She'd wait ten minutes, she decided. If this didn't work, she'd try something else. It might be—

The thought left her head at the sound of a step behind her. A surge of triumph flooded through her veins.

"I knew you'd come—"

Before she could turn, before she could raise the light, something struck the side of her head. The flashlight fell from her nerveless grasp.

She struggled, trying to deal with the wave of pain, trying to understand what was happening. But hands were pushing her, her shoes slipping in the wet mud. She couldn't get her balance, she was falling—

The water closed around her in a cold embrace, soaking through her clothes, muddying her face, her hands...

She fought to push herself up, getting her face out of the water. She had to breathe, had to scramble out of the water, but hands forced her down, weight on her back, water stealing her breath, heart pounding and then…nothing.

## CHAPTER ELEVEN

MEREDITH HATED TO SEE the evening come to an end, but as the lights of her house came into view, she knew it was time to return to reality. Zach pulled into the driveway, but when she reached for the door handle, he caught her hand.

"Don't go in yet." His smile was visible in the glow of the pole light at the end of the walk. "That's what I always said, isn't it?"

"Yes." She relaxed, making no attempt to get out. "Luckily I'm not as much of a frightened mouse as I was at seventeen."

Zach's eyebrows lifted, maybe mocking her just a little. "You sure?"

"Positive." She reached out to touch his cheek, her fingertips seeming ultrasensitive to faint stubble and warm skin.

"I'll consider that an invitation," he said, and kissed her.

Again. They'd pulled in at an overlook on the way home, one that was a favorite parking spot for teenagers. Any slight embarrassment she'd felt had slipped away quickly. They'd kissed, they'd talked, they'd embraced, only stopping when it became clear that if they didn't, they wouldn't be able to.

Now she nuzzled against Zach's shoulder, content to feel his arm around her. He squeezed her and then winced, drawing back a little.

"Have you noticed that the gearshift is in exactly the wrong place in this car?" It was a soft murmur of frustration and amusement.

"It does seem that way. Meant to discourage teenagers, maybe."

He grinned, stroking her hair. "No normal teenage boy would ever be discouraged by a minor hurdle like that."

"Amazing that..." She let the thought trail away, afraid she might be revealing more than was wise.

"That we still know each other so well?" He finished for her.

She nodded. Apparently she couldn't hide her feelings.

"I suspect that's because what we had was real," he said softly. "Not puppy love. Real."

And real love didn't die, did it? Being with Zach was like seeing something totally familiar and yet discovering wonderful new facets to it.

He still had that tough edge, but it was harnessed and controlled now. She'd seen that in the way he talked about the work he loved.

But his work was a reminder that this couldn't last. Even though it felt like pressing on a sore spot to be sure it still hurt, she asked the question she'd been avoiding.

"When will you have to leave?"

He gave her a quizzical look. "Eager to get rid of me?"

"No, just…trying not to be surprised."

"Yeah. You never did like surprises." He glanced down at their clasped hands. "My boss has hinted pretty strongly that he wants me back on duty next week."

Her heart sank. So soon. "I guess you'll have to leave then."

"Don't go sounding so final," he said. "You're not finished with me yet." He lifted her hand to his lips and spoke, his breath caressing her skin. "I'll come back to check on the progress of the house. Often. And you can come to Pittsburgh for a weekend now and then, can't you?"

She hesitated, glancing toward the house. The light was on in the living room, and she could see the flicker of the television screen. "I don't know if I can get away."

Zach moved, grasping her shoulders in a firm grip and holding her facing him. "Talk sense, Meredith. Your mother isn't helpless. As far as I can see, she's able to do everything she wants to do."

"Yes, but if she has an attack when I'm not here—"

"She can call 911 like any sensible person. And if that's not enough, you must know everybody in

Deer Run. Surely there's someone you can trust to keep an eye on her for a couple of nights. Just promise me you'll try, okay?"

With his face close to hers, there was only one answer she could make. "I promise."

Zach made it sound so easy. And with his lips on hers, she was able to convince herself that he was right.

After several long, breathless moments, she slid out of the car. Zach rolled down the window, leaning across the seat. "I'll see you tomorrow. Sleep well."

"Good night." *Good night, my love.*

The euphoria lasted until she put her key in the lock and opened the door. Meredith took a deep breath. Her mother was still up, and it was probably too much to hope that she wouldn't have something tart to say. She may as well get it over with.

"I'm home, Mom." She put her bag on the hall console and walked into the living room. The television showed one of the reality shows her mother typically watched. The ottoman was positioned in front of her favorite chair. But her mother wasn't there.

Meredith had had such an image in her mind of her mother sitting there, counting off the number of minutes Zach's car sat in the drive that for a moment she couldn't believe the evidence her eyes were seeing.

"Mom?" She walked through the dining room to the kitchen. Also empty, with the light on over the sink and the dishes her mother had used not in evidence. Meredith touched the dishwasher. Still warm.

She checked the laundry room, powder room and her office. Nothing. Apprehension rising, Meredith headed upstairs. Her mother might have gone to bed, of course, but she would hardly leave the television on if so.

A quick search of the upstairs turned apprehension to something approaching panic. Her mother wasn't in the house. She hadn't left a note.

Meredith scurried back downstairs, double-checking the kitchen to be sure she hadn't missed a message. She hadn't. Was this her idea of payback, going out without letting Meredith know? Possible, but unlikely.

Before she had time to talk herself out of it, Meredith picked up her cell phone and pressed Zach's number.

He answered immediately, his voice husky and intimate. "Want to say good-night again?"

"My mother's not in the house." Panic rose as she said the words out loud. "She didn't have any plans to go out tonight, and there's no note. I don't know where she is."

"Are you sure there's not a note?" Zach's voice had turned crisp and professional. "Or anything marked on her calendar or daybook?"

"Nothing." She checked the calendar hanging on the pantry door as she spoke. "The television was on. She wouldn't go out and leave it on. Besides, she hates to go out at night. Where could she be?"

"Stay put. I'll be right there."

She hung up the phone and stared at it, willing it to ring, to be her mother, calling to say that she'd gone out with friends unexpectedly. It didn't.

Was she overreacting? She didn't think so.

Meredith walked back through the downstairs again, knowing full well it was pointless. She reached the front door just as Zach knocked, and she rushed to open it.

"I don't understand." She grasped his arm. "Where could she be?"

"Take it easy." He took both her hands in a reassuring grip, but she could see that he was already scanning the area, looking for anything out of place. "She's a grown woman, not a child. You're sure she's not in the house?"

"I looked everywhere. Well, not the cellar or attic, but why would she go there?"

"Unlikely, but we'd better check, anyway." He was already striding toward the kitchen. Opening the cellar door, he switched on the light. "I'll take a look down here. Maybe you ought to start calling her friends."

Thank goodness he was taking her seriously. And she should have thought of that herself. She yanked open the drawer where her mother's address book lived, under the kitchen phone.

Zach came back up while she was on the phone with one of her mother's bridge cronies. He shook his head, and a moment later she heard him trotting upstairs.

By the time he was back, she'd called her way through most of the names in the book, and the faint embarrassment she'd felt on the first few calls had vanished.

"Nothing upstairs," he said when she hung up. "Have you called everyone?"

"All except Bennett Campbell. Do you remember him? Retired doctor?" She was punching in the older man's number as she spoke.

"Vaguely." Zach was frowning, his mind obviously churning. "Is the car here?"

"I didn't think of—" She broke off as Bennett answered. Without waiting for more, Zach went out the back door.

Everyone else she'd called had expressed concern. Bennett was alarmed.

"You're sure she hasn't fallen somewhere?" His voice was brusque, as if accusing her of not being there when her mother needed her.

"She's not in the house," she repeated.

"You'd better look outside," he said. "I'm calling the police."

He hung up before she could protest. Still, maybe he was right. Struck by a sudden thought, she pulled open the cabinet where her mother customarily kept her handbag, insisting it wasn't safe to leave it out where anyone might see it. The bag was there.

She heard the back door open and hurried back

to the kitchen. "Her handbag is still where she keeps it. The car?"

"Still there." Zach's frown had deepened. "Do you have a flashlight? I'll look around the outside."

She nodded. "Bennett said to do that. And he's calling the police." She yanked open the drawer and reached for the flashlight, only to discover that it wasn't there. "Zach, she must have gone outside. The flashlight we keep here is missing."

Zach gave an abrupt nod. "You have another one?"

"Yes, of course." She darted to the pantry and pulled two more flashlights from the emergency shelf. She thrust one into Zach's hand and switched on the one she held before running to the door. "She must have gone outside. But why?"

Her mother wasn't the type of person to go out in the dark to investigate a suspicious noise or a barking dog. She'd send Meredith or she'd call for help. But it seemed that was exactly what she'd done.

Zach was beside her when she reached the bottom of the porch steps. "The back porch light was on when I came out," he said. "Did you leave it on?"

"No. It was off when I left, I'm sure." She sent the beam of her flashlight spinning across the lawn, reflecting from the brave orange and yellow of the mums along the porch.

Zach's hand closed on her arm. "Let's be methodical about this. You walk around the house. I'll take the backyard and garage."

He was giving himself the more likely spot, she

realized, but she wouldn't waste time arguing. She nodded and trained her circle of light on the ground, looking for any sign as she went.

*Please, please.* The prayer was instinctive and very nearly wordless.

*Don't panic,* she repeated the words as she circled the house. *That won't help.*

Nothing had disturbed the mulch around the shrubs beside the house, nothing lay hidden beneath the overgrown lilac bush she kept intending to prune. She reached the front just as two cars pulled into the driveway, one after the other. The first was Bennett's dark sedan; the second the Deer Run police car.

Bennett was out first, hurrying toward her. "Any sign of her?"

"Nothing. Zach is checking the backyard now."

"Zach Randal, would that be?" Jim Burkhalter, Deer Run's burly, graying chief of police, followed Bennett more slowly.

"Yes." Meredith kept her voice even. Chief Burkhalter would have been the person to whom her mother had reported the theft that had torn Zach away from her. "We had been out to dinner. When I returned and found my mother missing, I called him to help me look for her."

"Instead of the police or your mother's friends?" he asked.

"Obviously I called my mother's friends, as well." She wouldn't let his question annoy her. He'd never been noted for tact. "And Bennett said he'd notify you. It's only been…" She paused to look at her watch. "It's been about twenty minutes since I went inside and realized she wasn't there. I was alarmed, because she didn't have plans to go out tonight. The television was playing. Her purse is where it belongs. The back porch light was on and the flashlight we keep in the kitchen is missing. I can't think where she's gone."

Zach rounded the house, switching off his flashlight as he approached them. "I checked the back. Nothing there." He nodded to the other two men. "Chief."

Burkhalter returned the nod with a long look. "Randal. I heard you were back in town. Heard something about you being in law enforcement, too." His tone expressed doubt.

Zach reached into his jacket pocket and pulled out a dark object, which he flipped open to reveal a badge. "Pittsburgh P.D."

The chief looked it over carefully before handing it back. "Good," he muttered. "Just bear in mind this isn't your jurisdiction."

Meredith couldn't remain silent. "Why are you wasting time? We have to find my mother."

"She's right," Bennett said. "It's clear something has happened to Margo. If she felt ill and she was alone…"

He let that trail off, but it was probably clear to everyone what he meant. Something had happened to her, and Meredith was to blame.

ZACH FELT FAIRLY SURE that Chief Burkhalter wasn't convinced there was cause for alarm, but also sure that he wasn't about to argue with the respected physician. Even retired, Bennett Campbell no doubt wielded a strong influence in Deer Run.

"Well, now, I don't think you should worry too much." Burkhalter patted Meredith's hand. "We'll do a search, but most likely we'll find she's visiting someone." He held up a hamlike hand when Meredith seemed about to protest. "Yes, I know you called people, but likely she's with the one person you didn't think of."

Meredith did not look soothed. "Without her car or her handbag? Or her keys, for that matter?" She swung to Zach. "Was the back door locked when you went out?"

"No. The porch light was on, and the door was unlocked."

Meredith rubbed her arms, and he realized she was shivering. He caught Bennett Campbell's gaze. If anyone would get Burkhalter moving, it would be him.

"This is nonsense," Campbell snapped. "Standing here muttering platitudes while poor Margo is lying ill or injured. I demand you call out enough men to mount a thorough search."

Zach saw Meredith wince at the image Campbell had planted. She needed something concrete to do.

"Meredith, have you looked to see what clothes

are missing?" he asked. "It might help to know what your mother has on."

The strain ebbed from her face. "I'll do that right now." She ran for the house. After a moment's hesitation, Zach followed her. Burkhalter would probably let himself be pushed more readily without an audience.

Meredith had already run upstairs by the time he reached the hall, and he went up two steps at a time, propelled by an urgency he didn't want Meredith to see. This was looking more serious by the moment.

He found Meredith in the largest bedroom, which was a masterpiece of pink and frills. She burrowed in the closet and then jerked out one drawer after another. Finally she looked at him, a frown drawing her eyebrows together.

"I don't understand. She seemed to be settled for the evening when I left, but apparently she came up and changed clothes at some point."

"Can you tell what she's wearing?"

Her frown deepened. "Yes, but it doesn't make any sense. She's put on her black slacks and a black sweater. That's all that's missing. Where would she go dressed like that?"

"I can't imagine."

Actually he could, but he didn't think it would be good to say so. If it weren't for the presence of the car in the garage, he'd think she'd set out to follow them. He could picture her creeping around, maybe peering into the vehicle when they'd been parked at the overlook.

He shook off the thought. The car was here. They couldn't get away from that fact.

Another vehicle pulled into the driveway, its headlights reflecting from the window. Maybe reinforcements had arrived.

They went downstairs. Deer Run's two patrolmen had arrived, and Zach realized that Ted Singer was eyeing him suspiciously. No doubt he'd be glad of an excuse to blame Zach for any malfeasance. Several other cars pulled up within moments. It looked as if word was spreading.

To give him credit, Burkhalter proved adept at organizing a search now that he had sufficient numbers. Several people were dispatched to search along the road in either direction, while others started knocking on doors and looking in neighboring yards.

Meredith still wore the dress she'd had on when they went out to dinner, but she'd pulled a coat over it. She looked as if she held on to her composure by a thread. He touched her arm lightly.

"Why don't you go inside? There's nothing you can do here."

"No, I can't—"

"Zach's right." The woman who spoke came to put an arm around Meredith. "We'll go inside and start coffee brewing. That's the most useful thing to do now."

To Zach's relief, Meredith seemed to listen. She let herself be pushed toward the back door.

Two figures had been standing quietly behind the woman. Now the older man moved forward. "Don't fret about her. Rachel will take care of her."

*Rachel. Of course.* "If she keeps her busy inside, that'll help," Zach said.

"I am Rachel's *daad.*" The tall, graying Amish man looked vaguely familiar. "This is her brother, Benjamin. We'll help search, *ja?*"

The teenage boy looked like most Pennsylvania Amish boys his age, with fair hair in a bowl cut, blue eyes and a general air of growing out of his blue shirt and black pants.

"Thanks. The more sets of eyes, the better." He switched his flashlight back on, seeing that the two of them had come prepared with their own. In fact, the father carried a battery lantern that cast a wider field than a flashlight.

"Where should we start?" The boy spoke for the first time. He sent a nervous glance in the direction of Burkhalter, making Zach remember Meredith saying that the Amish, though very law-abiding, preferred to avoid the police when possible.

"I was just going to scout along the tall grass at the far edge of the yard for any sign she went beyond the yard. You want to help with that?" Zach asked.

They nodded, separating to move slowly along the point at which mowed lawn gave way to a tangle of weeds and brush. Zach followed suit, trying to concentrate on each blade of grass as if it had a secret to tell him. Anything to keep himself from wondering and worrying.

When he straightened to stretch his back briefly, he could see the lights crossing and recrossing the surrounding properties, and hear voices calling Margo King's name. Where had the woman gone? This didn't make any sense. Margo was hardly the type to go out for a walk at night, not if she was in her right mind.

And if she'd had some sort of episode, become confused, wandered off? He suspected that was in everyone's thoughts. If so, Meredith was going to have a hard time forgiving herself for going out tonight. To say nothing of forgiving him.

A breeze swept down the valley, making the grasses sway and whisper. He spotted a light flash on and off and realized it was Rachel's brother, signaling him. He hurried to join the boy.

"You find something?"

"*Ja.* Maybe," he added cautiously. "See here." He knelt, focusing the light on the path that led back to the woods and the dam. "Someone has been here. And since that shower yesterday, ain't so?"

The boy was right. In a soft patch of ground was the smudged mark of a shoe.

"Could be nothing, but maybe we'd better have a look. Go slowly, in case there are any other prints."

"*Ja.*" Keeping his light trained on the path, the

boy moved cautiously. Zach kept pace with him, supplementing the kid's flashlight with his own.

At the place where the path entered the fringe of trees, Benjamin stopped. "There."

Zach bent for a closer look. The boy's sharp eyes had picked up the faintest smudge that might be another shoe mark.

"Good work spotting that. Could be someone else going to the pool, I suppose, but not that many people go there." And why on earth would Margo?

"No. It's a bad place," Benjamin said unexpectedly.

"Why bad? Because Aaron Mast died there?" He eyed the boy.

*"Ja."* The whites of his eyes showed.

"You don't have to come any farther," Zach said. "I can check it out."

Benjamin straightened, young face firming. "I will come, too."

"Right. Let's go, then."

The belt of trees ended in the cleared space around the pool. Zach paused as they stepped into the clearing. "Margo King," he called. "Can you hear me?"

Nothing. They swept the beams of their flashlights around the clearing slowly, the dark pool telling them nothing. Then the light hit an even darker shape at the edge of the water.

The boy gasped, and the flashlight shook in his hand. "Is it…"

"Stay here," Zach ordered, moving forward carefully, his logical mind telling him it could be a half-submerged log even as his instinct told him it wasn't.

He went closer—close enough to see that it was Margo, facedown in the water. Gone, he thought, but he had to make sure.

He came in from the side, avoiding the scuffed marks at the water's edge, and reached out to the form that rocked slowly with the movement of the water. A few moments later he stood.

"Sh-shouldn't we get her out?" It sounded as if the boy's teeth were chattering, but he hadn't run or screamed.

Zach retraced his steps. "It's too late," he said. "Benjamin, listen to me." He grasped the boy's arms, turning him so that he no longer looked at the body. "The police will want to see everything just the way we found it. I want you to go find Chief Burkhalter. Don't say anything to anyone else. Just tell him quietly. We don't want Meredith to hear until someone can break it to her properly. Understand?"

The boy gulped, nodded and spun to race back down the trail.

Zach stood, surveying the scene, knowing Burkhalter wouldn't thank him for interfering in a case of what might or might not be accidental death. He stared at the body, sympathizing with Benjamin's instinctive desire to pull it out. Pity moved through him. He couldn't pretend he'd liked Margo, but she shouldn't have died like this.

It could have been an accident, of course, but Zach found it hard to imagine a likely scenario.

Poor Meredith. She would grieve no matter how it had happened, but he very much feared the circumstances were going to double her grief.

## CHAPTER TWELVE

THE SECONDS TICKED BY. Zach pictured the frightened boy trying to explain the situation to Burkhalter without alarming everyone else. Would the chief understand?

Maybe he should have gone himself, but it had seemed wrong to leave Margo's body alone here. And he couldn't ask Benjamin to stay. The kid was scared enough already.

Voices pierced the night—a babble that grew in volume, with Burkhalter's bull-like roar foremost among them. A wave of flashlights swung this way, bobbing and flashing along the trail. Blast the man, he was letting the whole herd come stampeding onto what might be a crime scene.

Moving quickly, he positioned himself at the entry to the path. Burkhalter reached him first, thrusting him back when Zach tried to stop him.

"What's this nonsense?" He stopped in midroar as Zach trained his light on the body, muttering an oath under his breath.

"Better try to keep them from tramping all over the scene," Zach said quietly, wondering how likely it was that the chief would listen to anything he said.

Before Burkhalter could respond, Bennett Campbell tried to push past them.

"Get her out, man. What do you mean by leaving her there? You should have pulled her out the instant you found her."

Zach gripped his arm. "It's too late."

"You don't know that. I'm the doctor here, not you." He swung on Burkhalter. "I demand you let me treat her."

While Campbell's influence had worked in his favor earlier, it went against him now. Zach made eye contact with Burkhalter, and it seemed to him that there was a question in the older man's face.

"At least try to preserve the scene," Zach said.

Ted elbowed his way forward. "The chief doesn't need any advice from you."

Ignoring him, Zach kept his eyes trained on Burkhalter. Finally the chief nodded.

"Ted, help me get her out. Doc, you come, too. Nobody else moves any farther, got it?"

Nobody argued. The three picked their way across the clearing, avoiding the edge of the pool. They began the difficult job of getting the body out without disturbing the area any more than they had to. Silence hung heavy, broken only by the grunts and murmurs of the men. Zach suspected every person there had accepted the fact that Margo was dead.

He felt a tug on his sleeve. Benjamin stood there, shivering a little, his father behind him with a hand on the boy's shoulder.

"I'm sorry," he murmured. "I tried to tell him quietlike, but he wouldn't listen, wouldn't believe me."

"It's okay, Benjamin. I know you did your best. You're not to blame for Burkhalter's..." He mentally deleted several words he wanted to say. "It's not your fault he didn't listen."

"Rachel had Meredith in the house," the father said. "It could be that she didn't hear."

Zach nodded. It could be, but he didn't hold out much hope that she wouldn't catch on to the uproar. He ought to go and tell her himself, but someone had to try and ensure that Burkhalter handled this properly.

Flashlights bounced as a ripple went through the crowd. His heart sank. Too late to break the news gently—Meredith pushed her way forward with Rachel trying vainly to hold her back.

"Let me through. Mom—"

His heart contracting, Zach stepped into her path so that she ran right into him.

"Let me go." She struggled against the restraining hands, and he suspected she didn't even recognize him in that moment.

"Merry." He used the pet name without intention. "I'm so sorry. She's gone."

She stared into his face, her eyes dark with shock. "Gone," she repeated. "She can't be. She was fine when I left."

"Hush now," Rachel said gently, putting her arms

around Meredith. "Just listen to me. You can't get in the way. Let the doctor do his work."

The glance Rachel sent to Zach showed that she understood there was nothing the doctor could do, but she'd chosen the right approach. Meredith settled, shivering a little but no longer trying to rush forward. Her gaze strained toward the small group huddled around the dark figure on the edge of the pond. Someone switched on a strong battery lamp, and it cast the scene into sharp, black-and-white relief.

Bennett Campbell rose from his knees, moving as slowly as if he'd aged twenty years in the past few minutes. "Margo is dead." His face was ravaged in the harsh light. He seemed shaken by a spasm of emotion. "It never should have happened." He stared at Meredith. "You shouldn't have left her alone."

Zach felt Meredith recoil, as if each word was a separate stone striking her. Rage filled him, but before he could speak, Rachel did.

"That was unnecessary, Dr. Campbell." Her clear voice rang like a bell in the sodden silence.

Zach suspected he wasn't the only one looking at Rachel in surprise. Such an attack was unusual, to say the least, for someone raised Amish.

Apparently she got through to Campbell. He looked abashed, rubbing a hand across his face. "Sorry," he muttered. "Afraid I'm upset." He turned to Burkhalter with an assumption of something like his earlier assurance. "I'll sign the certificate and make arrangements with the funeral director. That's the least I can do for her." His voice trembled again.

Zach's heart sank. He was going to have to intervene again, and it was the last thing he wanted to do. Leaving Meredith with Rachel's arm securely around her, he picked his way toward Chief Burkhalter. Not that his caution was going to do much good. The ground would look like the proverbial herd of elephants had tramped over it by morning.

"You can't do that," he said, keeping his voice low.

Campbell flared up in a second, as he'd expected. "Stay out of this, Randal. I'm the woman's physician. I'm within my rights to sign the death certificate. It's a clear case of accidental drowning."

"What about the injury to the side of her head?" Zach could see the mark clearly now that the body was out of the water.

"Incidental," Campbell said. "She struck her head on a rock when she fell. It's obvious what happened. She must have had an episode with her heart. Short of breath, her heart racing, she tried to go for help and became disoriented."

The man couldn't possibly be as dumb as he sounded. It made Zach wonder how many of his former patients had died unnecessarily.

"First taking the time to change into dark clothes and collect a flashlight?" He let the sarcasm show in his voice.

"What are you suggesting?" Campbell demanded.

"I'm not suggesting anything." He hadn't reached

that point yet. He just knew this death couldn't be written off as another accident. "That will be up to Chief Burkhalter. He's required to order an autopsy in a case of unexplained death."

Campbell's face reddened. "I've just explained—"

"He's right, Doc." Burkhalter looked like a man who accepted his duty, now that it had been pointed out to him. He turned to the nearest patrolman. "Clear the area. Get all those people out of here. Take names and addresses and send them home. Ted, you secure the scene. I want crime scene tape clear back at the beginning of the path, and you'd best block off the other side of the creek, as well."

Now that Burkhalter had gotten a grip, he was doing what should have been done from the first. Zach regretted that it had taken his intervention to make it happen. Burkhalter was bound to resent that fact.

Maybe he should have let it go—let it be written off as an accident. But that was the trouble with being a cop. He couldn't turn off his profession when it was inconvenient.

Besides, in the long run, Meredith would have to know the truth. His heart wrenched. Otherwise she'd spend the rest of her life convinced that she'd caused her mother's death.

MEREDITH HUDDLED IN her chair at the kitchen table, trying to take what comfort she could from the familiar setting. There was the tea towel, hung up neatly after her mother had cleaned up from her supper. Above the table hung the clock her father had taken in trade from an Amish craftsman, a habit of his that had driven her mother crazy. Now they were both gone.

She shivered, wrapping her hands around the mug of tea Rachel had made for her, trying to absorb its warmth. A blanket dropped over her shoulders, and hands smoothed it around her. She looked up, grateful, into Zach's worried face.

For just an instant her heart was pierced by the knowledge that she loved him. Then, just as quickly, it was superseded by the conviction that if she hadn't gone out with him that night, her mother would still be alive.

She stared down at the amber liquid in the cup— chamomile, by the scent of it. She bit her lip. Zach, her mother…

"You're blaming yourself," Rachel said, sitting down across from her. "Stop it right now. What happened wasn't your fault."

Meredith shook her head. "If I hadn't gone out—"

"Rachel's right," Zach interrupted, his voice gruff. "We don't know enough yet to say how or why this happened to your mother. But it's obvious that she had formed some intention of her own. Changing her clothes, taking a flashlight… Those things show that she intended to go out, apparently to the pool. Why?"

Rachel nodded. She stood again, as if she needed

to keep busy, and began slicing the shoofly pie her mother had sent over at some point in the past hour.

"Until we know what Margo planned to do, we won't know how she died." She plopped the plate down on the table. "I was brought up to say that it was God's will when something like this happens. Maybe so. Maybe it was some plan of Margo's that went wrong, or maybe it was someone's evil intent. But it definitely didn't happen because you went out to dinner."

Meredith was almost convinced. Rachel had put it so compellingly. And maybe she was swayed by Rachel because Rachel so seldom told anyone else what to do or believe.

"I...I'll try to remember that." She managed a smile. "You should go home. Mandy—"

"Mandy is fine," Rachel said. "My sister is with her tonight, and she'll get her off to school in the morning. I'm staying with you."

Meredith had to fight back tears. "I can't let you do that."

"You have nothing to say about it," Rachel said with mock severity. "You can come to my house if you'd rather. We have a room ready for you. But I thought you might want to be here."

"Yes." She felt a wave of gratitude for Rachel's quick understanding. "I need to stay in my own house tonight." It would feel like desertion to go away now.

"So I'm staying, too." Rachel glanced at the clock

and then at Zach. "How long will Chief Burkhalter keep us waiting here? I think Meredith should lie down, even if she doesn't sleep."

"Hard to say." Zach didn't sound especially sure of Chief Burkhalter's methods. "I can try to hurry him up." He half rose, but Meredith caught his arm.

"Don't. It's all right." She felt an inward shudder at the thought of closing her eyes. All she'd see would be that dark shape at the edge of the darker pool.

"Someone's coming." Rachel nodded to the glass in the back door. "Maybe—" She cut off the words when the door opened and Bennett Campbell stepped inside.

Bennett seemed to hesitate at seeing the three of them watching him. Then he approached Meredith, still moving so stiffly that she felt a wave of pity for him. He'd been so attached to her mother that she didn't know what he'd do without her.

"Bennett, would you like to sit down?" She gestured to a chair.

He shook his head. "I won't take a minute. I must apologize for speaking so sharply earlier."

But not for his words, she suspected. "We were all in shock," she replied, not sure what else she could say in the face of his stiff manner.

"Yes, well…" He hesitated, eyeing Zach with suspicion. "Was that true, that Margo had put on dark clothing and taken a flashlight with her?"

"Yes." She couldn't avoid answering a direct question, whether it was really his business or not.

Bennett shook his head slowly. "Inexplicable," he pronounced. "Still, people can do the most extraordinary things when they're upset."

In other words, he didn't want to let go of his pet theory. Meredith felt a surge of impatience with the man. They wouldn't find out the truth of what happened by snatching at easy answers.

"Well, I must go. You'll let me know if there's anything I can do." Still shaking his head, he went back out, holding the door for Chief Burkhalter as he did.

Rachel already had a mug and the coffeepot in her hands by the time the chief reached the table. "You'll need some coffee by now, Chief Burkhalter. And maybe a piece of shoofly pie to keep you going."

Seeming thrown off his stride by this display of hospitality, Burkhalter let himself be ushered to a chair. He had a mouthful of shoofly pie by the time he tried to regain control of the situation.

He swallowed. "Maybe I'd better talk to Meredith alone," he said.

Rachel slid into the chair next to her, so that Zach was on one side of her and Rachel on the other. She reached over to squeeze Meredith's hand.

"Meredith is still in a state of shock. She needs to have her friends here," she said.

Burkhalter looked undecided for a moment, but then he shrugged. "Yeah, well, it doesn't matter, I guess. At this point, I just want to get the events of the evening clear in my mind. We can talk more tomorrow." He pulled a battered notebook from his uniform pocket and spread it open next to the plate of shoofly pie. "Now, I understand you went out this evening?"

Meredith nodded. There was nothing to be wary of in answering his questions. "Yes. I left at about six-thirty or so. My mother was sitting in her recliner in the living room, watching television. She seemed to be settled for the evening."

Burkhalter nodded. She realized that Zach was watching him closely, his dark eyes unreadable.

"And Zach here picked you up? You didn't drive separately?"

"No, he drove. We went to Williamsport, to the Peter Herdic House."

"I had made a reservation for seven," Zach put in smoothly.

"Your mother had no plans for the evening as far as you know?" Burkhalter looked at her, pen poised over the notebook.

"No, certainly not. I don't understand it. She seldom went out in the evening unless someone else was driving, and she never walked anywhere after dark."

"You don't go along with what the doc said about her getting confused?"

"I've never known her to show any signs of confusion." It really was inexplicable, but not for the reasons Bennett Campbell had advanced. "If my mother had started having rapid heartbeats when I wasn't here, she'd have called 911 immediately, not changed her clothes and gone out of the house."

"It's odd, that's for sure." Burkhalter mused for a moment. Or maybe he was trying to decide if he'd asked all the appropriate questions. "So what time did you say you left the restaurant?"

"We didn't," Zach answered for her. "It must have been about eight-thirty or quarter to nine." He looked at her for confirmation, and she nodded.

"And you got back here about...?" The chief paused, waiting for an answer.

"It was almost eleven." She had to expend some effort to keep her voice even. "I was surprised to see the television still on, because my mother usually goes upstairs by ten or so."

"Wouldn't take you that long to drive back from Williamsport," Burkhalter observed.

"We stopped on the way back to talk." She couldn't quell the heat that mounted to her cheeks.

"Where was that?" Burkhalter's gaze never left her face.

"Up at the overlook along the highway."

Burkhalter didn't comment, but he made what might have been a disapproving sound deep in his throat. "So you're saying Randal here was with you the whole time from six-thirty to eleven, that right?"

Her heart clutched, and the pulse in her throat hammered. "Yes. He was." She put everything she had in the words, but she knew what the question meant.

Burkhalter was thinking that if her mother had been killed, Zach might be the one person in Deer Run who had reason to want her dead.

Zach couldn't have done it. They had been together all evening. And he wouldn't have, even if he could have. He hadn't come back looking for revenge, and she wasn't a seventeen-year-old to be cowed by a parent's disapproval.

But one thing was abundantly clear. Once again, she was bringing grief to someone she loved.

ZACH CROSSED THE STREET to Meredith's house the next morning as early as he figured was reasonable. Not that he supposed Meredith would have actually gotten any sleep last night. Still, in a place like Deer Run, the proprieties had to be observed.

The orange crime scene tape behind the house was only too familiar to him, but obscenely out of place here. His stomach clenched. He had to protect Meredith, and he wasn't sure how that could be done.

Well, one step at a time. He rapped quietly on the door, not wanting to set the doorbell jangling.

Rachel opened the door and greeted him with a wan smile. "Zach. I thought it would be you."

He stepped inside. "How's Meredith?" Belatedly he realized it would have been polite to have asked how Rachel was doing, but all his thoughts were centered on Meredith.

"I'm all right." Meredith answered from the stairs. She came the rest of the way down, her hand on the railing as if she didn't quite trust herself. Her eyes were red-rimmed, but she seemed composed. "I keep telling Rachel she can go home, but she doesn't listen."

Rachel smiled and shook her head. "My sister got Mandy off to school, and I don't have any guests. Besides, you need someone to handle all the people who keep coming to the back door with casseroles."

"It's kind of them." Meredith pushed her hair back wearily. "But I'll never eat all that food."

"We'll start now," Rachel said briskly. "Come on, both of you. We'll all think more clearly once we've had some breakfast."

As if impelled by Rachel's calm good sense, Meredith let herself be hustled along the hallway to the kitchen. Zach followed. There were things they should talk about, decisions to make, but Rachel was right. That would go better with sustenance.

He paused in the doorway, surveying the baskets and casserole dishes collected on the counter. The women seemed to take it for granted, but he was startled by the sight. The food was a silent message of condolence and support from the community.

"There's a breakfast casserole ready. Rebecca brought it over from next door first thing this morning, and you'd better eat some or her feelings will be hurt." Rachel was working as she talked, spooning out portions of what seemed to be an egg and ham dish.

He steered Meredith to a chair. "You'd better listen to Rachel. She seems to have a will of iron behind that sweet exterior."

Rachel gave him a startled smile, and it occurred to him that Colin McDonald was a lucky man.

"Yes, all right. Don't both of you gang up on me," Meredith said. She sat down and obediently picked up a fork. Taking the chair next to her, Zach dove in himself, nodding when Rachel offered coffee.

Meredith toyed with her food for a few minutes and then fastened her gaze on his face. "The police didn't tell me anything about…about my mother's body. Do you have any idea when I can arrange the funeral?"

Naturally she'd be wondering. He had to answer, little though he wanted to talk about it.

"They'll have to wait until the medical examiner determines the cause of death. I should think they'd have an idea fairly quickly, although there may be some tests that have to be sent to a laboratory. There's no way of knowing exactly."

"You can still talk to the pastor and plan the service," Rachel said quickly. "At least you'll be ready when the time comes."

Meredith nodded, seeming reassured by the idea. "Mom had some favorite hymns and Bible verses." Her voice choked a little, and she cleared her throat before she went on. "You don't think it was an accident, do you?"

He frowned, trying to decide how to say what he

must. "There are too many things the theory of an accident doesn't explain."

"But why would anyone harm her?" Meredith gripped the edge of the table. "It doesn't make sense."

He put his hand over hers, wanting to offer comfort. Meredith drew her hand away from him as if she didn't welcome his touch. It startled him. He'd thought they'd moved past the barriers between them. But maybe this was her guilt in action—guilt that she'd been with him when her mother died.

"Look, if the medical examiner rules that it wasn't an accident, I think we have to talk to Chief Burkhalter about this business surrounding Aaron's death."

Rachel looked more startled than Meredith did. "How could Meredith's mother have been involved in that? Someone might be upset with Meredith for poking into it, but surely Margo didn't know anything."

"I'm not so sure," Meredith said slowly. "I didn't tell her about it, but she did seem interested in our scrapbook from the summer Aaron died." She rubbed her temples. "She said if anyone knew anything about that night, it would be her, because she was the only one of us home."

"Did you ask her what she meant?" Somehow Zach wouldn't have expected Margo to take an interest in an issue outside her own wishes, but maybe he'd been wrong.

"I tried, but she just slipped away from the subject. She always did that when she didn't want to talk about something." Meredith's frown deepened. "Can you imagine Chief Burkhalter's reaction if I tell him that we've been trying to find out what really happened to Aaron Mast? He'd be angry that anyone questioned his judgment, and he certainly wouldn't believe it could possibly relate to my mother's death."

"It makes more sense than him badgering you and Zach as if you had something to do with it," Rachel said. "That's just utter nonsense, and he's certainly known you long enough to know it's impossible."

That led right into the more difficult point he had to bring up. He couldn't let Meredith walk innocently into a meat grinder.

"You have to realize that the police can't look at individuals that way. The investigation may eventually involve the state police and even the county district attorney's staff. That's why I think we need to talk this over with an attorney."

"But—" Meredith looked as if she'd been hit. "No one could suspect me of harming my mother. And we were together all evening."

So she'd already considered that he might have a reason for wanting Margo out of the way.

"It's inevitable that the first people the law looks at are those closest to the victim," he said. "I don't want to scare you, but you have to be prepared. We both do."

He thought that might shake her, but instead it seemed to give her strength. Her color improved, and her eyes sparked.

"Then we can't just sit around and wait to be

blamed. If the attack on Mom had anything to do with Aaron's death, we'll have to find out what happened for ourselves. Maybe if I talked to Laura again—"

"You'll never get near her if Victor has anything to say about it," Rachel pointed out. "Let me do it. I can find some excuse to stop by."

"Would you?" Relief showed in Meredith's voice.

"Of course." Rachel glanced toward the back window and half rose. "Someone's out there."

Zach beat Meredith to the window in the back door by half a step. She leaned around him, apprehension filling her face at the sight of people moving through the tall weeds behind the garage.

"What are they doing?"

He measured the activity with an experienced eye. "That's a grid search. It looks as if Burkhalter has called in the state police crime scene investigators."

"I wouldn't have thought he'd let the investigation out of his hands," Rachel said, sounding as if she'd had previous experience with Chief Burkhalter. "Why would he call them in?"

"At a guess, it's looking less like accident and more like murder. At least these guys will do a thorough search, which is more than he could manage with his small force."

He looked at Meredith as he spoke, hoping she was reassured. But she wasn't staring out the window now. In fact, she seemed to be looking at the wall, where a row of pegs held a raincoat and a couple of umbrellas.

"What's wrong?" He wasn't sure he liked the expression on her face. She looked like someone who'd picked up a flower and discovered a spider.

"My jacket." She reached out a hand toward an empty peg. "My tan windbreaker isn't here." Her eyes widened. "Mom had it on. I didn't realize it at first—I didn't get a close look…" She let that die off.

She was right, he realized. He'd subconsciously recognized the sodden jacket Margo had been wearing, even stained and wet from the pool.

Rachel came to look at the hooks. "It was chilly last night. She must have picked up the jacket as she went out the door."

Zach's mind turned the fact over and gave it a good hard look. It could mean nothing at all. But it could also mean that Margo hadn't been the target at all. The killer might have thought he was attacking Meredith.

## CHAPTER THIRTEEN

FOR MEREDITH, THE DAY seemed to grind on endlessly. She couldn't stop thinking about her mother, imagining those last moments. Had she realized what was happening to her long enough to be terrified? Had she cried out for Meredith? With every question the knife of grief pierced deeper into her heart. And guilt. How did anyone get past the guilt? If her actions had somehow led to her mother's death, she would never forgive herself.

She couldn't rationalize away the implications of her mother having been attacked while wearing Meredith's jacket. The three of them had discussed it backward and forward, coming to no conclusions. Zach had left after about an hour, probably annoyed with her lack of response each time he tried to get close to her.

When the door closed behind him, Rachel turned to her, a question in her eyes. "You were a little hard on him, weren't you?"

"Maybe." She rubbed her forehead, wishing she could think clearly. "It would be too easy to lean on him."

"A man's strength is welcome sometimes." Her smile suggested she was thinking of Colin.

"Too welcome." She yearned to seek comfort in his arms, so much so that it was like a physical ache. "But just being close to me has brought him under suspicion."

"I don't think Zach minds that," Rachel said.

She could only shake her head. Loving her had nearly ruined Zach's life once. She couldn't let that happen again.

Rachel shrugged, apparently giving up for the moment at least. "It is worrying about your jacket. The light tan would show up, even at night."

"Yes, it would." She couldn't entirely suppress a shudder at the train of thought. "People are used to seeing me wear it. Mom even complained about it, saying I should get something new. And at night, the gray in her hair wouldn't show up." She stopped, not wanting to carry the supposition any further.

She shook her head, trying to shake off the thought. "Look, there's no reason for you to stay with me. I'm sure you have things to do, and people will probably be dropping by all day."

"All the more reason I should stay. You shouldn't have to keep going over it and over it with people."

"I'll be fine. Anyway…" The doorbell interrupted her. Her nerves jumped. If it was Chief Burkhalter coming back with more questions, she might welcome Rachel's presence.

But it was Rebecca Stoltzfus from next door, leaning on her cane with one hand while holding a basket in the other. Meredith found her eyes filling with tears at the sight of the lined, kindly face. "Rebecca." Her voice choked. "Come in."

Rebecca handed the basket to Rachel and put her arm around Meredith, holding her close and murmuring soft words of comfort in dialect.

Meredith didn't even bother to translate. She didn't need to. Love and comfort were the same in any language.

She drew back after a moment, mopping her eyes. "I thought I was done crying."

"That will take some time," Rebecca said. "You must not expect yourself to be strong always, ain't so?"

"I'd be disappointed if I did." She managed a watery smile and turned to Rachel. "Now, you see, I told you someone else would stop by. You don't have to stay with me."

"Maybe I will leave for a little while, now that Rebecca is here. I'll try to take care of that other thing we talked about."

Meredith's mind was blank for a moment, but then she nodded. Rachel had said she'd try to talk to Laura. "Be careful," she said.

"Always." Rachel gave her a quick hug and hefted Rebecca's basket. "I'll just put this in the kitchen on my way out."

"You didn't need to bring something else." Meredith led Rebecca into the living room and saw her settled into a comfortable chair. "We enjoyed your breakfast casserole already."

"Ach, it's chust a streusel cake. In case you want to give folks something with coffee when they come by."

"It's so kind of you." She sat down on the sofa facing Rebecca, her mind churning. She'd had the sense that Rebecca had held something back when they'd talked about the night Aaron Mast died. Maybe now was the time to press for the truth.

"You must give yourself time to adjust," Rebecca said, her tone matter-of-fact. "It is always more of a shock when someone passes suddenly."

Meredith hesitated, wondering how best to put this. "Yes. To see her like that—" She broke off, sure the Deer Run grapevine had carried the news of how Margo King died all over town. "The police think it may not have been an accident."

Rebecca looked saddened but not surprised. That news must have spread, as well. "It is hard to believe that someone would want to harm Margo."

If she were to gain Rebecca's help, she'd have to be honest. "We realized this morning that my mother was wearing my jacket last night. It's possible that whoever attacked her thought he was attacking me."

Now the shock filled Rebecca's face. She reached out to grasp Meredith's hand. "But who could do such a thing?"

"Rachel and I fear it might be connected with my trying to find out more about the night Aaron died."

Rebecca murmured something softly that might have been a prayer. "It is hard to believe there is so much evil in the world." She was quiet for a moment, her blue-veined hand still patting Meredith's. Finally she sighed. "When you asked me about that night, I did not tell you everything. I think you knew that."

Meredith nodded, waiting.

"Sometimes the past is better forgotten, but not if it puts you in danger now. I didn't see anything that night, but I did hear something."

Meredith's breath caught. "What?"

"It must have been just about dark. I stepped out on the back porch to see how cool it had gotten before I opened the windows."

Meredith nodded. Without air-conditioning, Rebecca would follow the country tradition of closing the house during the day in summer and opening it at night.

"I could hear that someone was down by the dam—you know how noise carries on a summer night. But I couldn't identify anyone just by the voice."

"How many voices? You must have had a sense of that."

"*Ja.* Two, I'm pretty certain." She hesitated for a moment. "It seemed like they were arguing."

Had Laura been there with Aaron, maybe breaking up with him? "Male or female?"

Rebecca looked startled, as if she hadn't questioned that. "Two men. Well, boys or men."

That blew up the theory that Laura had been there. Unless, of course, she had come later. Meredith's spurt of enthusiasm slid away.

"Was there anything else you could tell from their voices? Did you hear enough to know what they were arguing about?"

"No, no, not actual words, just the sound of the voices." Her eyes widened suddenly. "Ach, how foolish I am not to realize. They were speaking Pennsylvania Dutch. They were Amish."

For a moment they just stared at each other. Then Rebecca shook her head decisively.

"But it can't be. None of the *Leit* would do such a thing."

The *Leit*—the term the Amish used to identify themselves. Their opposition to violence was absolute. Naturally Rebecca couldn't believe an Amish person would strike down a brother.

But Meredith wasn't so sure. Hard as she tried to push the idea away, she couldn't help thinking of Samuel.


RACHEL HAD BEEN RIGHT—there had been a steady stream of visitors, including the pastor. Meredith hadn't known how to tell him that they couldn't make funeral arrangements until the police released her mother's body, but he seemed to anticipate that.

Maybe, after all the years he'd spent in the ministry, it wasn't possible to surprise him. He'd made some practical suggestions for decisions she could make, and left with a promise to help anytime, in any way. Meredith found herself soothed by his manner, reassured that the world had not turned entirely upside down.

When yet another knock came at the back door, Meredith found she had to drag herself to answer. It would be someone with still more food, she supposed, and much as she appreciated it, at this moment she needed rest more than calories.

Her cousin Sarah stood on the porch. The brisk wind that had come up made the strings of her black bonnet flutter wildly. She carried the predictable basket.

"Sarah." For some reason, her eyes filled with tears at each new arrival. "Come in. Thank you for coming."

"I'm so sorry for your loss." Despite the fact that she and Margo hadn't ever so much as spoken to each other, Sarah's pain was evident. She took off her bonnet and black coat quickly and turned to envelop Meredith in a warm hug. "You surely aren't here alone, are you?"

"Only for a few minutes." She stretched the truth a little to reassure her. "Rachel will be back soon."

"Rachel's a *gut* friend, *ja?*" Sarah began unpacking the basket. "This is chicken potpie ready for your supper. When you're hurting, you need something that slides down easily, ain't so?"

Meredith couldn't help but smile. Her cousin had

a way of seeing what other people didn't in the small things of life. "You're right, as always."

"That's because I'm your big cousin. I'm supposed to watch out for you." A shadow crossed her face. "Daad wanted to come, but he felt a little funny about it, I think, because Margo didn't like him. He sends his love, and says if you need him anytime, just send word."

Meredith's throat tightened. "My mother's attitude..." She let that trail off, because they both knew only too well what it had been.

Sarah set the casserole dish on the counter before she turned to answer. "It's all right. Your mother has moved beyond such concerns now."

Meredith tried to imagine her mother unburdened by her obsession with social position. She hoped it was so.

Sarah began filling the kettle with an automatic assumption of control in the kitchen. "Sit," she ordered. "You'll have a cup of tea, *ja?* And maybe some shoofly pie? That looks like Rebecca Stoltzfus's dish."

"It is. She's been over twice already with food." And with some troubling information. A chill went through Meredith. Samuel. How could she talk to Sarah about Samuel?

In a few minutes Sarah was seated across from her, obviously intending to stay there and see that Meredith ate and drank something, at least. She managed to choke down a small bite of shoofly pie and followed it with a gulp of hot tea. People pushed food on the bereaved because it was the only way to express their concern, she supposed.

Sarah stirred her tea absently, frowning a little. "I heard something I could hardly believe. When the milk truck driver came, he said that Margo had been attacked. Surely that can't be true."

"It looks that way." She'd better proceed cautiously if she intended to bring up the subject of Samuel. "The coroner hasn't ruled yet, but there was an injury…"

"Ach, I can scarcely take it in." Sarah shook her head. "Who would want to attack Margo?"

"It seems impossible." She was finding it easier to talk about with each retelling. "I can't imagine what took her out to the pool at night, but she was wearing my coat." She stopped, letting that sink in.

Sarah just stared at her for a moment, her blue eyes going dark with shock. "But why? It doesn't make sense."

Meredith had a moment of identifying fully with the sentiment. It didn't make sense, but it had happened.

"I… We…wonder if someone might feel that I'm getting too inquisitive about the way Aaron Mast died."

"Aaron…" Her face paled. "But no one could want to harm you over something that happened so long ago." She started off sounding sure, but the sentence slid into something that was almost a question.

"They might if they had something to hide about what happened that night. I know, it seems incredible, but what other options are there?"

Sarah put her hand to her mouth as if to hold back a cry. "I am the one who asked you to look into it. If you are in danger, it is my fault."

"No, don't think that." She reached across the table to grasp her cousin's hand. She should have foreseen that reaction, and she hadn't. "We started asking questions almost as soon as Rachel and I got back together. I think now that I've never been satisfied with the explanation of Aaron's death, even when I was a child."

"You can't make me feel less guilty so easily," Sarah said. "Tell me what I can do to help."

Meredith looked down at their clasped hands, trying to frame what she had to say. "Samuel really didn't want to talk to me about Aaron. Maybe he'd talk to you."

And if Samuel was guilty, was she asking Sarah to spy on her own brother? Still, she'd be safe with Samuel. No matter what he was hiding, he'd never harm Sarah, and no one else need ever know she'd asked questions.

"*Ja,* I can talk to him again about Aaron. What do you want to know?"

There was nothing but to come right out with it. "Maybe you can find out if he saw Aaron that last night. He claims he didn't, but someone—"

Sarah pulled her hand away. "You are saying that my brother lied to you?" Her voice was tart.

She had to tread carefully. "He loves you. He wants to protect you from being hurt. Maybe he thought that made it worth telling me less than the truth about seeing Aaron that night."

Sarah looked unconvinced. "You said someone said something about Samuel. What was it?"

"Not about Samuel specifically." She didn't want to cause a breach between Sarah and Rebecca Stoltzfus. "But Aaron was heard arguing with another man that night. They were speaking Pennsylvania Dutch, so the man had to be Amish."

"Samuel would never harm Aaron. They were best friends."

"I'm not saying Samuel had anything to do with Aaron's death." Wasn't she? "But if he saw Aaron that night, he might have seen something or might know something that would help."

Sarah nodded slowly. "I will talk to Samuel. That's all I can say."

"Thank you." It was an oddly formal little exchange that left Meredith's heart feeling battered. She had already hurt her relationship with Sarah. Who knew how much more damage she might do to it before this was over?

ZACH JOGGED ACROSS the road when he saw a car stopping in front of Meredith's house that afternoon. He'd hesitated to go over in case she was getting some much-needed rest, but with all this company, she might appreciate a buffer.

He reached the gate as a man got out, then hurried around the car to open the passenger door. A woman emerged, carrying a sheaf of roses. Victor and Laura Hammond. That was surprising. From what Meredith had said, he'd thought Hammond was doing anything possible to keep Meredith away from his wife.

Zach swung the gate wide for them. Laura passed through without so much as a glance, but her husband looked at him closely.

"Zach Randal, isn't it?"

He nodded. "Looks as if we're all coming to check on Meredith."

"Terrible thing, terrible." Victor's pudgy face seemed to sag. "Margo King, of all people. I can't believe it could happen here. They're saying she was attacked."

"That's apparently what the police believe."

Shaking his head, Hammond started up the walk. "Poor Meredith. She must be devastated. We felt we had to come and offer our support."

As they approached the door it opened, and Meredith stood there. He was struck by how fragile she looked. He had to be patient with her, but the fear of what the police might even now be thinking jabbed at him. They might not have time for patience.

"Laura, Victor. It's kind of you to stop by." The pleading glance she sent his way seemed to ask him to help her get rid of them.

"We just had to see how you're doing." Victor pressed her hand. "This is such an awful thing. We could hardly believe it when we heard, could we, Laura?"

He glanced at his wife as he spoke, and Zach followed the direction of his gaze. Then he looked a little closer. Laura was on something, he felt certain of that. The dilated pupils and the glazed expression both told a story. The woman frowned, not seeming to know the right response to the question.

"Laura wanted to bring you some flowers." He nudged her hand. This time she seemed to understand, because she handed the roses to Meredith.

"I'm sorry." Her voice was hardly more than a whisper.

"Thank you, Laura." Meredith hesitated a moment, and then she put her arms around the woman in a quick hug.

Laura clutched her tightly for a moment. Tears filled her eyes, and she didn't seem to notice when they spilled over onto her cheeks.

"There now, dear, don't cry." Victor detached her and stood holding her arm. "This whole thing just seems so impossible. I suppose it was some vagrant. Or someone high on drugs. Don't you think?"

Meredith shook her head, and Zach felt she'd reached the end of her rope. No matter how rude he had to be, it was time to get these people out.

"I'm afraid Meredith is still in shock." He nudged

them gently toward the door. "It was good of you to stop by, but she needs to get some rest now."

For a moment he thought Victor was going to rebel, but then he nodded. "Yes, of course. Meredith, you just call me if there's anything at all I can do. That's what friends are for at a time like this."

Meredith managed a nod, and Zach ushered them the rest of the way out. He closed the door on Victor's obvious expectation that he was coming, as well.

He turned back to Meredith, his heart wrung by the pain in her face. He touched her arm gently. "Come and sit down before you fall down, okay?"

"I'm all right." She murmured the words automatically, it seemed, and she let him lead her into the living room and settle her in a corner of the sofa.

He pulled a chair over so that he could sit facing her. For some reason, she looked even worse than she had earlier. "What's going on? Has something else happened?"

"When Rebecca Stoltzfus, my neighbor, was here earlier, I talked to her again about the night Aaron died." She looked at him as if to be sure he understood. "I was right about her. She had been holding something back."

"What?" His instincts clicked on alert. Were they finally going to have something solid to work on?

"Rebecca said she went out on the back porch right around dark that night. She heard voices coming from the direction of the pool."

"Did she recognize them?" That would probably be too much to hope for.

"No, but they were both male, and they were speaking Pennsylvania Dutch. And they were arguing."

"Samuel," he said. It would explain Samuel's reluctance to talk to Meredith about that night.

"She didn't know who it was," Meredith repeated, sounding as if she were grasping at straws. "But when my cousin Sarah came, I said something about it." Meredith rubbed her arms as if cold, making him long to do it for her. "She was upset, and no wonder. I shouldn't have said anything."

"You had to," he pointed out. "If we're ever going to get to the truth…"

"I'm not a very good detective, I'm afraid. Anyway, I told her that if Samuel was there that night, he might have seen or heard something useful. I'm not sure she believed that's what I was driving at, but she agreed to talk to him."

"The police would get better results." He was getting impatient already.

"No!" Alarm flushed her face. "You can't tell the police. The whole family would never forgive me if the police came knocking on their doors."

"Okay, no cops. But there's one thing we should have done before this, and that's searching your mother's bedroom for any hint as to why she went out last night." Was it only last night? It felt as if an eternity had passed. He'd never been on this side of an investigation before. "Or have you done that already?"

"I looked around to see if she'd left a note anywhere, but I didn't actually search." Meredith pushed a strand of hair back from her face. "You're right, of course. We'll have to do that now."

She got up, heading for the stairs. She was so pale that he took her arm. "You look as if you'd be better off lying down," he said.

"I'm fine." Meredith's answer was predictable. Stubborn, but predictable.

But when they reached the doorway to her mother's room she stopped, hanging on to the door frame with one hand.

"Do you want me to do it?"

She shook her head again. "I'll take the closet and the dresser. I know what should be there."

"Just look for anything that seems out of place." He could understand her not wanting him to go through her mother's clothes, cop or not.

He started with the bedside table, searching quickly and methodically. Maybe Margo hadn't left a note, but she might well have forgotten or ignored some indication as to why she'd gone outside. After all, she'd expected to come back.

Unfortunately, that didn't seem to be the case. Zach worked his way around the perimeter of the frilly pink bedroom, checking every piece of furniture without success. He glanced at Meredith, who was going through the dresser drawers, examining each garment before returning it to its place. "Anything?"

"Only what I saw last night. She came upstairs at some point in the evening and changed into slacks and a sweater. The skirt she wore earlier is hanging on the door, and her slippers are lying by the bed. Nothing else."

He approached the delicate white drop-front desk that stood next to the window. "What did she keep in here?"

"Writing supplies, mostly. She didn't care for the computer."

Zach opened the front. The inside, like the room, was fairly neat despite all the frills.

Meredith came to stand next to him, looking. "That's the notepaper she used." She indicated a compartment filled with folded note cards.

He pulled one out. It was expensive stuff, heavy cream paper embossed with Margo's initials.

"My mother used that for all her correspondence." Meredith touched the stack of matching envelopes, printed with the return address. "She wrote notes for everything—thank-you notes, complaints, reminders—always on her special notepaper."

"What's this, then?" He picked up the plain, cheap tablet of lined writing paper that lay in the center of the desk. A box of envelopes sat next to it, open. It looked as if a few envelopes had been removed.

"I don't know." Meredith looked at it, frowning.

"That paper and those envelopes are definitely out of the ordinary for my mom."

He flipped open the tablet. Cheap stuff, the kind you could pick up at any supermarket or discount store. Several sheets had been torn out. Curious, he counted the envelopes in the box. "Three missing," he said. "Why would she use this cheap paper and plain envelopes instead of using her special stationery? Did she pay the bills?" That might be an answer.

"No, never. I took care of all the bills and any business concerning the property." Meredith looked at him, troubled. "What does it mean?"

"I'm not sure." Maybe he was building something out of nothing in his need to find answers, but it did seem odd. "Who would she write to that she wouldn't want to use her special stationery for?"

"I can't imagine." She rubbed her forehead. "My brain seems to have stopped working." She looked around the room, as if looking for something. "I just realized—the scrapbook isn't in here, is it?"

"Scrapbook?" His brain failed him for a moment, too, and then he caught up. The scrapbook Meredith had told him about, the one the girls had kept the summer Aaron Mast died. "It's not here. Don't you keep it in your room?"

"I noticed it was missing this morning." Her voice was tight. "My mother had seemed interested in it. I thought she might have brought it in here. But if it's not here, then where is it? Someone else must have taken it."

## CHAPTER FOURTEEN

MEREDITH COULD SEE that Zach wasn't convinced the scrapbook was missing, but after they'd gone through the whole house, he had to agree.

"I don't understand why anyone would want to take it." Meredith sagged onto the sofa, feeling as if she'd run a marathon. "It wouldn't even make sense to anyone but the three of us."

Zach nodded, somewhat grimly. "That's the interesting thing about this scrapbook. What could possibly have been in it to generate such interest?"

"Nothing. Or at least, nothing I can think of. I've been through it dozens of times."

Zach sat down opposite her, studying her face. "Sorry. I know you're beat, but we have to try and figure this out."

"I understand. I just don't know what I can say that will help."

"First off, how could someone get into the house to take the scrapbook? It's the only thing missing, so we have to assume the thief knew about it and thought it was a threat to him. Or her."

She hadn't really thought all of that through, but Zach was right. "As for getting in, that wouldn't be hard. Mother was paranoid about locking up at night, especially when she was home alone, but she often left the door unlocked when she went out in the daytime."

Zach frowned. "You ought to have dead-bolt locks on all the doors. Anyone could break in, even if she hadn't conveniently left the place open."

She couldn't help defending her mother. "Everyone in town leaves their doors unlocked during the day. It's hardly the big city. Neighbors would notice if a stranger was hanging around."

Zach shot her an impatient look. "The person we're interested in isn't a stranger, Meredith. You have to accept that. If someone killed your mother because of Aaron Mast's death, it's someone you know."

She knew that, intellectually. But emotionally, she couldn't picture anyone she knew striking down her mother. She struggled with the idea, trying to fit a familiar face on the image in her mind of a dark figure creeping up on Margo.

"I know. It's hard." Zach seemed to read her thoughts. "But I don't think we're going to find that this was done by a wandering nutcase. Okay, so just about anyone could have gotten into the house. When was the last time you saw the scrapbook?"

She shrugged, feeling useless. "I don't know. Last week, maybe? I found Mom looking through it, and I took it away and put it in the drawer of my desk."

"Why was she looking at it?" The question

snapped at her, as if Zach had forgotten who she was for the moment.

"I don't know." She tried to remember what her mother had said at the time. "It seemed to be curiosity. I think she'd overheard me talking to Rachel about it, and she always wanted to know what was going on."

Zach drove one hand through his hair. "The whole thing is so nebulous. What could someone want with a kid's scrapbook? Describe it to me."

She wasn't sure where to start. "Rachel and I made the scrapbook the summer Aaron died. Along with Lainey, Rebecca Stoltzfus's great-niece. She was staying here that summer. I think it might have been Lainey's idea to begin with. She created this fantasy game that we played all summer. Aaron was our perfect knight, and Laura his secret love. We knew about their romance, you see. We followed Aaron around, so we saw them together."

"It's a wonder he didn't chase you away. Or tell your folks. Unless he didn't know."

"He knew, all right. But he was kind. Aaron was always kind." She could see him so clearly in her mind's eye, always young, hopeful, in love.

"So what exactly was in the scrapbook?" Zach brought her back to earth.

"Drawings, mostly. Sketch maps we made of our mythical kingdom. Bits and pieces of a story we made up."

"It doesn't sound like a threat to anyone," he said.

"That's why it doesn't make sense. We certainly didn't know anything about how Aaron died. Only that it happened, and our parents clamped down on where we went and what we did. Lainey was sent back to her mother, school started and it all slipped away like a dream."

"So why…" Zach let that trail off, staring out the front window.

She followed his gaze. A police car had pulled up in front of the house.

Meredith's stomach clenched at the sight of Chief Burkhalter walking toward the house, his two patrolmen trailing along behind. "What do you think they want?"

Zach stood. "This looks like more than follow-up questions. I suspect this means the medical examiner considers it a case of murder."

Meredith fought back a powerful surge of anxiety. Now was not the time to give in to the powerful combination of grief and panic. She had to rely on the calm, rational thinking that had always been her strength.

Zach made a move as if to go to the door, but she waved him back, getting up. This was her home, and she felt the need to assert that fact.

"Chief Burkhalter." She held the door wide to allow them to enter. The younger patrolman looked embarrassed, as if he couldn't quite decide what to do with himself. But Ted… There was a cat-that-ate-the-canary expression on his face that raised her hackles in an instant.

She focused on Chief Burkhalter. "It's good of you to come by. I was about to call to see if you had any idea yet about when I can schedule my mother's funeral."

Burkhalter's gaze shifted away from hers. "I'm afraid I... We really can't say, yet. The medical examiner called with his preliminary report. Still some test results to come back yet, but the long and short of it is that it looks like your mother was murdered."

She'd thought she was prepared for it. Apparently she wasn't. The room seemed to swim around her.

Zach and Burkhalter reacted simultaneously, each taking an arm to help her to the sofa. "Put your head down until the dizziness passes." Zach's hand pressed on her nape, guiding her head down. He sat next to her, and it seemed she could feel the tension in every cell of his body.

"I'm all right," she murmured. She started to raise her head, found the room was still spinning and put her head down again.

"What were you thinking, blurting it out like that?" Zach's angry question was obviously directed at Burkhalter.

"Sorry," Burkhalter muttered. He patted her arm. "Davis, what are you standing there for? Go to the kitchen and bring Ms. King a glass of water."

Hurried footsteps moved toward the kitchen. Cabinet doors opened and closed, water ran. Presently a glass appeared in her range of vision, the hand that held it shaking so that water sloshed over the side and dripped on her lap. She grasped it before he could do any more harm and raised her head slowly to take a sip of water.

"There, you're looking better now." Burkhalter sounded relieved.

"Thank you." She handed him the glass. "I'm all right. It was just a shock."

"Shock to everybody in town, I guess." Burkhalter looked harassed. "I don't know how the news got out, but seems like it's all over town already." He glared at his officers. "People calling up, thinking there's some kind of maniac on the loose."

"That doesn't make sense." The words were out before Meredith considered that maybe it would be better not to argue with the prevailing opinion. Still, she'd never been much good at lying, and she'd better not start now.

"What makes you say that?" Burkhalter's gaze sharpened.

"Because I can't understand why my mother changed her clothes and went out to the dam at night."

Burkhalter nodded. "That's the question, isn't it? If she saw something or heard something suspicious…" He let that trail off, as if inviting her to provide an answer. Zach's arm pressed against hers, expressing tension.

Well, Burkhalter surely knew that one as well as

she did. Mom had called his office often enough. "If that were the case, my mother would call 911. Or possibly call me, if it wasn't too alarming. She certainly wouldn't change her clothes and go out to investigate on her own."

"That's what I figured, too. I suppose you looked for a note."

"That's the first thing I did." She waved toward the kitchen. "You're welcome to have a look yourself. We always leave…left notes for each other on the bulletin board next to the fridge."

"Well, the thing is, I'd appreciate it if you'd let my people have a look around your mother's bedroom," Burkhalter said, his tone making it clear it wasn't really a request. "Maybe there's some indication of what took Margo outside."

She was about to say that they'd just searched, but the pressure of Zach's arm on hers stopped her. "Of course. Please, go ahead and look."

Burkhalter nodded to Ted, and the two patrolmen headed for the stairs.

"It's the room to the left at the top of the steps," Meredith called after them, suppressing the thought of how her mother would have hated the idea of strangers looking through her things.

"There's one odd thing that Meredith thought you should know." Zach sounded as if he'd been quiet as long as he could manage. "About the jacket Margo was wearing."

"The jacket?" Burkhalter frowned.

"I didn't realize it at first," Meredith said. "But that light tan jacket my mother was wearing was actually mine."

Burkhalter's frown deepened. "Where did you keep that jacket?"

"On the peg by the back door. I suppose she might have decided she needed a coat and just grabbed it as she went out."

"Depend on it, that's what happened." Burkhalter looked relieved. "It got pretty chilly last night after the sun went down."

That was the logical explanation. She found herself hoping Zach wouldn't repeat his obvious fear that she had been the intended target.

"And Meredith discovered today that something is missing from the house," Zach said instead.

Unfortunately that was just about as bad in terms of subjects she didn't want to discuss with Burkhalter. It was going to lead inevitably to telling him what she'd been doing, and she knew what his reaction would be.

"Well, that's more like it." Burkhalter brightened at the thought of a thief. "What was taken? Money? Silver?"

"Nothing like that," she admitted. "It was a scrapbook. An old one that I had from the summer Aaron Mast died."

Chief Burkhalter looked as like a man who'd missed a step in the dark. "An old scrapbook. Well, now, don't you think you might just have forgotten where you put it? I mean, that was a good twenty years ago. It could be stuffed away in a box—"

She shook her head. "You don't understand. I've had it out recently. Rachel Mason and I kept it together." She decided to leave out mention of Lainey for the moment, fearing it would confuse the issue further. "My mother had been interested in it, as well. I know exactly where it was in my room, and today I discovered that it was missing."

Burkhalter ran a hand through his graying hair, making it stand on end. "I don't get it. Why would anyone want an old scrapbook a couple of kids made? Why all the interest in it?"

Meredith took a breath, trying to arrange her thoughts. "The thing is, we... Well, we kind of had a crush on Aaron Mast that summer. We used to follow him around. We knew all about his secret romance with Laura."

"Well, yeah, guess that never was as much of a secret as those two thought. Sad business." He shook his head. "What happened last night kind of brought it back to me."

Burkhalter had been chief then. He'd have been one of the ones who'd pulled Aaron's body from the pool, most likely. And he'd been the one to announce that it was an accident.

"When Rachel came back to town, we started talking about that summer. That was when I got the scrapbook out. We realized that we...had questions about Aaron's death. When Rachel found that note in the covered bridge that had been left for Aaron, it made it look as if he had killed himself."

Burkhalter's face had grown steadily redder as she talked. "It was ruled an accident. Everybody accepted that. Don't you think I had my suspicions of suicide at the time? Never leads to anything good, a relationship like that one. Laura broke it off, the boy was despondent and he killed himself. I did the kind thing and ruled it an accident. You should have let it alone."

She felt herself wilt under his glare. If she'd never started looking into Aaron's death, Sarah and his parents might have been content with a soothing lie. And her mother might still be alive.

"How do you know Laura broke up with him?" Zach's question probably took both of them by surprise. "Did she say so?"

"I didn't question her. She was upset, under a doctor's care." Burkhalter's face was an alarming shade. "I did what was best for everyone concerned."

"Did you?" Zach ignored the warning she was trying to convey through the pressure of her hand on his. "What if it wasn't suicide? What if someone doesn't want Meredith snooping into what happened to Aaron? What if that same someone was responsible for Margo's death?"

Burkhalter shot to his feet—not an easy feat for someone of his girth. "Maybe the Pittsburgh P.D. deals in fantasy. I don't. When someone gets killed, the killer is usually someone a heck of a lot closer than that."

He jammed his cap on his head and stamped off toward the stairs. Meredith listened until the thud of his footsteps had faded. Then she let out a long, shaky breath.

"He didn't believe me."

"Us." Zach's hand closed warmly over hers. "I made things worse. But his mind is so closed it would take a stick of dynamite to open it."

"What can we do?" The situation closed around her like quicksand.

Zach's face tightened. "We start looking for that stick of dynamite."

ZACH WAS NOT in the best of moods when he headed for the King house the next day. The sense of helplessness gnawed at him. He had to be doing something to help Meredith, whether she wanted him to or not.

After the cops finally left, he'd tried to comfort Meredith, but she had withdrawn again. He wanted to get back to the closeness they'd reached before Margo's death, or even the sense he'd had of Meredith relying on him when Chief Burkhalter was questioning her. But Meredith had given him a frozen look and said she was tired. In other words, go away.

Rachel was standing at the gate, talking to a man leaning against a late-model sedan. This must be Colin McDonald. They were engaged, Meredith had told him. Lucky Colin, given the way Rachel was looking at him.

She turned her smile his way when she saw him approaching. "Colin. You remember Zach Randal, don't you?"

"Sure thing." Colin stuck out his hand, and Zach had a quick impression that the mischief-maker of their childhood had matured into solid strength. "Zach and I have been talking about getting his property ready to sell."

"Colin's been a big help." Though the house was the last thing on his mind now. "By the way, congrats, Colin. I hear you convinced Rachel to marry you."

"It took some doing, but I wore her down." Colin's grin was the one he'd always worn when he'd pulled off a particular piece of mischief.

"Colin knows what's going on." Rachel cut short the casual conversation. "He wants to help."

Zach's initial reaction was that if there was really anything to be done, he'd do it. But it would be stupid to push away any offers of help.

"Good. Meredith needs as many people as possible on her side."

"You do, too, I'm afraid." Colin's face hardened. "The gossip is going around already."

"It's wicked, that's what it is." Rachel looked outraged. "Zach couldn't have done anything to Margo because he was with Meredith. And anyone who suggests Meredith would lie about that is just plain *ferhoodled.*" Rachel resorted to the Pennsylvania Dutch of her childhood to find a word strong enough.

"Some people will believe anything, and the worse it is the better they like it," Colin said. "Ordinarily I wouldn't pay much attention, but this time it was Kristie James telling someone in line at the post office that the police suspect you. With a lot of embroidery, of course."

"Kristie?" The name didn't ring any bells.

"Hasn't been here that long—she works at the Brass Bell."

The Brass Bell was the local bar.

"She's also Ted Singer's girlfriend," Rachel added. "I'm sure it's against the rules for him to be talking to her about the case." Rachel looked ready to take on anyone on her friend's behalf.

"True, but things get out." Zach was realistic about that. No matter how much Chief Burkhalter might want to keep a lid on the case, rumors would leak.

"That's exactly why I was just telling Rachel that Meredith should talk to an attorney," Colin said.

Rachel looked troubled. "But wouldn't that make her look guilty?"

"Better to be prepared no matter how it looks." Zach suspected it was going to be an uphill battle to convince Meredith. "We need to talk to her about it."

Rachel nodded reluctantly. "At least Jake Evans is a friend. Nobody would think it odd if he stopped by, I suppose." She glanced at him. "If you're going to be here awhile, I have a few things to do."

He nodded. "Meredith isn't going to thank us for hovering over her anyway. Did you have a chance to see Laura Hammond yet?"

"I tried." She made an expressive face. "I think I could have talked my way past the housekeeper, but Jeannette Walker was there. She's like a mother tiger where Laura is concerned."

"The woman is never happy unless she's manipulating people," Colin said.

"I figured she was just a garden-variety gossip," Zach said. "You should hear her trying to get information out of me."

Colin grinned. "I'm sure that's the only reason she hasn't kicked you out yet."

"True. She wants me there because she figures I'm a pipeline to information, and I want to stay because my bedroom gives me a good view of Meredith's house."

"Well, if you can't stand it, I have a room for you anytime," Rachel said. "But I'd better be going."

"Yeah, me, too." Colin gave her a light kiss. "I'll be around, Zach. Anything I can do, just say the word."

Zach nodded, but his attention had already shifted away from them. He had to see how Meredith was holding up.

She opened the door almost before he knocked.

"What were you and Rachel and Colin scheming about?"

Maybe he'd better not push his luck by trying to kiss her. He settled for a smile. "Hi. Nice to see you."

Meredith flushed slightly, and it was good to see some color in her face. "I'm sorry. That was rude. I just—"

"You don't want us talking about you behind your back." Since she didn't make any move to take him farther than the hall, he walked on into the living room. "It was nothing important. Rachel told me about her attempt to see Laura."

Meredith moved toward the sofa and then seemed to change her mind. She took the rocking chair instead. To keep him from sitting next to her?

"Victor and Jeannette seem determined to keep Laura from being upset. I was surprised he actually brought her to the house yesterday."

Mentally shrugging, he subsided into the wing chair. "He must have figured she wouldn't be upset by you, doped up as she was. Do you still think she knows more than she's ever told?"

"I'm not sure what I think anymore." Meredith pushed her hair behind her ears. She clearly hadn't put on makeup, and she looked pale. "It's just so confusing. What was my mother doing at the dam? I've been over it and over it and I can't even imagine an answer."

Zach frowned, not liking the defeated tone in Meredith's voice. That wasn't like her. "It seems clear enough to me. She went out either to spy on someone or to meet someone."

The blunt comment brought the brightness to her eyes again. "You can't know that."

"The logical answer is usually the right one. You've already said you can't think of another reason, so what's wrong with mine?" If challenging her was the only way to make Meredith fight, that's what he'd do.

"Who would she be spying on? It's ridiculous."

Interesting that she didn't immediately deny that Margo would spy on anyone. He didn't have any illusions about Margo, but he suspected Meredith still cherished a few.

"You mentioned having seen lights moving there a couple of times. She might have decided to investigate."

"She wouldn't. She'd be too afraid to."

"Maybe not if she thought she knew who it was. But I agree, the other is more likely. She went to meet someone."

"But why there? Why at night?" Meredith flung out her hands in a gesture that suggested she was pushing his ideas away. The movement stung.

He hitched his chair a little closer to hers, reaching out to clasp her hands. For an instant she gripped them, her eyes widening. Then she snatched her hands away and clasped them in her lap.

Zach bit back an instant response. "Look, I know it's hard to believe, but Margo was there. She did something you believe is foreign to her nature. So think. We can't resolve this without knowing what took her out of the house, and the police are already—" He stopped, not sure he wanted to go there.

"The police are already what?" Meredith was alert in an instant, face flushing, eyes frightened.

"Apparently Colin overheard some gossip, coming from our friend Ted Singer's girlfriend. She's spreading it around that the police think I did it and you're covering for me."

The fear turned to panic. "It's happening again."

He'd expected her to jump to denial, and her response threw him. "What do you mean? What's happening again?"

Meredith's eyes filled with tears, but when he reached toward her, she shook her head. "Because of me you were labeled a thief and chased out of town. And now you're being blamed again for something you didn't do. Because of me."

"That's ridiculous." He grabbed her hands despite her effort to pull free. "Listen to me. What your mother did years ago was her fault, not yours. And what's happening now is caused by Chief Burkhalter's blindness, nothing else. We both know we didn't harm your mother, and we're going to prove it."

"If it weren't for me—"

"Stop it," he snapped. "You're not a martyr, so don't act like one."

That brought a flare of anger to Meredith's face.

Good. He'd rather have her mad. Then they could fight their way to the truth.

He tried to ignore the little voice in the back of his mind that commented on the irony of the situation. Margo had parted them once before. Now that she was gone, she still seemed to stand between them.

## CHAPTER FIFTEEN

MEREDITH GLARED AT ZACH, anger swamping every other emotion. "How can you talk to me that way? All I want—"

"All you want is to find some way to make yourself responsible for everything that goes wrong."

He held her by the wrists, and she could feel her pulse pounding against his fingers.

"That's not true." Wasn't it?

*Ach, my little Merry, don't fret yourself so much over other people. They must find their own happiness.* Her father's voice, speaking softly in the Pennsylvania Dutch he'd used only when they were alone together. What would he say to her now?

"Isn't it?" Zach's intense gaze held hers, challenging, demanding. "Don't feel responsible for me. That's not what I want from you."

The very air in the room seemed charged with emotion. She couldn't look away from his face. *What do you want, Zach?* If she said the words aloud, what would he say?

A siren wailed outside and then cut off. It had both of them spinning to look outside as a police car pulled into the driveway and stopped.

Zach released her. "This isn't good. If he asks you anything that makes you uncomfortable, say you want your attorney present. Promise me."

His urgency compelled her to nod, but wasn't it far more likely that he'd be the one who'd be asked the tough questions? Another glance out the window told her it was Ted Singer, not Chief Burkhalter, and her stomach churned.

The doorbell rang at what seemed unnecessary length. Meredith took a deep breath and straightened her shoulders. Coming on top of that emotional exchange with Zach, a visit from the police was less than welcome.

She opened the door, hoping her face expressed nothing more than her ordinary composure. "Ted. What can I do for you?"

He jerked a thumb in the direction of the patrol car. "You can get in. Chief wants to see you."

For a moment she couldn't speak. Had it really come to this, that Chief Burkhalter was sending someone to pick her up?

"If Burkhalter wants to see Ms. King, he can come to the house." Zach stood, feet apart, shoulders tense as if ready to spring.

"My business isn't with you, Randal." Ted gave a thin smile. "Yet. Chief wants me to bring her in."

"Then I'm coming." Zach was close enough to touch if she reached out her hand, and she could feel the fury radiating.

"Not with me, you're not." Ted's big hands curled

into fists. He'd like nothing better than for this to turn physical, she realized, and she couldn't let that happen.

"It's all right." She managed a smile for Zach, even though there was nothing to smile about. "I'll ride with Officer Singer, and you can follow in your car."

*Please, don't make a scene. Don't make this worse.* She willed him to get the message.

He gave a short nod. "Right. I'm also calling your attorney. He'll meet us at the station."

Singer took her arm, as if to force her away from Zach. She froze, giving him a glare that should make him think twice.

"Excuse me. I need to get a jacket and my bag and lock the house," she said firmly.

He met her eyes for another second, and then looked away and let go of her.

Meredith took her time putting on her jacket and double-checking the door as they went out. She found her confidence rising. Annoying as Singer was, it was gratifying to know that she could make him back down, even a little. Or maybe it was Zach's comment about calling her attorney that had done the trick.

Zach followed them down the walk, his cell phone already at his ear. He must be calling Jake, who she supposed was her attorney, not that he'd ever had occasion to do much legal work for her.

Zach touched her arm lightly as they reached the car. "Remember what I told you."

She nodded. Singer held open the back door of the patrol car. So she was meant to ride in the back, like an arrested felon. It was too much to hope that the neighbors weren't noticing. She could see the front curtain twitch at Jeannette's house as Singer slammed the door.

Meredith leaned back, clasping her hands in her lap. It was too late for worrying about what the neighbors would think. She had a bigger worry right now.

The three blocks to the police station were too short to come up with any kind of strategy for answering questions. The smart thing was probably to do as Zach said and refuse to say anything until her attorney was there. Unfortunately that felt like an admission that she had something to hide.

Singer opened the car door and reached out to take her arm.

She pulled back. "I'm perfectly capable of walking inside without your help." She stalked toward the double glass doors of the station without waiting to see what he would do.

The door swished open and closed gently behind them. Too bad. Now that she was fired up, she'd have taken some pleasure in slamming it.

Burkhalter was leaning on the counter that bisected the front office, apparently talking to the department's secretary and dispatcher, Josie Welsh. He turned, opening his mouth to speak, but she got in first.

"If you wanted to talk with me, Chief Burkhalter,

all you had to do was call. It certainly wasn't necessary to have an officer bring me in like a Saturday-night drunk."

Burkhalter closed and opened his mouth a couple of times. "I didn't—" He stopped, turning a fulminating look on Singer. "Sorry, Meredith. There must have been a misunderstanding. I surely didn't mean you had to come in right this minute, but as long as you're here…" He seemed to run out of steam. "Josie, bring some coffee and a couple of those crullers to my office."

"Coming right up." Josie, who'd been in chorus with Meredith back in high school, gave her a reassuring wink.

Burkhalter led Meredith back to his office and fussed over pulling up the most comfortable of his chairs. Once she was settled, he backed toward the door. "Josie'll be right in with the coffee. Excuse me for just a minute."

He closed the door, but Meredith had no trouble in hearing his voice.

"What the devil did you mean by that? I told you to contact Ms. King and say I'd appreciate her stopping by, not go drag her out of her house."

"I thought…"

"You didn't think, that's your trouble. Going out and rousting a respected citizen like that—you'll be lucky if she doesn't have you fired."

"Listen, she's the one who's a suspect, not me."

Singer sounded as sulky as if he'd been called on the carpet by the principal.

The door opened just then, and Josie came in carrying the promised coffee and crullers. She wore a grin as she kicked the door closed behind her.

"Chief's giving it to Ted, and he deserves every bit of it. Always throwing his weight around, just like he did in high school." Josie set the tray down on the desk. "Listen, don't you worry. Anybody who knows you knows you couldn't have hurt your mom. Truth is, the county attorney was on the phone first thing this morning, and Burkhalter's scared to death he's going to get shoved out of the investigation unless it looks like he's doing something."

Several of the knots in Meredith's stomach unraveled. "Thanks, Josie. I appreciate the support."

"Don't let them bully you." The door rattled as it opened, and Josie slipped out as Burkhalter came in.

"There, now, that's taken care of." He rubbed his hands together and looked at the plate of crullers in obvious anticipation. "Now, don't you worry about this visit. I just have to make sure I have a complete record of everything that happened, that's all. You understand, don't you?"

Meredith hesitated, remembering Zach's advice. But it was natural that the police would need a record of the events of that night, and she didn't have anything to hide.

"Yes, I understand."

"Good. Milk? Sugar?" He held up a mug of coffee.

"One sugar, please." She concentrated on arranging the events of that evening in her mind while Burkhalter fussed over the refreshments as if he were presiding at a ladies' auxiliary tea.

Finally Burkhalter lowered his bulk into the swivel chair behind the desk, which creaked in protest. "Now, then." He took a bite of cruller and pulled a notebook toward him. "I think we have all the times down already, and we've checked with the restaurant, just as a matter of routine, you know. That all seems straightforward."

She nodded. So what was she doing here if he already had the information?

"Was there any…well, unpleasantness with your mother about you going out with Randal that night?"

The coffee turned to acid in her mouth. So that was what the police were thinking.

"I'm thirty years old, Chief Burkhalter. I don't ask my mother's permission when I go out."

"Well, no, of course not. But to be honest, I remember how she felt about him back when you were teenagers. She can't have been glad to see him back in town again."

Meredith's mind raced. She could deny that her mother had been upset by Zach's return, but Mom had probably talked to half the town about her feelings. It would be only too easy to prove.

"She wasn't happy about Zach's return, no." Meredith picked her words carefully. "But she knew he'd be leaving again soon. And she didn't raise any objection to my going out that evening."

Now that she thought about it, her mother's complaints had been very mild. If she'd wanted to keep Meredith at home, she was capable of working herself up into a state, but she hadn't. Maybe because, as Zach said, she had an appointment with someone herself?

"So you really expect me to believe your mother was okay with you going out with Randal, despite the fact that she knew he was a thief?"

"He was not a thief." Meredith tried to control her voice. "I'm sure you realize my mother made that whole thing up just to get rid of Zach when we were teenagers."

"Well, I have to admit I thought as much at the time." Burkhalter leaned forward. "But it seems like the kind of thing a man wouldn't forget easily. The kind of thing someone might want revenge for."

She could feel the blood drain from her face. She'd been wrong. Burkhalter was more devious than she'd given him credit for. He'd been after Zach the whole time, and he was trying to use her against him.

"That's ridiculous. Zach didn't harbor a grudge against my mother. And he couldn't possibly have attacked her. She was fine when I left, and we were together the whole evening."

Burkhalter raised his eyebrows, managing to look doubtful. "Were you?"

"Yes." She was frightened now, really frightened.

Josie had been wrong. Jim Burkhalter, someone who had known her all her life, thought she would cover up for her mother's murderer.

Voices were raised in the outer office, loud enough to penetrate the door. A moment later it flew open. Zach and Jake Evans jostled each other as they erupted into the room.

"Chief Burkhalter, is my client under arrest?" Jake was at his most formal, a side of him she'd seldom seen.

"What? No, of course not. Ms. King's just answering a few questions. She doesn't mind. Isn't that right, Ms. King?"

She felt, rather than saw, Zach move behind her. He put his hands on her shoulders. Strength and protection flowed through them.

"I don't believe I care to answer anything else." She kept her voice firm.

"Good," Jake said. "We'll just be leaving."

"Now, wait a minute," Burkhalter protested.

"No." Jake leaned forward to plant his fists on the edge of Burkhalter's desk and glare at him. "Your actions are way out of line, and you know it."

"This isn't going to go away." Burkhalter's face reddened. "A woman's been killed, and it's my job to find out who did it. And I'm not going to go chasing fairy tales about Aaron Mast, either."

"Fine. Investigate. But you don't talk to either of my clients unless I'm present."

"Either?" Burkhalter said.

"I also represent Mr. Randal." Jake's tone was firm. "Call me the next time you want to have a little chat with either of them."

Meredith couldn't get out of there fast enough. She sent a quick thankful glance toward Josie in the outer office, and then Jake was pulling open the door.

Once outside, she sucked in a breath. "Thank you. Both of you."

Jake shook his head. "Don't thank me too fast. Burkhalter might be slow, but he's stubborn. This isn't over."

Meredith nodded, realizing she was clinging to Zach's hand. She ought to let go, but she didn't want to. Little though she might want to believe it, this situation was real.

AT JAKE'S SUGGESTION, they'd come back to Meredith's house to have what Zach was mentally classifying as a council of war. He'd had his doubts about Jake at first, but he found his opinion rising as they talked over the coffee and cinnamon rolls Meredith insisted on setting out.

That was probably as much a defense mechanism on her part as any desire for food. If she treated this as a social situation, maybe she could handle it better.

Jake had patiently led Meredith through every word that had been exchanged in Burkhalter's office. Zach listened, trying to push down the urgent desire he felt to flatten most of Deer Run's police force.

"What part of 'Don't say anything until your attorney is present' didn't you understand?" he asked.

Meredith sent an annoyed glance his way. "All right, I was wrong. You don't need to keep harping on it. But I've known Jim Burkhalter since I was a child. I just couldn't believe he thought I might be involved in my mother's death."

"If it's any consolation, I'm the one he has in his sights, not you." He hadn't been particularly surprised to learn the aim of Burkhalter's little interview.

"Meredith is the stumbling block to his building a case against you," Jake said. "Unless he can get her to say you weren't together all evening, the only way he can proceed against you is to presume she's covering for you."

"How can he even think that?" The words burst out of Meredith. "Why is he focusing on us instead of trying to find the person who attacked my mother?"

Zach shrugged. "If I were in charge of the investigation, I'd start with the people who were closest to the victim, too."

"That's always going to be the police reaction," Jake said. "Combine that with the fact that Burkhalter is more used to drunk and disorderly and petty theft—well, it's not surprising. Though I confess, I'm surprised that he'd move against Meredith so quickly and so publicly."

"It must be because of the district attorney." Meredith frowned, pushing a strand of brown hair behind her ear. "Josie said that he'd called the chief this morning, pushing him on the investigation."

"Josie?" Zach tried to remember someone by that name and came up empty.

"The department's secretary, receptionist, office manager and dispatcher," Jake clarified.

"She shouldn't have told you any such thing, but I'm glad she did." Zach pictured the instant dismissal that would come to any member of his department who leaked such information. But this was Deer Run, not Pittsburgh.

"She was just trying to help. She said nobody who knew me would believe I could do something like that." Meredith was clearly comforted by that vote of support. Unfortunately, it wasn't going to make much difference.

He exchanged a look with Jake, relieved to see that the attorney was as skeptical as he was.

"I'm sure that's true," Jake said carefully. "But it will be the district attorney who decides whether or not to take the case to trial, and he doesn't know you. And if it should come to that, chances are slim that anyone from Deer Run would even be on the jury."

It was much of what he'd already tried to tell Meredith, but it was good for her to hear it from Jake. Maybe now she'd be able to accept it.

He sat still for a moment, unable to take his gaze from Meredith. There had to be a way to protect her.

"Look, Jake, there are a couple of things you don't know." He spoke abruptly. "For one, Margo was wearing a jacket that belonged to Meredith when she was killed. Almost anyone who spotted someone in that jacket in the dark would think it was Meredith."

Jake looked at Meredith questioningly. "Your tan windbreaker?" he asked, proving Zach's contention.

Meredith nodded. "It was hanging by the back door. She must have slipped it on when she went out."

"So you're thinking Margo was attacked by mistake. That the target was Meredith?"

Zach nodded, avoiding Meredith's eyes. The possibility that Margo was attacked by someone aiming at Meredith would just increase her sense of guilt, but it was crucial that Jake understand.

"Same question applies, then," Jake said. "Who would want to attack Meredith?"

Zach hesitated. Where to start in explaining their suppositions about Aaron Mast's death? "Meredith and Rachel Mason have been trying to find out what really happened when Aaron Mast was killed."

"I know," Jake said. "The whole town must know that by now, and Colin's a good friend of mine. And I grant you, there's no doubt that a thorough investigation wasn't done at the time. Burkhalter opted for the easiest explanation and the one he thought would cause the least grief. But even so, is it likely someone would attack Meredith after all this time?"

He knew, only too well, how thin it sounded. But what other explanation was there? "A person who'd been hiding a big enough secret for twenty years might well have a lot to lose if the truth came out now."

Jake nodded slowly. "Okay. I'm not sure I buy that, but let's assume it's true for the moment. What has Meredith found out that would make her a threat?"

Meredith flung her hands out. "Nothing. At least, nothing that seems very significant."

"We don't know what is or isn't significant," he pointed out. "If we assume someone who was involved in Aaron Mast's death attacked Margo, that means it's one of a fairly small group of people who are still in Deer Run."

Jake nodded, scribbling something on a legal pad. "So who does that include?"

"Laura Hammond," Meredith said. "She's said odd things to me a couple of times about Aaron. And I found her down at the dam one night not long ago."

Jake wrote down Laura's name. "Is she as unstable as people say?"

Meredith rubbed her arms. "I don't know what people are saying, but she was almost incoherent that night. She's clearly haunted by Aaron's death."

An idea swam to the surface of Zach's mind. "So she's unstable. Maybe because of drugs, maybe for psychological reasons, maybe both. She's been known to come to the dam at night. Suppose she showed up there, startled to see a figure standing by the pool. Is she unstable enough to see that as a threat and act?"

Meredith's lips trembled, as if he'd painted too

vivid a picture. "I don't know, and I'm not sure any-one else does."

"Okay, Laura Hammond," Jake said briskly, with an air of pulling the conversation to practical ground. "And by extension, I suppose we add Victor Hammond."

Meredith nodded. "He had a crush on Laura that summer. He followed her around like a puppy dog, and he certainly knew she was meeting Aaron."

"Who else?" Jake tapped the point of his pen on the pad.

Meredith rubbed her forehead. "Jeannette warned me to forget about Aaron. She implied that my father was interested in Laura." She pressed her lips together for a moment. "And my cousin Sarah said that she'd heard that my father also warned Aaron away from Laura. If so, I think he was only trying to keep Aaron from making…from making his mistake. But still—"

Zach wanted to touch her in support, but she looked so fragile it seemed she might shatter. "But you and your mother would be the only people who'd try to protect his memory."

Relief washed over Meredith's face. "That's true, isn't it?" He had a feeling she hadn't realized how much that suspicion had been bothering her.

"On the other hand, your cousin Samuel would have every reason to protect himself."

"Samuel King?" Jake raised his brows. "Do you

know how slight the odds are that an Amish person would commit murder? Why do you suspect him?"

"I don't," Meredith said, with a quelling look for Zach.

"Samuel's sister, Sarah, was Aaron's sweetheart, and he dumped her to chase after Laura." Zach ticked the facts off on his fingers. "Samuel had been Aaron's best friend, and it caused a lot of hard feelings. To put it mildly, Samuel was opposed to Aaron's relationship with Laura. He's reacted almost violently when questioned about Aaron's death. And Meredith's neighbor overheard Aaron at the pond on the night he died, arguing with someone she said was another Amish boy."

"You've questioned him about this?" Jake was frowning.

"We tried. He refused to answer any questions, nearly knocked Meredith over and warned her to forget about Aaron."

"You make it sound worse than it was," Meredith protested. "I certainly wasn't frightened of Samuel."

"Maybe you should be." Meredith was a little too naïve where people she cared about were concerned.

"He should certainly be questioned," Jake said, heading off what might have turned into a quarrel. "Maybe the police—"

"No!" Meredith's voice rose. "You can't. My father's family would never forgive me if I led the police to one of them. They're the only family I have now."

Zach had to harden his heart to the pain in her voice. "Samuel has to be made to tell what he knows, Meredith. You know that."

"Sarah said she'd talk to him." She wrapped her arms around herself protectively.

"Sarah is his sister. She's going to protect him no matter what."

She knew that. He could see it in her face. But as to admitting it...

"I'll talk to him, then," she said.

His reaction was instantaneous. "Not alone."

"You can both do it," Jake said. "As soon as possible. If there's another avenue for Burkhalter to explore, the sooner we divert him from you, the better."

It took a moment, but Meredith finally nodded. Zach studied her. How long was she going to hold together? And what would it do to her if she had to turn Samuel over to the police?

## CHAPTER SIXTEEN

MEREDITH PULLED HER SWEATER closer around her as she and Zach approached her cousin's sawmill. They'd driven straight to Samuel's farm from the meeting with Jake. Probably Zach was afraid she'd change her mind if they didn't come right away. Or maybe he feared they had no time to spare before the worst happened and they found themselves charged with murder.

Samuel's wife had directed them to the small sawmill. She'd eyed them with curiosity, but she hadn't asked questions.

Like plenty of Amish, Samuel found it necessary to do something to supplement his income from farming. The mill wheel swung, creaking, and the noise from the saws ripped through the air as the blades ripped through the wood.

"Let me handle questioning him." Zach's shoulders were stiff, his hands clenched. He looked ready to vent his frustration with the legal system on Samuel.

"Samuel is my cousin. He's more likely to talk to me."

"That's what you said before," Zach reminded her. "It didn't work."

She'd argue the point, but Zach pulled the mill door open just then. The noise assaulted her—so fierce that she longed to clap her hands over her ears. How did Samuel stand working in here?

Samuel was guiding a log into the saw, wearing protective goggles and a pair of black earmuffs, presumably to cut the noise. He glanced up at the movement of the door, his face turning wary when he saw who it was.

Zach advanced to within a couple of feet of Samuel. "We need to talk." He had to shout to be heard over the buzz of the saw.

Samuel shook his head. "Can't. Busy." He turned his back on them.

Zach reached out to grab his shoulder. Samuel attempted to brush his hand away, but Zach didn't release him. Zach jerked his chin toward the saw. "Turn it off."

Before Samuel could react, Meredith moved. Samuel must have forgotten that she'd been here many times as a child, but she hadn't. She found the switch that controlled the saw and flipped it. The resulting silence was deafening.

Both men looked at her. Then Samuel pulled off goggles and earmuffs and tossed them aside. "Meredith, I am sorry for your loss."

"*Denke,* Samuel."

Her use of the dialect brought a smile to his face, but it disappeared as quickly as it had come.

"I have an order I must finish. We can talk later."

"No." Zach's voice was flat. "We're talking now."

Samuel swung toward him, his shoulders stiff. "I don't know what you're doing here. I don't have to say anything to you."

"You do unless you want to talk to the police." Zach was uncompromising.

"The police?" Samuel seemed honestly dumbfounded for a moment before his anger flared. He shot a fierce glare at Meredith. "This is how you treat family? To threaten them with the police?"

"What about how you treat family?" Zach shot back. "Margo is dead, and you're still refusing to tell us what we have to know about Aaron."

"Aaron?" Samuel's forehead furrowed, and he shook his head as if to clear it. "What do you mean? What does Aaron have to do with Margo King's death?"

Seeing an opening in his confusion, Meredith took a step closer, trying to see the big cousin who'd been kind to her instead of the man who sometimes seemed a stranger. "My mother was wearing my jacket, standing at the dam when she was attacked. I'm afraid she might have been killed being mistaken for me." The words had become easier to say, but not easier to bear.

"You mean because you were trying to find out about why Aaron died? But that is *ferhoodled, ja?*"

"Not so crazy," Zach said. "If someone has been hiding a secret about Aaron's death all these years, that person might see Meredith as a threat."

"You mean me?" Samuel's voice rose in disbelief. "You think that I would harm my cousin? Or my friend?"

"You didn't see him as such a good friend when he broke your sister's heart, did you?" Zach was pressing, trying to push through Samuel's resistance. "We know you've been hiding something about Aaron. We just don't know whether it's something guilty. Like I said, you can tell us or tell the police."

Samuel shook his head, his stubborn jaw set. "I don't know anything about Aaron's death."

"Don't you?" Zach's voice expressed disbelief. "You were with Aaron that night at the dam. You were overheard."

Samuel turned his face away so fast that just the movement told Meredith it was true. He had been there.

"Aaron was meeting Laura that night," he muttered. "Maybe they were arguing."

"It won't work, Samuel." Meredith's heart hurt as she said the words. Obviously she wouldn't have made a good cop. "Aaron was heard talking to another man. In Pennsylvania Dutch."

Still, Samuel didn't speak. Zach closed in on him, his face set. "Aaron was your best friend, and he dumped your sister. You were angry with him. You argued with him over it that night."

"No!" Samuel rubbed his head, looking baffled and angry. "You're getting it all wrong. We didn't argue about that."

"It was you there that night." Zach pounced on Samuel's words. "You admit it."

Samuel's face twisted with pain. "*Ja,* it was me. I saw him going to the dam, and I knew he was going to meet Laura. I tried to talk him out of it—show him how foolish it was. But he said…" His lips clamped.

"He said what?" Zach pushed.

"He said Laura was going to have his baby."

Meredith's mind reeled. Laura had been pregnant? But no one had ever even suggested that. How could she have kept that a secret?

"They were going away together. Aaron would give up his family, his faith, everything for her." Samuel looked at Meredith. "Your *daad* tried to talk to them—to show them how wrong it would be. But they wouldn't listen to him, either."

At some level Meredith felt relief. Her father had only wanted to help them.

"So you figured it was all over then." Zach's focus never shifted. "You fought, struggled, maybe, and he fell into the dam."

"No." Samuel's grief and pain veered back to anger. "I did no such thing. I would not raise my hand against a brother. I told him he was a fool, and I went away and left him there." His face twisted. "He was my friend, and that was the last thing I said to him."

Meredith's heart caught in a spasm. She knew

a little about that kind of regret. "Samuel..." She reached out to him, but he shook her hand off.

"Are you satisfied now?" he demanded. "How much more trouble will you cause?"

"It's not Meredith's fault," Zach shot back. "She's the innocent one in all of this."

Samuel turned his back on them. He walked stiffly to the saw and switched it on, and it came to life with a metallic roar.

Zach started after him, but Meredith caught his arm.

"Don't. It doesn't matter." She shivered. "Let's get out of here."

"I STILL CAN'T quite believe it." Meredith grabbed the corner of the sheet Rachel had been taking from the clothesline in her backyard when she'd walked across the backyards to tell her what they'd learned. "If Laura had been pregnant, how could we not have heard anything about it?"

Rachel gave the sheet a flip to straighten it against the pressure of the wind. The day had darkened, and dark clouds massed over the ridge to the west of town.

"We were only ten," she reminded Meredith. "I don't know about your mother, but mine never mentioned the word *pregnancy* in my hearing. Now that I think of it, she still never actually says it."

Despite the worry that rode her, Meredith had to smile. "I know. Amish babies just suddenly appear, without anyone actually hinting that they're about to arrive."

Rachel put the folded sheet in the basket and reached for the next one with a quick glance at the sky. "The women chatter about who's expecting among themselves, but it's just not brought up in mixed company. And I certainly never would have heard a word of it if an *Englisch* girl found herself expecting."

"Even if the father was Amish?" Meredith grabbed the hem of the next sheet. It billowed out in the wind like a living thing.

"Especially then." Rachel shook her head. "I'm not sure how Laura's pregnancy affects the truth about Aaron's death. What does Zach say?"

"We didn't actually talk about it much." Her lips tightened.

"Why not?" Rachel stopped what she was doing to stare at her. "He was with you when you talked to Samuel, wasn't he?"

"Yes." She focused on the sheet, smoothing it out as she folded it. "He thinks I'm trying too hard to protect Samuel."

And maybe the reason that bothered her so much was that the way he'd visualized the scene had seemed only too real.

"Is that the only thing that's come between you?" Rachel's blue eyes were fixed on her face, demanding answers.

She shrugged. "I don't know. It... I think Zach expects more from me than I can give."

"Did he say that?" Rachel's persistence was one of her strengths. At the moment, Meredith could do without it.

"No, not exactly. He's not pushing me—not about our relationship, anyway. But he just won't admit that the closer he is to me, the more it feeds the idea that he's guilty."

"I don't see that at all." Rachel grabbed the last sheet just as the first fat raindrops fell. "It's already too late to pretend you two are casual acquaintances. And how can he help you if you hold him at arm's length?"

The clouds opened, saving her the necessity of coming up with an answer she didn't have. They grabbed the basket and the last sheet and ran for the back door, rain pelting them.

They plunged inside the house as the first clap of thunder rumbled overhead. Rachel dropped the basket, laughing a little, and tossed a terry-cloth dish towel toward Meredith. "Another minute and my laundry would have been soaked."

Meredith toweled her hair. "I hate to point out the obvious, but you're not Amish any longer. Why don't you just throw the sheets in the dryer?"

"I like it when they smell like sunshine." Rachel pulled out a chair. "You'll stay for a bit, won't you?"

She hesitated, looking out at the rain slanting across the grass. "Maybe I should get on home."

She was beginning to feel as if she carried some terrible disease, spreading suspicion to everyone who got too close.

"Are you going to shut me out now, too?" Rachel said. She shook out the last sheet and began folding it.

"I'm not trying to shut you out. I just think…"

"You think you're protecting other people by not letting them get too close," Rachel said firmly. "You might as well admit it."

"Maybe that's the best thing I can do." She hung the towel on the rack. Why was Rachel bugging her about this now? "I can't let other people suffer because of me. Zach's already been through that. He should understand."

Rachel gave her an exasperated look. "I'm sure it seemed like the end of the world when Zach was chased out of Deer Run. But was it? Does he see it that way? It seems to me leaving here might have been the best thing that ever happened to him. He didn't just survive. He thrived."

"I know, but…" She couldn't get rid of her burden of responsibility so easily.

"Look, I'm not suggesting the two of you run away together." Rachel gave a wry smile. "Not that you'd be able to anyway. But you can't help Zach by pulling away from him when he's trying to clear both of you. At least cooperate with him. You owe him that, don't you?"

Meredith nodded, not entirely convinced but not

wanting to argue about it, either. "I suppose the police already think we're involved with each other. You should have seen the way Ted Singer looked at me. I felt as though I needed a shower."

"From what I remember, Ted always was a bully. I'm sure Chief Burkhalter doesn't think that way."

"Burkhalter was okay, I guess, but it's still obvious that he has his sights set on Zach. And you know how stubborn he is."

"True." Rachel dropped the last sheet into the basket. "He's always going to look for the easiest answer. You can't really blame him, since most of the time that's the right answer. Anyway, once he knows about Laura's pregnancy, he may feel differently."

"Maybe." Meredith was doubtful. "He seems convinced that Aaron's death has nothing to do with what's happening now. And I'm not sure that her pregnancy adds much to the equation."

Rachel seemed to consider that for a moment. "I'm not sure, either," she admitted. "But it seems as if it must mean something. What happened? Did she have the baby? If so, she must have gone away, or people would know. Did she lose it, or...?" Her startled gaze met Meredith's.

"You're thinking she might have ended the pregnancy." Meredith turned that over in her mind. "It's possible, I suppose. It's even possible that she'd already decided to do so and told Aaron that night."

"That might give Aaron a reason to kill himself,"

the umbrella back so that she could see, getting a face full of rain in the process. Someone or something had moved there, in the shadows between the garage and the toolshed.

Heart thudding, she took a step back before common sense washed over her. Was it Zach, taking a look around while he waited for her to come?

Something man-sized shifted in the dark space. "Zach?" Her voice cracked slightly on his name.

No answer, but the shadows seemed to move again, coalescing into a shape even as her vision wavered in the steady rain. It wasn't Zach. Zach would speak.

She spun and ran toward the house. The wind caught the umbrella and tore it from her wet hand. She ran, blinded by the rain, afraid to look back and see who or what chased her—

She barreled into Zach, knowing him the instant their bodies touched, before he could even speak.

He grabbed her by the arms. "What's wrong? What happened?"

"Nothing. I…" She sent a glance toward the toolshed and saw no one. "Maybe my imagination working overtime. I thought I saw someone over there, between the garage and the toolshed."

His grip tightened, and then he shoved her toward the steps. "Go inside. I'll have a look."

Meredith shook her head. What was she thinking, acting as if she needed to be rescued? She wasn't the helpless princess in the tower, any more than Laura had been in their childhood imaginings.

"I'll go with you." She said the words firmly, daring him to argue.

Zach gave her a look that suggested he knew just what she was doing, but he shrugged, pulling a businesslike flashlight from the pocket of his jacket. "All right. Stay behind me. Please."

She nodded. The rain seemed to slack off a little as they approached the toolshed, not that it mattered. She was so wet already that she could hardly get any more drenched. She nodded toward the flashlight. "You came prepared."

"I'm not tramping around in the dark with a murderer on the loose. And neither should you." He flashed his light toward the garage, but the doors were closed, just as she had left them. With the automatic opener, there'd be no easy way for someone to get in without leaving a trace.

"It was still light when I went over to Rachel's." She was probably talking just to hear the sound.

The beam of Zach's torch illuminated the narrow space that ran between the garage and the toolshed. It was empty now, but someone could easily have slipped away behind the structures while she and Zach were talking.

"Is the toolshed locked?" He moved toward the door, and she followed.

"No. I don't even think we have a key for that door."

Zach reached for the latch, then turned and moved her back a few feet. "Stay out of the way." This time he didn't bother adding please. Tough, competent... Zach's boyhood rebellion had matured into the qualities that made him a strong man.

She nodded, shivering a little, her brief spurt of courage fading.

Holding the flashlight high with his left hand, Zach yanked open the door, and the inside of the toolshed flashed into view. Small, cluttered with the accumulation of years—there was no place anyone could hide.

"Is this the way it should be?" Zach was focused, sending the beam of his flashlight into every corner. It caught the delicate gray shape of a spiderweb in the corner and illuminated the wooden tool chest that had belonged to her father.

"I guess so. I haven't been out here in ages." She took a step inside, relieved to be out of the rain. "I keep a few small tools in the house, and the lawn mower is in the garage, so there's not much reason to come in here."

"You're sure you saw someone?" He turned to her, face intent.

Meredith blew out a breath, trying to relax taut muscles. "I'm sure I saw something moving." She closed her eyes for a moment, trying to visualize that quick glimpse. "It wasn't a small animal—something big, the size of a person."

"There's no sign anyone was in here, but it would

be a good spot from which to watch the back of the house." His face was lean and remote in the dim light, focused on the problem, not on her.

Her mind scrambled through possibilities. "Watch the house—you mean, like the police?" She could hear the note of incredulity in her voice. Really, she had to get over the illusion that this situation with the law was some sort of macabre joke.

"Could be." He focused on her, frowning. "That call from Jake—it's my turn to go in and talk to the cops tomorrow morning. But Jake found out there's going to be someone from the district attorney's office sitting in on the interview."

Her throat clenched, making it difficult to speak. "They're serious about us, then."

"They always have been. That hasn't changed." He suddenly seemed to see her, taking in her wet, bedraggled condition. He clasped her arm. "You're soaked. I can't keep you standing here in the cold talking."

She shook her head. "That's not important. Zach, what are we going to do? If they arrest you…" She faltered, unable to go on.

"Don't, Merry." His voice lowered with emotion, and he cupped her face with his free hand, his palm warm against her skin. "It's going to be all right."

"How?" she demanded, torn between longing and pain. "How is it going to be all right? They think we did this terrible thing, and they're not even looking for anyone else."

Something moved in his eyes. "I told Jake what Samuel said about Laura."

"You shouldn't—"

His fingers tightened, as if he'd shake sense into her. "Wake up, Meredith. You can't protect other people at the cost of your own life. Or mine, if that means anything to you."

"Of course it does." All the passion she'd tried to contain seemed to pour into the words. "But what can we do?"

"Jake thinks we have to tell Burkhalter all of it— Samuel, Laura, the works. Even if he doesn't take it seriously, maybe the D.A. will."

A shudder went through her. "My family..."

Zach released her, his face hardening. "Face it, Meredith. It might come down to me or Samuel. Which of us will you try to protect?"

## CHAPTER SEVENTEEN

ZACH TOOK A deep breath of cool, damp air when he finally stepped out of the police station the next day. The string of bright fall days had ended, but freedom felt good no matter the weather.

"Glad to have that over with?" Jake paused beside him, buttoning his suit coat against the chilly breeze.

"There were moments when I didn't think I'd be leaving that place." Zach jerked his head toward the faded brick of the police station.

"They don't have enough evidence to hold on to you. You know that." Jake was giving him credit for knowing the law, if not all the politics. "A motive based on rumors and hearsay, and an opportunity only if Meredith King is lying about her mother's death? I doubt they'd even get a search warrant on that, unless they had a very friendly judge in somebody's pocket."

"Yeah. But they won't give up." Zach shoved his hands in his pockets. "I wouldn't, if it were my case."

Jake eyed him with an air of sizing him up. "I've never had a cop for a client before. You have a unique perspective for a person of interest in a homicide."

"Can't say I get a lot of pleasure out of that." He

hunched his shoulders and then realized he was echoing the bad-boy stance of his teen years—the look of someone who knew that if there was trouble in the offing, the blame would fall on him. He straightened. He wasn't that kid, and he wouldn't let Deer Run do that to him.

"No, I guess not, but if it were your case what would you do?" Jake was assuming the role that seemed to fall so easily to him—the leader, the one in charge, figuring out what to do next.

He'd been that way in high school, too. The natural choice for captain of the football team, president of the student council, the senior class, the honor society. Well, that need to succeed of Jake's was on Zach's side, at least for the moment.

Zach forced himself to consider the case in the abstract. "I'd try to find someone who saw the car that night, first off. Try to prove we came back to Deer Run earlier than we said. Try to link me to the weapon." His gaze sharpened on Jake. "It's a safe bet they haven't found it yet. If they had, there'd have been questions in that area, but neither Chief Burkhalter nor that assistant D.A. ever went in that direction."

"Good point." Jake frowned. "That means they're still looking, and until they identify it, they can't tie it to anyone."

"If the killer's smart, it'll be at the bottom of the river by now," Zach said. "If not... Well, maybe they will locate it, but whatever it is, they can't link it to either of us."

"I suppose I don't have to tell you not to let anyone search your car or your room without a warrant?"

"No, you don't. But maybe you'd better stress that to Meredith."

"I will." Jake hesitated. "Burkhalter wants to see Meredith again this afternoon. And Reilly, from the D.A.'s office, will be sitting in."

"It figures." He had to unclench his jaw to speak. "That's the other thing I'd be doing if it was my case. Trying to break down the alibi witness."

"I've known Meredith King since kindergarten," Jake said. "She always tells the truth. The problem is going to be to keep her from saying more than she should."

"Yeah. Well, she'll listen to you, I think." Now it was his turn to pause. "You know she didn't want us to mention Samuel to the police."

"We didn't have a choice." Jake was firm on that subject. "The whole story about Meredith looking into Aaron Mast's death had to be told for there to be any other possible motive for Margo King's death."

"Burkhalter still didn't believe it." Zach stepped back on the sidewalk to let a couple of women pass and noted that they gave him a wide berth. Deer Run had no doubt already made up its collective mind about him and his connection to Margo King's murder.

"I didn't expect him to, but Reilly did listen and

make notes. If he's any good at his job, he'll do some sort of follow-up."

Zach nodded. It was their best chance, and they both knew that. But he couldn't help wishing it hadn't been something that was going to hurt Meredith as much as this would.

"You'll be with her the whole time she's in there, right?" He knew Jake would, but it hurt that he couldn't be.

"I will." Jake looked grim. "Trust me, I won't let them push her too hard."

WINDBLOWN RAIN STREAMED against the windshield as Meredith drove back to the house after her interrogation, making Deer Run look blurred and unfamiliar to her eyes. Or maybe her perception of the village that had always been home was changing.

The whole questioning routine had seemed futile to her—the same questions asked over and over again in a slightly different way. Maybe that was some sort of interrogation technique, an attempt to frighten her and catch her in a lie.

She rubbed the back of her neck, feeling the tension knotted into cords. She hadn't been scared, exactly, since Jake had been sitting next to her the entire time. He had interrupted often enough that she could catch her breath and think through her responses.

The assistant district attorney had put some of the queries to her. Afterward, Jake said that hadn't happened when Zach was interviewed. She wasn't sure what to make of that development.

Meredith took a cautious glance in the direction of Jeannette's bed-and-breakfast as she turned onto her driveway, hoping Zach wasn't watching for her return. *Please don't let him come over right now. Just give me a little quiet space.*

She stopped by the front porch, not eager to drive to the detached garage and then dash through the pouring rain to the house. This way it would only be a few steps.

She'd usually stopped here to let her mother out— the pain hit even as she thought the words. Grief wasn't just emotional; it was physical, as well. She'd learned that when her father died. Then she'd had the luxury of mourning. Now… Well, now she had to keep pushing the grief down to deal with cloud of suspicion that thickened around her and Zach. It seemed wrong to focus on anything else at a time like this.

She put up her umbrella as she stepped out of the car. The wind promptly caught it, turning it inside out. Giving up, she raced for the porch and stumbled inside, slamming the door behind her.

The house was dark and quiet. She hadn't realized how loud it had been in the car with the rain pelting down.

It was dark. Hadn't she left the hall light on? She flipped the switch up and down. Nothing. Apparently the power was off.

Walking into the living room, she touched the back of her mother's favorite chair, letting her hand linger there for a moment. Jake had said he'd press the authorities on releasing Mom's body, so she could proceed with the funeral. He seemed to understand the importance of the rituals of grieving. Maybe that came from spending a lifetime in the same small town.

A quick glance out the window told her that the lights were on farther down the block. That meant a power surge had probably tripped the circuit breaker, a routine occurrence with their antiquated wiring. She'd have to go down to the cellar and flip the switch.

Automatically she headed toward the kitchen. Her hand was on the door when something creaked, loud in the silent house, and her heart was suddenly pounding. She froze, straining her ears for a repetition, but none came.

Finally she let out a shaky breath. She was getting spooked. Not surprising, maybe. The kitchen was even darker than the living room had been, since its windows faced west, toward the storm. She took a step and bumped into a chair, then put her hand on its back. Funny, how things seemed to switch position in a darkened room—like waking up at night and walking into the closet instead of the hall.

The flashlight was usually kept in the top drawer to the left of the sink. Meredith had pulled it open before she realized it wouldn't be there. Mom had taken it out the night she died.

She swung away, blinking back the sudden tears that filled her eyes. There was a flashlight upstairs in her bedroom for just such emergencies, but her cell phone would surely give her enough illumination to make it down the cellar steps and find the circuit box. She took it from her bag.

Yanking the cellar door open, she paused. The dim kitchen was nothing compared to the utter blackness of the cellar, and the glow from her phone lit only the first two steps. Going down would be like stepping into black water. She shuddered at the image. Maybe—

The floor creaked behind her, sending her heart into her throat. She half turned, raising the light, but something black was coming at her, like a black bird swooping down, grazing her head, striking her shoulder. She cried out, ducking away from the blow, he'd hit again, she couldn't protect herself and then she was stumbling backward, feet slipping, falling—

Steps striking her, blackness surrounding her, nothing to grab on to— She hit the floor, stunned.

It took a moment for her brain to start working. She'd landed on her right side on the heavy mat she'd placed at the bottom of the stairs. Not sure she could move, she took a tentative breath. Her lungs still worked, it seemed, although pain seemed to rico-chet through her ribs.

Not moving seemed the best idea. If he thought she was dead, so much the better. Surely he couldn't see her from the top of the stairs. He'd go away, satisfied…

But he wasn't. Deliberate footsteps sounded on the stairs. He was coming down to make sure. He'd find her, he'd finish the job.

Meredith's fingers clenched, and she realized she was still holding the cell phone.

Relief flooded through her. She raised it so that she could see to key in the numbers. "I'm calling 911. The police will be here in minutes."

She could almost feel the indecision emanating from the dark figure. Then the dispatcher was speaking, and even as she stammered out the information she heard the quick withdrawal. Back into the kitchen, an odd thud and then the back door slamming.

"I think he's gone."

"Stay on the line with me." It was Josie's voice, instantly reassuring. "The car will be there in minutes. Stay on the line, Mer."

"Thanks." She muttered the word and clicked off, heedless of the advice. Zach. She had to call Zach.

She pressed his number, relief flooding through her at the sound of his voice. "I'm in the cellar." She stammered the words. "Somebody attacked me."

"On my way." He didn't waste time asking questions. Crazy, that just the sound of his voice was enough to make her feel safer.

ZACH FIGURED HE broke the land speed record getting across the street. He hoped the front door was unlocked, or he'd have had to break it in. He tore through the house, calling Meredith's name, heart pumping with fear.

"Here. In the cellar." Her voice was shaky but strong.

He reached the door and plunged downward, led by the glow of Meredith's cell phone. She was sitting at the bottom of the steps, hugging her knees to her chest, her hair swinging forward to half hide her face.

"Merry?" He knelt beside her, lowering his voice, trying to call up the detached sympathy he'd learned on the job. But this was Meredith, not a stranger. "Tell me what happened. Did he hurt you?"

She looked up at him then, and he thought she was making an effort to hold herself together. "Just bumps and bruises, I think." She rubbed her shoulder. "He swung something at me, but I was turning or it would have hit my head. And then he pushed me down the stairs."

"It was a man?" He couldn't help the way his voice sharpened.

She seemed to hesitate. "I…I'm not sure. I just assumed it was, but I didn't really see anything. Just a dark shape."

Zach resisted the urge to swear. He touched her head gently. "Sure he didn't hit your head?" He studied her eyes, looking for any sign of concussion.

She shook her head, still rubbing her shoulder. "If I hadn't moved… It was just like my mother." Her voice broke, and the need to take her into his arms nearly overwhelmed him.

"It's okay. You're safe now. I'd better call the paramedics to take a look at you."

"I already called 911. That was what scared him away." She managed a shaky smile. "Can't believe I held on to my phone while I was falling."

She'd called the cops. That was the right thing to do. Sure it was. But under the circumstances, he'd like to have a look around before they got here.

"Why is it so dark in here?" He couldn't very well try to take the cell phone. She was clinging to it like the lifeline it was.

"The circuit box." She gestured with the cell phone, and he spotted the gray metal box on the wall. "There must have been a power surge from the storm."

He rose and went to the box. A flip of the switch later, the lights went on.

In the harsh overhead light, Meredith's face was pale. She moved slightly, as if to get up, and winced.

He was at her side instantly. "Maybe you'd better stay put until the paramedics get here. Did you tell the 911 operator you needed medical help?"

"Not exactly, but I said I'd been attacked. It was Josie. I'm sure she'd send EMTs." She grasped his arm. "I'm okay. Just help me up the stairs."

Clearly she wasn't going to take no for an answer.

He lifted more than helped. Meredith wobbled for a minute and then steadied. She managed a wan smile.

"See? I'm okay."

"I doubt it." He put an arm around her. "I'd carry you up, but that stairwell is so narrow you might end up in worse shape than you are."

"I'm fine." Gripping his arm, Meredith moved, wincing again.

"Sure you are." He put his arm around her waist and helped her up the first step. "This is a piece of cake." He looked over his shoulder, scanning the cellar for any sign that someone else had been there. "You really think the storm knocked out the power?"

"What else…" She paused and then looked at him. "You think the intruder turned it off?"

"I think it's possible." And if it did happen that way, he'd just put his fingerprints on the circuit box. Great.

When they finally reached the top, Meredith was shaking.

"Sit down." The lights were blazing throughout the downstairs now. He lowered her to one of the kitchen chairs. "I want to make sure he's gone."

"He went out the back. I heard the door slam."

He was halfway to the door already. "Maybe he left some trace."

"What's that?" Meredith murmured the words, almost to herself.

He turned to see her bend, reaching for something under her chair.

"Don't touch it!" His exclamation came too late. Meredith had already picked up the object.

She held it, staring at it with a frown. "What's a hammer... Oh. I heard something hit the floor before I heard the door slam. He must have dropped it."

"Or left it behind deliberately." He snatched a dish towel from the rack and used it to grasp the hammer. Small, with a smooth wooden handle that looked as if hands had gripped it for generations. He held it to the light, his stomach churning. Those might very well be bloodstains on the head.

"This must be what he swung at me. It's a good thing he didn't get my head—" She stopped, her eyes widening, and he saw her thoughts land on the truth. "My mother."

"Probably." He wrapped the towel around the hammer, hiding it from her sight. "And unfortunately now it has your fingerprints on it." First him, now her. Anyone would think they'd set out to incriminate themselves.

The wail of a siren galvanized him. His fingers clenched around the hammer. "If Burkhalter gets his hands on this, he's going to use it to tie you to your mother's death."

He'd have thought she couldn't get any paler. It seemed she could.

"I don't know what to do." Her voice shook. "We need time to think."

The siren's wail moaned to a stop in front of the

house. There was no time, and she realized it as well as he did.

"Hide it. Please." Meredith's eyes widened with panic.

"I can't hide evidence. I'm a police officer." Everything in him rebelled at the thought. But if Burkhalter walked in and saw it, he'd arrest Meredith on the spot.

"Then I will." She took it from him, staggered a little when she rose, and then took two steps to the counter. She yanked out a drawer and shoved it inside.

"Merry—"

"Not for long, just until we have a moment to think. Please."

The cops were coming in the front door.

He nodded, taking her arm and helping her back to her chair. He'd just have to pray the hammer wasn't found until he had time to decide what to do about it.

# CHAPTER EIGHTEEN

MEREDITH'S HEART STUTTERED when Chief Burkhalter and Ted Singer barreled into the kitchen. She tried not to look as guilty as she felt.

"What are you doing here, Randal?" Ted Singer eyed him with obvious suspicion.

"Ms. King called me." Zach clamped his mouth shut on the words, a silent indication to say as little as possible.

"What happened here?" The chief looked annoyed, as if things were not proceeding as he expected.

"Someone was in the house when Ms. King returned." Zach moved to stand close to her. Not touching, but near enough that she seemed able to feel his warmth. "He or she pushed Ms. King down the cellar steps."

Burkhalter scowled. "Let Ms. King tell it. Please," he added, as if he hadn't decided on the proper protocol for addressing people he'd known for years and now suspected of murder.

"Just trying to spare her," Zach said, his tone mild. "She's had a shock."

"These stairs?" Singer grabbed the cellar door

and yanked it open, thereby adding his fingerprints to whatever else was there.

Meredith nodded and then regretted doing it. The right side of her neck was stiffening by the minute. She massaged her neck and saw Zach's fingers move, as if he wanted to do it for her.

"When I came back, the power was off." She tried to organize her thoughts into what to say and what not to say. "I thought the storm had tripped the circuits. That happens fairly regularly."

Burkhalter nodded. "Ought to have this whole place rewired with a bigger service entrance, that's what you ought to do."

For a moment Meredith thought he was going to mention his brother, the electrician, but he seemed to recall himself to the work at hand. "So you went down the cellar. Then what?"

"I didn't get that far. I came in here to get a flashlight. It was dark, and I groped my way over to the drawer. And then I realized it wasn't there." She paused. By this time, Burkhalter must realize what flashlight she was talking about. "I thought maybe my cell phone would give enough light to get down to the basement, but when I opened the door, I realized how black it was down there." Her voice trembled at the image of that darkness below her, like the dark pool that had claimed her mother. "I heard someone behind me, started to turn and something hit me on the shoulder. It knocked me down the steps."

Burkhalter looked from her to the cellar door.

"You sure you didn't just trip? Or maybe knock something off a hook in the cellar-way?"

"It was a person," she said, making her tone low and firm because she wanted to scream at him. "I saw the figure, but it was dark enough that I couldn't be sure whether it was a man or woman. It—he—came down a couple steps. That's when I hit 911 on the cell phone. He ran." She nearly stumbled over the thing she mustn't say. "The back door slammed."

Burkhalter looked at her for a long moment, as if deciding how much to believe. Then he jerked his head toward the cellar door. "Go down and have a look around, Singer. The lights are on now," he observed.

"I turned the power on at the circuit box," Zach said. "There was no way of knowing if it tripped because of the storm or because somebody threw the switch."

"So you've messed up any prints that were on it. You're a cop. You should know better than to touch it."

She could practically hear Zach grit his teeth. "I had to see if Meredith was all right. Did you send for paramedics?"

"I don't need—" she began, but he cut her off.

"You should be checked out."

"Josie sent for them. They should be here soon. Or Bennett Campbell is right down the street," Burkhalter pointed out.

"No." That came out more sharply than she intended. "Don't bother him. I'll wait for the paramedics, but I'm fine." She wasn't going to have Bennett checking out her bruises while thinking she was responsible for her mother's death.

Singer thumped back up the stairs. "Nothing to see down there, Chief. Just the mat rumpled up a bit."

"Then go out back and see if you can find any trace of an intruder," Burkhalter snapped.

Something about the way he phrased that made Meredith feel as if he didn't believe her account of what had happened. Was he picking up on the fact that she hadn't told him everything? Or did he imagine she'd staged the whole incident to gain sympathy and divert suspicion?

"So you figure this intruder was already in the house when you came back from the station." Burkhalter pulled out a much-thumbed notebook. "Anything missing?"

She managed not to shake her head, fearing the effect on her neck and shoulder. "I haven't had a chance to look."

"You surely don't think this was a burglar," Zach said. "It's obvious he came to attack Meredith."

Burkhalter shrugged. "Maybe so, but it's not that obvious to me. Supposing you let us have a good thorough look around the house for anything missing."

"No." Zach spoke before she could, and he put a warning hand on her shoulder. "Ms. King will have a look when she feels able, and she'll call you if anything's missing."

Burkhalter glared at him. "I might have to listen to that from Jake, on account of him being her attorney, but not from you."

By that time Meredith had caught up, and she wasn't sure where her wits had gone. There was little point in Burkhalter searching the house for missing items, since he wouldn't know if they were missing. Zach obviously thought he was using this to give himself another chance to search for evidence against them. And that evidence was five feet away from him in the kitchen drawer.

"I'm the only one who would know if something's missing," she said firmly. "Zach is right."

Burkhalter gave Zach a fulminating look and then returned to his notebook. "So why do you suppose someone would want to push you down the stairs?"

"Surely that's obvious, even to you." Zach's temper had apparently frayed to the breaking point. "Someone killed her mother, mistaking her for Meredith. Now he's trying to finish the job."

Surprisingly enough, Burkhalter didn't seem riled by Zach answering for her. Instead he turned to Meredith. "That how you have it figured, too?"

"I don't see what else it could be." She wrapped her arms protectively around herself. "Someone is afraid of what I might find out about Aaron Mast's death."

"Well, I suppose that's one way of looking at it."

Burkhalter snapped his notebook closed. "Thing is, as far as I can tell, you've been nosing around Aaron's accident for months now. And nothing happened to anybody until Zach Randal came back to town."

ZACH WAS STILL fuming over Burkhalter's attitude the next morning, but that was a minor annoyance in comparison with his worry over Meredith. At least, once the paramedics had checked her out, Burkhalter seemed convinced that her injuries were real. Whether he believed the rest of what they'd told him—well, that was doubtful.

He hadn't wanted to leave Meredith last night, but Rachel had insisted she'd stay, and he had to admit that it was probably better for Meredith that way. He'd spent the night feeling queasy every time he thought of that hammer stuffed in a kitchen drawer. A dozen times he'd gotten up, wanting to slip over under cover of darkness and retrieve it. But a glance out the window deterred him.

Like he'd thought, news of the attack on Meredith had spread quickly. Deer Run was on alert all night. Outside lights were on at every house on the street, and an unwary prowling dog knocking over a trash can had brought lights flashing in windows and one man, armed with a shotgun, out into the street.

No, it would be far safer to go out during the day, when kids were in school and the neighbors had relaxed their vigilance. Daylight eased everyone's fear.

But first he'd check on Meredith. He tapped on

the door, and Rachel answered so quickly she must have been watching for him.

"How is she?" he said, stepping inside. Judging by Rachel's face, she hadn't slept much.

"Hurting, but she won't let me take her to the doctor. I finally persuaded her to take a pain pill, and she got a little sleep, at least."

"Will you two please stop talking about me as if I'm not here?" Meredith's voice came from the living room.

He exchanged glances with Rachel and reached the living room in time to see Meredith grimacing as she tried to get up from the sofa.

"Stay put." He reached her in a few steps, his heart twisting, and eased her back against the cushion.

"You don't have to treat me as if I'm a china doll." Her voice was tart, but she clasped his hand. "I've got a spectacular collection of bruises, but they'll heal."

He held her hand in both of his, longing to embrace her but afraid to try. The dark shadows under her eyes looked like bruises themselves. "There's nothing wrong with taking it easy while that happens."

"We don't have time for that." Meredith squeezed his hands and then pulled hers free, as if needing to assert herself. "We have to decide what to do about the hammer."

He couldn't help an involuntary look at Rachel, but Meredith shook her head impatiently. "She knows. I told her."

Rachel came to sit on the other side of Meredith. "We're in this together." Her voice was firm.

He couldn't hold out against the two of them. "Okay. We have to do something about the hammer." He'd struggled with this all night long, and he still wasn't comfortable with his decision. "The police have to have it, but not with Meredith's fingerprints on it."

"That's why he left it behind, isn't it?" Meredith said.

He should have known she'd realize it. "Most likely."

"And I played right into his plan by picking it up. Or her plan." Meredith rubbed her forehead, as if that might help her think. "I still couldn't tell you for sure if it was a man or woman. Just a figure, that's all."

Rachel patted her hand. "The important thing now is to get rid of that hammer before the police find it. What should we do?" This last was addressed to him.

"If we get rid of it entirely, we're destroying the one piece of physical evidence." He was dizzy with going over and over it during the long hours of the night. "But we can't let it point to Meredith. The best bet might be to wipe it clean and then leave it somewhere in the woods or the stream, where the police can find it. I'll take it—"

"No." Meredith clutched his sleeve as he started to get up. "The police could be watching both of us. If you go wandering toward the woods, they're sure to stop you. That's true, isn't it?"

"Possible," he admitted. "But we can't just wait for Burkhalter to find it."

"I'll take it," Rachel said. "No one is watching me."

"It's too dangerous. I can't let you do that." Meredith's sense of responsibility obviously extended to Rachel.

"Don't be silly. I'll put it in my bag when I go over to the farm to pick up Mandy. I can drop it in the weeds by the creek. Now, don't argue. You know I'm right."

Meredith looked from his face to Rachel's. Finally she nodded. "Okay. We'd better do it quickly, then."

"I'll get it." But he paused, knowing he had to tell her something, no matter how much it hurt. "I had a look at the hammer when I picked it up."

"And?" Wariness showed in her deep brown eyes.

"It's old, and it's not mass-produced." He hesitated, but it had to be said. "There are two initials scratched into the base of the handle. SK."

It took a moment to sink in, and he saw realization dawn in her face. "Samuel King. You think it's Samuel's."

"I think it could be," he said, trying to soften the words. "Meredith, you can't ignore the evidence."

"There's more than one person around with the initials SK," she protested. "You might as well suspect Onkel Simon. Those are his initials, too."

"Your uncle didn't fight with Aaron on the night

he died." Her refusal to accept the truth about Samuel was wearing on his patience.

"Tools get passed around," Rachel said. "Even sold at flea markets. The hammer could have been kicking around for years."

He'd rather not have to argue with Rachel as well as Meredith. "Okay, but even so, we can't ignore the initials."

"My grandfather's name was Simon, as well." Meredith's eyes seemed to widen. "His tools had his initials scratched on the bottom. I remember my dad showing it to me. He was a carpenter, and when he passed, his tools were shared among his sons."

He processed that. "So you're saying your father had some?"

She nodded.

"Where were they kept?" He had a suspicion he knew the answer.

"In the shed."

"Where anyone could get at them. Including you." He ran his hand through his hair. "Okay. Well, that widens the field."

"Does it really change anything?" Rachel's practical common sense was a relief. "Get the hammer, and I'll dispose of it."

He nodded, not seeing any other option. He rose, but Meredith caught his arm.

"Wait. I moved it."

He stared at her. "Moved it? Why? Where?"

She stood, a little shaky but determined. "I

couldn't stand the thought of it there in the kitchen. When Rachel went home to get her things, I put it under the back porch steps, behind the pot of mums." She grimaced. "Maybe that was stupid, but I just couldn't handle having it in the house, thinking of my mother—"

She broke off, and he clasped her hand. He didn't approve, but he understood.

"Okay. Stay inside. I'll get it."

The two women followed him to the kitchen. He went onto the back porch and took a leisurely look around. No one was in view. It was as safe as it was going to be.

He went down the steps and bent, moving the pot of flowers, reaching under the step. Nothing. His palm touched damp earth. The hammer was gone.

MEREDITH SAW ZACH'S FACE when he turned, empty-handed. Grim, stark, frozen. In a few steps he was back inside, closing the door.

"It's not there."

Meredith discovered that she felt as frozen as Zach had looked. "How could it be gone?"

Zach shook his head, his jaw clenched. "Last night. Someone must have seen you put it there and taken it during the night."

His obvious guilt broke through her frozen state, and she reached out to touch his arm. "It's not your fault. You couldn't know."

"I should have guessed." He turned away slightly,

as if he didn't want to look at her. "I thought it would be safe until today."

"If the police have it…" she began, struggling to think this through.

"That's not likely." He swung back, frowning, and she could see him focusing on the problem instead of his guilty feelings. "Without a search warrant, anything they found wouldn't be admissible in court."

"Then the person who attacked me came back again." She shivered. "He was watching. He saw me put it there, and he took it." She shivered. "Why? Wouldn't he be better off to leave it there?"

"He couldn't be sure the police would find it before we removed it. I'm more worried about what he plans to do with that hammer now."

"You think he'll try to frame one of you with it," Rachel said, her arm tightening around Meredith's waist.

"Yeah. Maybe."

Or he might use it to attack again. She knew that was what Zach was thinking, and she couldn't let him see her fear.

"So what do we do? Should we tell Jake?"

Zach rubbed the back of his neck. "I guess so. It's not right to keep it from him if he's going to defend us."

"Should I call him?" She didn't relish the idea of trying to explain this business to Jake.

"No. I'll go over and see him. Better to explain in person." Zach didn't look as if he liked the idea much, either. "Meantime, I don't want you to be alone."

"I'll stay," Rachel said instantly.

"No." She put as much force as she could into the word. "I'm not going to put you at risk. You have a child to consider."

"I have a friend to consider, too." Rachel could be determined when she put her mind to it. "I'm staying with you."

"Not at night," Zach said. "I'll be here at night."

"Zach, you can't. People will talk. The police will think—"

"It doesn't matter what anyone thinks. I'm not leaving you here alone."

He spun away, moving quickly probably because he didn't want to argue any further. "I'm heading out to find Jake. There are a couple of other things I want to check on, too. Stay here."

He was gone in a moment, leaving her to exchange looks with Rachel, who smiled. "I would say that's a man who cares for you."

Meredith shook her head. "I…I can't think about anything like that. Not right now."

"Maybe not," Rachel said. "But soon, I hope. Now, why don't you lie down and take it easy for a bit? You must be sore."

"I feel as if I've been used as a piñata, to tell the truth. But I was thinking I should pick out the clothes for my mother, for the funeral." Her throat closed.

"Later," Rachel said, urging her toward the living room. "You'll feel more up to it later."

RACHEL HAD BEEN RIGHT about the benefits of a rest. By afternoon Meredith was still stiff and sore, but at least her outlook had improved somewhat. Zach would have talked to Jake by now, and she felt better for having Jake on their side.

Rachel, coming through from the kitchen, stopped to glance out the window. "There's a buggy pulling up. Looks like Sarah's come to visit."

Meredith managed a smile, just because Rachel looked so pleased. Rachel still reflected her Amish background in many ways. To her, family included anyone who was related, and they would all rally around in case of trouble. She'd never understand just how tenuous Meredith's place was in the King family.

"I'll put the kettle on," Rachel said, and vanished in the direction of the kitchen. Another Amish habit—a guest was always welcomed with food or drink or, more likely, both.

Meredith reached the door by the time Sarah knocked. She opened it quickly. "Sarah, it's good of you to come." Word of her fall must have spread quickly. "Let me take your jacket and bonnet."

Sarah shook her head, her face white against the black bonnet rim. "I cannot stay, but I must tell you what I am feeling." Her lips pressed together for an instant. "You brought the police down on Samuel."

"What…" For a moment her mind scrambled for understanding. The police didn't know, couldn't know, about the initials on the hammer.

"Why did you do that? I told you that I would talk to my brother, but you couldn't wait. First you go and question him yourself, and then we learn that the police have been at his door. How could you?"

The police. That must mean that someone, maybe that assistant district attorney thought enough of their story to investigate.

"Sarah, I'm sorry. I didn't know the police would do that. But don't you see—"

"I see nothing except that you have treated your family badly. Samuel is so upset, so ashamed, to have the whole community know that the police asked him about Aaron's death. I don't know how he will ever hold his head up again. And I don't know how I can ever forgive you."

Not giving Meredith time to say anything, Sarah turned and marched out. The click of the door seemed a death knell to Meredith's relationship with her father's family.

## CHAPTER NINETEEN

"DID JAKE UNDERSTAND about the hammer?" Meredith's voice contained traces of the strain she was under.

"I think so." Zach was lying, but he figured Meredith looked as if she'd had all she could handle at the moment. "My report can wait. What's going on with you? Not trying to be insulting, but you look like you've been pulled through a knothole."

Rachel had tactfully retired to the kitchen after she let him in, and he sat down next to Meredith on the sofa, enjoying the momentary illusion that this was any ordinary afternoon.

She was silent for a moment, staring down at their clasped hands. Finally she shook her head.

"I should have expected it, I guess. Sarah stopped by. It seems the police called on Samuel, asking questions."

He studied her face, reading the pain she was trying to mask. Unsuccessfully, at least from him.

"How did she seem?"

"Upset. Angry." She shot him a look that contained a spark of anger of her own. "What else would you expect? To have her brother questioned like that—well, it's just unbearable to her."

"Well, I guess she'll have to stand it. You have." He'd pretty much run out of sympathy for Samuel, who'd done everything he could to obstruct their learning the truth.

"Samuel is like a twin to Sarah. She'd told me she'd talk to him, and the way Sarah sees it, I betrayed her by questioning Samuel and giving him up to the police. Things can never be the same between us."

Her voice trembled on the final words, and his heart twisted. Nobody else could affect him that way, making him want to move mountains to make her pain go away. Trouble was, this particular mountain couldn't be moved.

"I'm sorry." He squeezed her hand. "But we didn't have a choice. Maybe eventually she'll be able to understand that."

"Maybe." She met his eyes, and he could see that she didn't believe it. "What did Jake have to say? And please don't try to sugarcoat it for me."

Since he planned to do exactly that, he assumed his best poker face. "I told him about the hammer. He wasn't happy with us for hiding it, but he understood why we did. As to who took it… He's confident the police don't have it. He says Burkhalter would never bend the law that way. He may be stubborn, but he'll do everything by the book."

"What does Jake think of our chances? Honestly."

Meeting her gaze, Zach realized that he didn't have it in himself to lie to her further. "If the hammer never turns up, he thinks the D.A. will be unlikely to prosecute, based on what they have now. But that doesn't mean they'll stop looking for more evidence."

"And we'll have to live with that cloud of suspicion over us." She drew the obvious conclusion. "What if the hammer does turn up with my fingerprints on it?"

He sucked in a long breath. "In that case, he suggested we consult a high-profile criminal attorney. He gave me several names of people he'd recommend."

She paled. "Does that mean Jake thinks I'm guilty?"

"No, no. He was afraid you'd think that, so he wanted me to explain to you. He's never defended so much as a felony case. He just wants us to have the best defense, that's all."

"I still can't believe this is happening." Meredith managed a smile. "I know, that's stupid. But every time I try to take it in, my mind just seems to run up against a brick wall."

"I understand." He did understand, but he also knew that feeling could be dangerous. They couldn't just wait for the axe to fall.

"You surely weren't talking to Jake all this time, were you?"

"I did a little door-to-door of the route we took coming into town the night your mother died. If someone saw us, that would establish when we returned. Not much of an alibi, obviously, since it wouldn't prove we hadn't returned earlier and then come back again, but it would be something."

"Judging by the way you look, I assume you weren't successful."

"Deer Run's habit of minding everyone else's business let us down this time. Nobody along the route remembered seeing the car. If only we'd stopped for gas—"

"Don't, Zach. That doesn't do either of us any good."

Now she was the one talking common sense, and he managed a grin. "What makes you so sensible, Ms. King?"

"I've always been the practical one." Her eyes misted suddenly. "Except when it came to you."

He felt as if he couldn't breathe. "Yeah. Same here." He shouldn't speak, not when a trap was closing inexorably around them. He shouldn't. But even as he thought that, he was touching her shoulder, turning her more fully toward him.

Meredith's eyes darkened. She leaned forward, lips parting, and he couldn't hold back any longer. His lips found hers, and he pulled her against him, kissing her as if he'd never get enough of her.

And Meredith responded, drawing him even closer, so that he wasn't sure if the heartbeat he felt was hers or his own. This wasn't a shy seventeen-year-old any longer. This was, literally, the woman of his dreams.

The kiss could have lasted an eternity as far as he was concerned. But Meredith drew back...reluctantly, he thought.

"Meredith—"

She stopped him with her fingertips on his lips. "Wait. Let me say this." She sucked in a breath. "I...I think I know what I feel. But we haven't been living in a normal world since you came back."

"That doesn't mean it's wrong to feel this way." Maybe he'd never really stopped loving her. Seeing her again had just lit the spark to something that had been there all along.

"Not wrong, no." Meredith seemed to be struggling to put it into words. "But we can't let this go any further right now. Not with my mother dead and all of this hanging over us." Tears filled her eyes. "Understand, Zach. Please."

"I do." He planted a kiss in her palm. "I wish I could say I didn't. If—"

A flurry of footsteps stopped his words. Rachel hurried in, her face white. "The police—I saw them from the side window. They're coming to the house."

Meredith blanched. He gripped her hands tight. "Remember. No matter what anyone says, you don't say a word unless Jake is with you."

Meredith nodded, her eyes wide and frightened. He wanted to hold her against him one more time, but someone was already pounding on the door.

At a nod from him, Rachel opened the door. Ted Singer was in first, closely followed by Chief Burkhalter. They passed Rachel without a look and headed straight for the two of them.

Burkhalter's face was expressionless. He stopped in front of Zach.

"Acting on information received from an anonymous caller, we've just completed a search of the Willows bed-and-breakfast. In the course of said search, we discovered a hammer in a trash can that appears to be bloodstained." Burkhalter stopped to draw a breath, looking like a man who's memorized his lines and is in danger of forgetting them.

"Never mind the rest of the spiel." Zach rose. "I know it."

Singer seized his arm, pulling it behind his back to put the cuffs on. Zach barely noticed, because he was looking at Meredith.

He could read her face so clearly. She was seeing all her worst fears coming true. She felt she was responsible for ruining his life again.

But it wasn't his life he was worrying about right now. As soon as the police lab tested that hammer, they'd identify Meredith's fingerprints, and this would happen to her.

She stood, fighting for control. "I'm coming with you."

"No, you're not." He kept his voice low and steady. "You're going to remember exactly what I told you.

Call Jake, tell him what's happened and do just what he says. Promise me."

Singer was pulling him away, but he held eye contact with Meredith until he saw her nod.

MEREDITH FOUND SHE was staring at the door when it closed behind the men, hardly conscious of Rachel speaking to her. It was her fault—

She stopped that thought before it could swamp her. This was no time for self-pity. She had to do what she could for Zach.

"I have to call Jake." She'd barely said the words before Rachel handed her the phone.

"Jake will know what to do." Rachel's fingers twisted together, and Meredith realized she was praying.

Thank goodness Jake had given her his cell number so that she could get through directly. She held her breath while it rang, trying to think how to compress what she had to say if she had to leave a message.

But Jake answered in seconds. "Meredith? What's wrong?"

"The police were here. They arrested Zach. They found the hammer in the trash can at the bed-and-breakfast."

"An anonymous tip, I suppose." Jake was quicker to understand than she had been, but then, she'd been numb with repeated shocks. "I can leave right now.

I'll be with him the whole time they're questioning him, I promise."

"I want to go—"

"Absolutely not." Jake's response was sharp. "Meredith, listen to me. You don't go anywhere near the police unless they come with a warrant."

"I should be there for Zach."

"Is that what he said?" Jake paused a moment. "No, I'm sure he didn't. He told you to stay clear, and that's the right advice. As far as the cops are concerned, you're Zach's motive as well as his alibi. If you go rushing to his defense, it just makes matters look worse. Got it?"

"Yes." She didn't like it, but she understood. "The person who planted the hammer has to be the one who killed my mother. But why plant it on Zach? Why not me?"

"Impossible to say." Judging by the background noise, Jake was already on his way. "It's possible he or she wiped off your fingerprints. If not, as soon as the hammer is processed…" He hesitated, but she could finish the sentence.

"The police will arrest me."

"Yes. I'm not going to minimize the situation, Meredith. I think you'd better be prepared for that to happen. But don't lose heart. The guilty person is getting desperate, and that should work in our favor. Got to go."

She tried to cling to that scrap of hope as she clicked off the phone. If Chief Burkhalter weren't so blind, surely he'd see that things weren't as they seemed.

"Jake told you to stay here, didn't he?" Rachel watched her, face anxious.

"Yes. He'll be with Zach, and he'll let me know as soon as there's something to tell. But that hammer…" She rubbed her forehead, trying to make herself concentrate. "As soon as they find my fingerprints, they'll arrest me."

"They can't. You'll see. Jake will do something." But Rachel didn't sound as if she believed herself.

Concentrate on the next thing. That was what she had to do. If she let herself look too far ahead, she'd give in to despair. "I think I'd better email my clients and let them know I'll be unavailable for the next week or so. People will understand. They'll have heard of my mother's death."

They'd probably heard she was under suspicion, as well. It was a wonder she hadn't started losing clients.

Rachel glanced at the clock. "Mandy will be home from school soon. I'll meet her and take her over to the farm, and then I'll be back. Will you be all right here alone that long?"

Meredith nodded. "I'll be fine."

"Lock up after me. And don't let anyone in."

She sounded as if she were talking to Mandy, and that actually made Meredith smile. "Will do."

She followed Rachel to the door and flipped the dead bolt once she'd gone out. The reminder hadn't really been necessary. She wasn't going to open herself up to another attack like yesterday's.

Meredith gave one longing glance toward the sofa and then headed for her office. She could rest later. Right now she'd best communicate with her clients. Leaving them in limbo was a sure route to losing them, if they weren't already gone.

It was a relief to be doing something so mundane as checking her email and running through her list of currently active accounts. Nothing was crucial at the moment, and thank goodness it wasn't tax time.

She labored over constructing a message that would be brief but reassuring. By the time a week had passed, she'd surely know where she stood. She'd either be under arrest, in which case her clients would flee, or the situation would be cleared up. Maybe that last was an irrational hope, but she had to think something positive.

Once the messages were sent, she reached into the drawer where she kept scrap paper. Making lists was second nature to her, even, it seemed, when under suspicion of murder. She ought to contact the minister again, and there were distant relatives and some friends of Mom's who might not have heard. They'd have to—

She stared at the sheaf of papers she'd just pulled from the drawer. They weren't all blank. Several of them bore writing. And not just any writing—her mother's handwriting.

Meredith's heart gave a painful lurch. It wasn't

unusual for Mom to raid her office desk for supplies, but she hadn't generally left things behind.

Meredith bent over the paper, frowning. It looked as if her mother had been writing a draft of something, trying out different ways of saying something, crossing out unsuccessful attempts.

*...sure you don't want people talking about...you know how gossipy Deer Run can be...I'm not sure it's right to keep silent...*

And then...*meet at Parson's Dam at nine p.m. We'll talk.*

Meredith's fingers tightened on the paper, and she put it down carefully. There was no name, but the meaning was clear enough. Her mother had invited someone to meet her at the dam the night she died.

Her thoughts spun crazily and then settled. This was evidence—evidence that could prove someone else was involved. She had to call Jake.

Yanking out her cell phone, she punched in the number and held her breath. If he was already in the interrogation room, he might not be able to answer.

But he picked up quickly. "What is it, Meredith?"

"I found something. Notes, in my mother's handwriting, in with the scratch paper in my desk drawer. They read as if she was threatening to tell something, and she was making an appointment to meet someone at the dam. Don't you see? This proves someone else was involved."

Jake gave a low whistle. "About time we were getting a break. Listen, put the papers back exactly the way you found them. I want Burkhalter to see them in situ. It may take some time to convince him to come over, but I'll manage it somehow. Just wait for us."

Wait. She was getting tired of that word. Stay there, wait, don't do anything.

Putting the papers back the way she'd found them, Meredith closed the desk drawer. Wait. She paced to the front windows, peered out for any sign of a police car, then stood looking out, willing it to appear.

Apparently police cars, when wanted, were like watched pots unwilling to boil. Who had her mother written to? What had she known?

A shiver ran through Meredith. Her mother had made an appointment with a killer—a killer they knew. She couldn't have realized how dangerous that was.

Still no sign of the police. Forbidding herself to stand staring out the window, she went back to the kitchen, only to find she was craning her neck to see out the window on the side of the house.

Her breath caught. Laura Hammond hadn't been seen in public in days, but there she was, walking down the sidewalk toward Meredith's house, alone. Alone, with no Victor or housekeeper or Jeannette to keep her from talking.

Meredith hurried to the front door, her bruised ribs protesting at the speed. She swung it open.

Nothing. There was no sign of Laura. Frowning, Meredith stepped out onto the porch, hugging herself against the chilly breeze. It was yet another gray day with a touch of rain in the air, an odd day for Laura to be out for a walk. She'd felt sure Laura was coming to see her. It seemed she'd been wrong.

Meredith went back inside, shivering a little, and pulled a cardigan from the hall closet. By the time she'd figured out how to get the sweater on without further aggravating her shoulder or her ribs, she was thoroughly exasperated.

Where were the police? Why was it taking so long? Surely when Jake told Burkhalter what she'd found, he'd realize how important it was. Wouldn't he?

She'd left her cell phone in the office. Maybe she should call Jake again....

But before she'd gone more than a few steps, there was a knock at the door.

Laura, she thought. She spun, hurrying to open the door. Victor Hammond stood there, his hand raised as if to knock again, his round face drawn, eyes worried.

"Is Laura here?" He tried to peer around Meredith into the house. "Is she?"

"No. I'm sorry," she added, seeing his disappointment. "Is something wrong?"

He half turned away, shaking his head, and then he turned back. "She's been so upset. Talking about Aaron again. I thought maybe she'd come to see you."

She should be wary. Zach's warning that the killer

was someone she knew rang in her mind. But Victor looked so lost that it tugged on Meredith's heart. She certainly knew what it was like not to be able to help the person you loved.

"I saw her a few minutes ago from the window. I thought perhaps she was coming here, but by the time I got to the door, she'd disappeared. Maybe she's gone back home."

Victor looked as if he were going to cry. "I'm afraid…afraid she's going to…to do something to herself."

"You think she might try to kill herself?" Her mind seemed to switch into gear. "The dam. If she means to harm herself…"

"She'd go there. Where Aaron died." Victor was already trotting down the steps.

Meredith hesitated in the doorway for a moment. Stay inside, keep the door locked—that was the sensible thing to do. But how could she be sensible when someone she'd known all her life might be dying.

She pulled the door closed and hurried after him as quickly as she could move. Poor, lost Laura. Her mind seemed to tick away the seconds as she hurried toward the path. If they didn't get there on time, the dam might well claim another victim.

## CHAPTER TWENTY

MEREDITH COULD HEAR the water rushing over the dam as she raced toward the clearing. The sound jacked up her fear. Two days of rain, and the creek was high. If Laura ventured into the pool—

*Don't think that. Just hurry, hurry.*

She'd lost sight of Victor on the path, but when she burst into the clearing he was already there, standing right at the base of the dam, peering into the churning water. The noise was so loud it reverberated in her head, making it hard to think. She scanned the surface of the pool, afraid of what she'd find. But there was nothing.

Relief washed over her. "She's not here. She must have gone—"

But Victor shook his head. He pointed to the base of the dam, where the water roiled like some monstrous boiling stew. His arm shook.

"There. Is that her? Laura?"

Meredith ran toward him, stumbling over a fallen branch. If Laura was submerged they'd never get her out, not without help.

"Where?" She reached the edge of the pool next

to him, straining to see anything in the foaming, churning water. "I don't see—"

The push came without warning, hands on her back, propelling her forward. She stumbled, trying to catch her balance, but she was already knee-deep in cold water.

"Victor!" Even as she cried out, turning, he swung a thick branch at her, his face contorted.

She jerked away, heart pounding. "What are you doing? Help me."

His only reply was to swing the branch again. She stumbled backward, away from its deadly arc. He was mad, he must be—

Her foot caught and she tumbled, off balance, ending up on her knees, the water rushing around her chest. Shock immobilized her for a moment.

She couldn't let that happen. She had to get up, find a way to get out. The water wasn't that deep here, if she could just get to her feet....

But even as she fought to get up the current caught at her, grabbing her like hungry jaws, pulling her toward the dam. Fight it, she had to fight it. She grabbed for something, anything to hang on to. If she let herself get pulled any farther it would be too late, she'd never get out—

Her hand caught a submerged rock, caught and held. The current pulled at her, trying to wrench her free, but she managed to get her other hand on the rock, clinging tightly. She could hold on—

"Why did you have to be so nosy?" Victor swung

wildly at her. "You and your mother. And Zach. I had to stop you."

The branch struck at her, knocking one hand loose. She fought to find the rock again, but she was numb, cold, the water soaking her clothes, dragging her down. Her vision blurred.

"I'm sorry." Victor's voice was clogged with tears. He loomed over her, standing ankle-deep in the water, raising the branch for another blow. "I have a gun, but I don't want to use it. Just let go. It'll be over in a few seconds."

The branch swung toward her head. Sucking in a breath, she ducked under the water. *Hang on, hang on, don't give up, don't ever give up.*

She came up sputtering, gasping for air, water streaming in her face, blurring her vision. If he swung again, if he hit her—

"Victor!" A voice screamed the name, and he halted in midswing, giving Meredith another precious second of breath.

It was Laura—Laura standing there, crying, screaming. "Don't, Victor, don't!"

"I have to, don't you see?" Victor's voice had turned pleading. "Her mother knew something. I had to do it. Now she knows. You should have stayed in the car, the way I told you. I have to do it now."

Meredith's numbed mind tried to put it together. Victor. It had been Victor all along. He'd used Laura to play on her sympathy and lure her out of the house.

"I have to protect you, Laura. I always did. Aaron would have ruined your life."

Aaron. Meredith clung to the name, trying to force her scrambled thoughts into order, but she couldn't. If he killed Aaron or if Laura killed Aaron, it didn't matter, because she couldn't hold on, and Victor was turning back toward her, raising the branch, and Laura was screaming, and it was the last sound she'd ever hear—

"Drop it!" Burkhalter's voice, shouting, people rushing toward them. Help… Too late, her fingers slid off the rock, the water took her…

And then hands grabbed her, pulling her back, dragging her away from the dam, choking and shaking but alive. Alive, wrapped in Zach's arms.

"Stop him!" Burkhalter shouted. Someone lunged toward Victor, but he had already scrambled free.

He ran out onto the top of the dam and stood teetering there for an instant. "I did it," he cried. "Not Laura. Me."

Before anyone could move, he'd pulled a handgun from his pocket. He put it in his mouth. The shot echoed, mingling with Laura's screams.

"I THOUGHT ZACH was under arrest." Meredith obediently slid into the fleece robe Rachel was holding for her. "But he was there, at the dam. I wasn't imagining it, was I?"

Given how confused she was about the aftermath of Victor's suicide, that seemed entirely possible.

She'd lost large swatches of time, only beginning to think coherently again when Rachel helped her into a hot bath.

"He was there." Rachel toweled her hair, as if Meredith couldn't be trusted to do it alone. Or maybe that was Rachel's maternal instincts coming to the fore. "He pulled you out. Another second and—" She stopped.

"And it would have been too late. I know." She shivered, and Rachel put a comforting arm around her.

"We weren't too late. Concentrate on that, and be thankful. Especially to Rebecca."

"Rebecca?" Meredith pushed her face back, wondering if she looked as bad as she felt. What did her elderly neighbor have to do with any of this?

"Rebecca saw you and Victor running toward the dam. It worried her, enough that she came to find me. We called the police." Now it was Rachel's turn to shiver. "Anyway, you've got an audience waiting downstairs if you feel able to talk. If not, they can just wait."

The police, probably. And Zach? "No, let's get this over with." She shoved her feet into slippers. "I'd better not look in the mirror."

"You look fine." Rachel led the way to the stairs. She kept a cautious arm around Meredith's waist all the way down.

Rachel had been right. There was an audience— Chief Burkhalter, Jake, even the assistant district attorney whose name had escaped her at the moment. But she only had eyes for Zach, who came immediately to help her to a chair.

"Are you sure you're up to this?" His eyes were dark with worry, his hair still damp, like hers. He'd changed, at some point, into dry jeans and a sweater.

"I'd rather do it now," she murmured. She wanted to ask if he was all right, but she might betray too much emotion in front of the others if she did.

She sat down, and Rachel tucked the afghan from the back of Mom's chair over her. Rebecca emerged from the kitchen with a steaming mug, which she put on the end table next to Meredith. After a searching look, she pressed her cheek against Meredith's.

"God has protected you," she murmured.

Meredith blinked back tears.

Burkhalter cleared his throat. "We don't want to bother you, Meredith. But it would really help if you'd just confirm what we all saw. For the record. Victor Hammond attacked you?"

She nodded. "He came to the door. Said he couldn't find Laura and thought she was suicidal. We went to the dam to look for her, and he pushed me in."

She discovered her voice was shaking and stopped for a breath. Maybe it was a little soon to relive it.

"Did he say why? Give you any indication as to what was in his mind?" This came from the county attorney—Reilly, that was his name. Her brain must be functioning again.

"Not to me, exactly." She frowned, trying to be sure she had events in the right order. "He said he had a gun, but this would be better. That I should just let the water take me."

She shivered again, despite her best efforts, and Zach took her hand firmly in his.

"Can't this wait, Chief?" His voice rasped with emotion.

"No, it's all right. Let's get it over with. I guess it was when Laura showed up that he said he had to get rid of me, like he'd gotten rid of my mother, because we knew too much. That he had to protect her." She shook her head. "You have to realize he was swinging a branch at me, trying to knock me into the dam. I was just trying to hang on, but I thought he meant that he'd killed Aaron. Or that Laura had, and he was trying to protect her." She frowned again, looking at Burkhalter. "What does Laura say?"

"Not much." His face seemed to sag with the weight of all that had happened. "She was nearly raving. She did say that her parents wanted her to… well, have an abortion. And Aaron was trying to get her to marry him."

"About then her attorney and her doctor showed up," Reilly said. "She's hospitalized now, out of reach." He looked dissatisfied. Maybe he'd been hoping for a big case to push his career along.

"I doubt anything she said could be taken seriously as evidence." Jake spoke for the first time.

"And after all this time, you're not going to find any other proof as to who killed Aaron Mast."

"That's for sure." Burkhalter sounded relieved. Unlike Reilly, he had to go on living here in Deer Run. He'd be happy to close things out quickly. "We heard what amounted to a deathbed confession from Victor. And he was seen around the Willows at the time when that hammer must have been planted. As far as I'm concerned, that ends it."

The two attorneys started talking simultaneously, with Jake upholding Burkhalter's viewpoint and Reilly arguing. Under cover of their voices, Meredith turned to Zach.

"I thought you were under arrest. How did you get there to pull me out?"

His grip tightened on her hand. "Jake was making a pretty good argument about the papers you'd found. Burkhalter was already shaken when Rachel called, terrified that something was happening to you. He pretty much dropped protocol at that moment, and we all rushed over here." His face twisted a little. "In time."

"Yes." In time. The danger was over, the past buried for good this time.

"Well, it's a sad business." Burkhalter stood, shaking his head. "And needless. The way I see it, Victor's guilt drove him a little crazy. Attacking Margo like that—well, she couldn't have known anything that would really incriminate him. Maybe saw him or Laura the night Aaron died, but that wouldn't be enough to bring charges after twenty years."

"She wouldn't have made it public, whatever she thought she knew." The words her mother had scribbled made sense to Meredith, now that she knew who their target was. "She… Well, she always felt that people like the Hammonds looked down on her. At most, she would have wanted to prove she was as good as they were."

It wasn't a particularly appealing side of her mother's nature, but Meredith felt confident that her analysis was the right one. Her mother might have wanted attention, but not at the cost of being involved in a murder trial. That would be the wrong sort of attention entirely. Ironic, that her actions had nearly put her daughter in the role of prime suspect.

"She was always dissatisfied, poor woman," Rebecca said, her face gentle as she looked at Meredith. "But nobody could have done anything to change that—not your *daad,* and not you."

Meredith let the words sink into her heart, finding them healing. Rebecca was a wise woman.

"I'm sorry for all this trouble." Burkhalter stopped in front of her, turning his hat in his hands. "Glad it's over. You'll want to get on with the funeral. I'll see to it the funeral home is notified to move ahead."

He gave her an awkward nod and went out, the other men trailing behind him. Jake paused long enough to bend and kiss her cheek.

"Congratulations on still being alive," he said. "I'll talk to you soon."

Rachel escorted them to the door. After a glance at Meredith and Zach, Rebecca carried cups to the kitchen.

Zach stood, and Meredith looked at him in surprise. "You're going?"

"You need to rest." He touched her cheek, his fingers gentle. "Burkhalter was actually right about one thing. You need to do a proper job of mourning your mother. Afterward, there will be time for other things." He bent and kissed her lightly. "I'll be around."

MEREDITH MOVED THROUGH the people who crowded the living room and dining room after the funeral service, trying to speak with everyone who'd come. She'd been overwhelmed with offers of help—a reaction, perhaps, to the revelations about her mother's death. So much food had been brought that she hadn't had to do a thing for the traditional reception at the house, and there was probably enough in the freezer to last her for a month or two.

Rachel and her sisters had shown up early this morning to set everything up, leaving her with nothing to do but concentrate on, as Zach had said, mourning her mother properly. For someone who had shed small-town ways years ago, he'd been surprisingly wise about that.

He'd been around for the past couple days, dealing

with the police, helping to tie up loose ends. They'd traced the anonymous call about the hammer to Victor's cell phone. He must have been desperate to get Zach out of the way so he could deal with Meredith. The ironic thing was that she'd never seriously pictured soft, ineffectual Victor as a killer.

Laura had apparently collapsed entirely after witnessing Victor's death. She was in a residential facility, and Jeannette seemed to be taking responsibility for her. Little though Meredith liked Jeannette, she had to admit the woman had proved a faithful friend to Laura.

Reminding herself of her duties, Meredith thanked the members of her mother's garden club for the beautiful arrangements and agreed that Margo would have loved them. She glanced around, spotting Zach talking to Jake. He'd made no effort to talk to her privately in the past two days, giving her space, she thought, to get on with burying her mother before looking ahead.

But when she thought about the future, it seemed oddly blank. *There's plenty of time,* he'd said, but what did that mean?

She stopped at the sight of a group of soberly dressed people congregated in a corner of the dining room, and then went forward to greet her Amish relatives. It was unusual for the Amish to attend something like this, and none of them had ever been in the house before, due to her mother's attitude.

"I'm glad you're here." She clasped Onkel Simon's hand. "Thank you for coming."

"We thought you might need us," he said. *"Da Herr sie mit du."*

*The Lord be with you.* Yes, she did need to have her family here.

Sarah made a move as if to hug her and then drew back, her face expressing uncertainty. "Can you forgive me? I was so unkind—"

"Let's forget the past, all right?" Meredith put her arms around her cousin, grateful for the warm hug in return. "We both made mistakes, but it's over."

*"Ja."* Sarah's eyes were misty.

Samuel gave her a jerky nod. "I am sorry for your loss," he said carefully.

"Thank you." Samuel didn't come to forgiveness as readily as his sister did, judging by his stiffness.

When she would have moved away, he touched her arm, surprising her.

"I blamed myself," he said, his voice low. "I thought my harsh words had driven Aaron to take his life. You were right. The truth is better."

"Yes." She managed a smile. "It is."

ZACH WAITED PATIENTLY until the crowd left, busying himself with helping Rachel in the kitchen, not that she and her sisters seemed to need any help. Finally, as the house grew quiet, she flapped her dish towel at him.

"We'll finish up in here. Go and talk to Meredith. You know that's what you want to do."

He did. He just hadn't figured out what he wanted to say. Well, maybe it was time he did.

He found Meredith in her office, of all places, sitting in front of the computer. She looked up when he came in.

"Just making sure it's still there," she said, closing down. "A few days ago I thought my business was probably on the verge of collapse. Nobody wants an accountant who's involved in a murder case."

"But they all hung in there?" He moved to stand behind her, resting his hands on her shoulders. He could feel the tension in the tight muscles, and he smoothed his hands over them gently.

"Yes, they did." She seemed to stare at the blank computer screen. "I…I guess I'll have to get back to work soon." She hesitated. "And I guess you will, too."

Was that a question? He wasn't sure.

"I'll have a few things to say to my sergeant when I do. The old man was right, as usual."

Meredith focused on him, a faintly puzzled frown wrinkling her brows. "Right about what?"

"He told me I should come back to Deer Run and face whatever I was trying so hard to forget." He grimaced. "At first I figured that advice was backfiring. I came back here, and I was right back to being that kid no one respected."

She put her hand over his where it rested on her shoulder. "Zach…"

"It doesn't matter. That's what I finally figured out. All that ever really mattered was respecting myself." He shook his head. "I wasted a lot of years thinking people were looking down on me."

Like Meredith's mother, with her constant need to prove she was better than others.

"I'm glad," she said simply, her eyes warm. "If it took coming back to Deer Run to prove that to you, maybe it was meant to be."

"There's something else that was meant to be." He was bone-deep sure of it now. "I was too young to really understand what loving you meant back then. But not now. Now I know, and I still feel the same."

Tears shimmered in her eyes. "I—"

He put his fingers to her lips. "One more thing, first. I know everything's been crazy since I came back. I know you're still getting used to the fact that your mother is gone. I'm not trying to rush you. We have all the time in the world, and no one standing in our way." He managed a smile. "It's not that far from Pittsburgh to Deer Run. I could make it in a couple hours if I bent a few speed laws."

If she loved him, they'd work it out. If not, then it didn't matter.

Meredith took his hand in both of hers. "You're right. It has been crazy, and frightening, and tragic. But I don't want to be like Victor and Laura, forever caught in the mistakes of the past. I love you." She smiled, but a tear spilled over onto her cheek. "The rest of it we can work out." She echoed his thoughts.

"That's enough to go on with." He drew her up from the chair and into his arms, and she nestled against him with a little sigh, as if she'd come home at last.

He pressed his cheek against her and held her gently. There was time, he thought again. Time for grieving, time for planning, time for passion. This time around, their love was strong enough to survive anything.

* * * * *

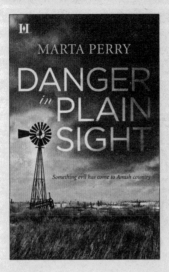

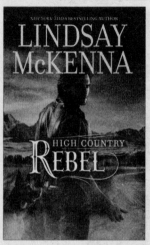

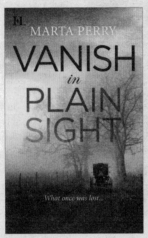

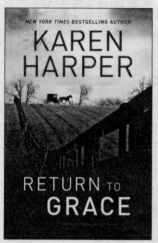

# REQUEST YOUR FREE BOOKS!

## 2 FREE NOVELS
## FROM THE SUSPENSE COLLECTION
## PLUS 2 FREE GIFTS!

**YES!** Please send me 2 FREE novels from the Suspense Collection and my 2 FREE gifts (gifts are worth about $10). After receiving them, if I don't wish to receive any more books, I can return the shipping statement marked "cancel." If I don't cancel, I will receive 4 brand-new novels every month and be billed just $6.24 per book in the U.S. or $6.74 per book in Canada. That's a savings of at least 22% off the cover price. It's quite a bargain! Shipping and handling is just 50¢ per book in the U.S. and 75¢ per book in Canada.* I understand that accepting the 2 free books and gifts places me under no obligation to buy anything. I can always return a shipment and cancel at any time. Even if I never buy another book, the two free books and gifts are mine to keep forever.

191/391 MDN F4XN

| | |
|---|---|
| Name | (PLEASE PRINT) |
| Address | Apt. # |
| City | State/Prov. | Zip/Postal Code |

Signature (if under 18, a parent or guardian must sign)

**Mail to the Harlequin® Reader Service:**
**IN U.S.A.:** P.O. Box 1867, Buffalo, NY 14240-1867
**IN CANADA:** P.O. Box 609, Fort Erie, Ontario L2A 5X3

**Want to try two free books from another line?**
**Call 1-800-873-8635 or visit www.ReaderService.com.**

* Terms and prices subject to change without notice. Prices do not include applicable taxes. Sales tax applicable in N.Y. Canadian residents will be charged applicable taxes. Offer not valid in Quebec. This offer is limited to one order per household. Not valid for current subscribers to the Suspense Collection or the Romance/Suspense Collection. All orders subject to credit approval. Credit or debit balances in a customer's account(s) may be offset by any other outstanding balance owed by or to the customer. Please allow 4 to 6 weeks for delivery. Offer available while quantities last.

**Your Privacy**—The Harlequin® Reader Service is committed to protecting your privacy. Our Privacy Policy is available online at www.ReaderService.com or upon request from the Harlequin Reader Service.

We make a portion of our mailing list available to reputable third parties that offer products we believe may interest you. If you prefer that we not exchange your name with third parties, or if you wish to clarify or modify your communication preferences, please visit us at www.ReaderService.com/consumerchoice or write to us at Harlequin Reader Service Preference Service, P.O. Box 9062, Buffalo, NY 14269. Include your complete name and address.

SUS13R

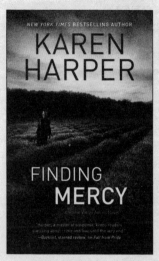

# MARTA PERRY

| | | |
|---|---|---|
| 77735 HOME BY DARK | ___ $7.99 U.S. | ___ $9.99 CAN. |
| 77576 VANISH IN PLAIN SIGHT | ___ $7.99 U.S. | ___ $9.99 CAN. |

*(limited quantities available)*

TOTAL AMOUNT                                                          $ _____
POSTAGE & HANDLING                                                   $ _____
($1.00 FOR 1 BOOK, 50¢ for each additional)
APPLICABLE TAXES*                                                    $ _____
TOTAL PAYABLE                                                        $ _____

*(check or money order—please do not send cash)*

To order, complete this form and send it, along with a check or money order for the total above, payable to HQN Books, to: **In the U.S.:** 3010 Walden Avenue, P.O. Box 9077, Buffalo, NY 14269-9077; **In Canada:** P.O. Box 636, Fort Erie, Ontario, L2A 5X3.

Name: _____
Address: _____ City: _____
State/Prov.: _____ Zip/Postal Code: _____
Account Number (if applicable): _____

075 CSAS

*New York residents remit applicable sales taxes.
*Canadian residents remit applicable GST and provincial taxes.

**HARLEQUIN**®HQN™
www.Harlequin.com

PHMP1013BL